THE HOLY WARRIOR
The Power of Faith

by

R.L. Spears Jr.

In loving memory of Carol Joann (Jody) Spears
09/24/1965 – 12/23/2021
I will miss you forever

This work of fiction is dedicated to our Lord, God in Heaven.

I want to thank all of the men, women and children in my life who have inspired me to create it. Special thanks to my wife and partner Jody, who also edited the book for me.

And there came a day when a child was born with a distinctive trait given exclusively for the sole purpose of reminding the world's people of almighty God's promise. For the scripture says, "and Jesus, answering, saith unto them, Have faith in God. For verily I say unto you, that whosoever shall say unto this mountain, be thou removed, and be thou cast into the sea; and shall not doubt in his heart, but shall believe that those things which he saith shall come to pass; he shall have whatsoever he saith." Mark 11 22-23 KJV Most people don't believe the words are meant literally, feeling they are more of a metaphor. More importantly, they miss the pure truth in the words. Jesus, the living embodiment of God on Earth, was not speaking figuratively. The life of this incredibly powerful man, Gabriel, would be a testament to the unlimited power of true faith in God.

PROLOGUE

On a bright, sunny Sunday morning, in the spring of the year
Gabriel Adams turned 12 years old, the boy sat quietly in
church as he did every week. His parents, Richard and
Cynthia sat attentively beside him along with his two younger
brothers, three older brothers, his younger sister and his three
month old baby sister, fast asleep, cradled in his mother's
loving arms. Gabriel's undivided attention was totally
focused on his elderly pastor standing ramrod straight behind
a wooden lectern with a raised depiction of Jesus on the cross
centered on the front of it. Gabriel always enjoyed his
pastor's sermons because the devoted older man had a true
gift for painting a vividly clear picture of the ancient world
described in the Bible. Sporting a thick unruly shock of snowy
white hair cut short on the sides, Pastor Reynolds was short
and rail thin. He couldn't have weighed more than 130
pounds, and his pastoral robes hung loosely from his tiny
frame no matter how the church seamstress tried her best to
improve their fit. But what truly stood out about Pastor
Reynolds was his startlingly clear blue eyes which burned
with an intensity that belied his advanced years. On this
particular Sunday he was speaking on the subject of man's
faith. His normally calm quiet voice amplified by a
microphone mounted on the lectern mellifluously rose and fell
as he spoke, almost hypnotic in its rhythmic cadence.
Gabriel's belief in God had always been uncommonly strong
and his parents were unwaveringly diligent in teaching him
and his siblings about God's holy word and making it clear to
each of them that they and all of God's children are special
and
singularly precious.

Then came a point in the sermon that seemed uncharacteristically pointed. As the pastor came to a passage about the infinite abilities of God's people if they only had enough faith, the diminutive clergyman seemed to focus exclusively on young Gabriel. The rest of the congregation seemed to gradually fade away along with the church, his family, and indeed the rest of the world. Nothing existed except the young boy and his earnest pastor. The little man's intense gaze seemed to penetrate the boy's very soul as he told Gabriel that a man or woman could literally move a mountain if he or she only had unshakeable faith that God would make it so.

The pastor appeared to be aware that there was no one else in the church but him and Gabriel. His normally steady but subdued voice gradually increased in power and volume until it resonated with an awesome quality, filling the space inside the small church like a premium surround sound system. Pastor Reynolds asked Gabriel, "Do you believe God will make what you ask in his name become reality?"

Gabriel heard his own voice clearly answer, "Yes." The voice sounded like his but different somehow...older, more mature. He wasn't consciously aware he had spoken out loud, but the pastor smiled, seemed satisfied with the answer and a flickering flame appeared in the pupils of his clear blue eyes. The fire grew continuously until the sockets appeared to contain no eyes at all, only a bright, burning blue and yellow flame.

Gabriel felt intense heat radiating from the burning orbs in the pastor's face, but there was no pain or discomfort at all. The flames grew and grew until they were all

Gabe could see. They surrounded him, enveloped him and filled him with their incredibly intense heat and pure bright light. Instead of fear, Gabriel felt great calm, comforting warmth, and a serenely peaceful stillness. He floated up from his seat on the church pew, contentedly suspended within the all-consuming flame, completely disconnected from the physical world.

A powerful, beautiful voice spoke to him, clearly neither his nor the pastor's. It was a gentle voice, even with such great power, yet deep and commanding.

Seemingly coming from everywhere and nowhere, the voice filled his young mind carrying with it an undeniable sense of immense power and supreme majesty, and Gabe knew without a doubt it was the voice of the Lord.

The voice told him, "*MY PEOPLE NEED YOU. THEY HAVE LOST THEIR WAY. THEY NEED TO BE REMINDED THAT I AM THE LORD, AND MY WORD IS TRUE. THEIR FATHERS AND MOTHERS KNEW OF ME, BUT THE CHILDREN AND THE CHILDREN'S CHILDREN HAVE FORGOTTEN ME. YOU WILL SHOW THEM THAT NOTHING IS BEYOND THEM IF THEY WILL ONLY BELIEVE, AND THEY WILL KNOW THAT NOTHING IS IMPOSSIBLE FOR THOSE WHO BELIEVE IN ME.*"

Gabriel heard his voice say, "Yes Lord." Then he felt as if he were an empty vessel that slowly began to fill with a thick, red liquid that he instinctively knew was sacred blood. The blood slowly replaced the flame, filling his mind, his thoughts and his very being. Then there was only complete, blissful darkness.

****

"Gabe? Gabe!" his mother's frightened voice came, penetrating the serene stillness. He opened his eyes and found himself lying on the church floor in the center of a circle of men and women, all of whom were fervently praying. "Mom?" he asked, a little disoriented, "What's happened?" Cynthia's face, or Cindy as she was commonly known, flooded with blessed relief, and Gabe turning his head saw the same expression on his father's face. "I think you had a seizure, Baby." Cindy said.

"I did?" Gabe asked. Nodding, she pulled him close and hugged him fiercely, tears rolling down her cheeks. "I don't feel bad though," he said. Everyone around them chuckled with shared relief, and Gabe's parents helped him to his feet. The choir began singing, and a joyful, celebratory mood filled the little church.

The family uncharacteristically left service, and as a precaution, his parents took Gabe to the local hospital. There he began several hours of exhaustive tests. Blood work, CT scans, MRIs, urine samples, stool samples, tissue samples, and a host of other tests he'd never heard of. All of the test results were negative.

The doctors could find absolutely nothing wrong, no evidence of or any residual sign of a seizure or any other abnormal condition. After that momentous day, his grateful parents showed him their love more than ever before. Everything returned to normal, but Gabriel knew, without a doubt, that his life had been forever changed and nothing would ever be as it was before. He had been shown his unique purpose....his calling....his holy mission. Gabe knew now that when the time came, he would be completely willing and humbly ready to do whatever was needed to complete that mission.

Throughout the rest of that pivotal year, Gabe went to school and happily played with his brothers and sisters just as he had before, but he knew deep in his heart that his days of being a normal child were over.

FIRST CHAPTER

"What do you want to do today?" Gabe's oldest brother, Andrew or Andy as he preferred to be called, asked. "I was thinking we could go down to the river and do a little fishing." Gabe greatly enjoyed spending time with his brothers and sisters.

They all had such different personalities and traits but he loved them all and he would do anything for any one of them. Andy had become his unofficial mentor in a way because, of all of his siblings, Andy's love of the Lord was the strongest next to their parents. Possessing an exceedingly kind heart and a deep genuine consideration for others, his eldest brother would unselfishly go out of his way to help anyone in need. Andy volunteered at the homeless shelter and spent countless hours just sitting and talking with the many less fortunate men and women who lived on the streets with no safe haven to call their own. He never "preached at them", which was one thing most of them despised, but was always willing to offer honest answers and sound advice which was always rooted in scripture.

One warm summer afternoon, Gabe had been greatly moved by an interaction between his brother and sister. It began when his younger sister, Allison, asked Andy why he spent so much time with "the nasty people" as she called them. Wrinkling her delicate nose in distaste, she wanted to know wasn't he afraid of them?

Andy answered, with his ever-present patience, "Alli," he began, his voice taking on the measured tone of a wise teacher speaking to a curious student, "The only difference between those people and us is that we have been blessed to be loved and protected by our parents who sacrificed their own wants and desires to care for us.

It would take very little, just a small change in our lives to put us in the same place those people found themselves in."

Alli looked truly skeptical and replied, "I would never just give up like that. They live like animals. They're dirty and they stink. They're scary too."

Andy smiled, squatting down to look her in the eye and lovingly cupped his little sister's chin with his right hand. "You stink sometimes, when you've been out playing all day," he chuckled, playfully flipping his index finger at her nose, which she deftly avoided, giggling. "But we all still love you, right?" Alli's brow wrinkled, her soft, brown eyes grew thoughtful, and she nodded. "God loves us too, even when we stink." His little sister smiled back up at Andy and nodded again although he could tell she didn't fully understand. His brother's perpetual kind, patient wisdom affected Gabe in a much more profound way than Andy would ever know. It went a long way towards shaping the man his younger brother would become.

Over the course of the next few years, as Gabe went through school with his siblings and childhood friends, those closest to him began to notice, at first subtle, then more profound changes taking place in the rapidly maturing young man. Physically, he changed a great deal with the advent of puberty, but the more significant alterations were in his spirit, his demeanor, and the way he interacted with others.

Gabe had always possessed a keenly sharp wit and an easy natural ability to find good natured humor in even the most serious situations. Most of his brothers and sisters, even those older than him, instinctively sought Gabe out whenever their spirits were low. Always ready with a joke or a witty remark, the hazel eyed young man never failed to brighten their outlook or put things in a better perspective.

In the summer between eighth grade and his freshman year of high school, Gabe grew over a foot in height and put on more than fifty pounds of solid muscle, largely because, with Jimmy, another one of his brothers, he began going to a gym and working out in his last year of middle school.

Jimmy was starkly different than any of Gabe's other siblings. He was invariably quiet, even somber at times. He obediently did his assigned chores, and even though he was always an above average student in school, his mind always seemed to be elsewhere. Where Andy, second only to their father, was Gabe's role model, Gabe always considered Jimmy to be his given charge to protect.

Jimmy's primary reason for taking to the gym was that he had been a favorite target of a group of particularly cruel bullies. These boys, all on one or more school sports teams, considered it great sport to taunt and victimize the smaller boy. Jimmy would frequently come home from school with fresh bruises or soaking wet from being dunked in the boy's room toilet, commonly known as getting a swirly. The quiet teenager never uttered a word of complaint or gave in to the urge to cry. He would simply shower, change into fresh clothes and sequester himself in his room. Gabe knew it broke his mother's heart to see the stubbornly concealed pain in her son's eyes but she let him have his space, having made clear to all of her children they could come to her at any time with any problem they had.

Gabe's father was tall, several inches above six feet. He was thin but not skinny, and his muscles were still well defined even many years after his discharge from the military. He worked long hard days on two different jobs to provide for his family even though his wife worked from home on her computer, making good money. Her ability to do that gave the family additional income while allowing her to be home for the kids. His hairline had begun to recede, not being a man of excess vanity, he cut it short and kept it that way. Since his wife liked facial hair on a man, he allowed his beard to grow along with his mustache, but he kept it neatly trimmed.

Richard knew his youngest son was quietly struggling with something and had approached him, more than once, in an attempt to get him to open up about what troubled him. Jimmy never admitted to any problems, and his father secretly admired the young man for facing his trials without complaining or whining. Besides, he saw Gabe's self-imposed role of his younger brother's protector and left well enough alone.

What made matters worse for Jimmy though was that, as Gabriel grew like the fabled beanstalk, Jimmy's own body seemed determined to remain more middle school sized. Even though the solitary young man greatly increased his muscle tone and mass, his height increased only by a few inches, leaving him still much shorter than most of the other boys in his class.

Conversely, the biggest benefit of Gabe's more impressive stature was that he rarely had to actually DO anything to fend off his brother's persistent tormentors.

His mere physical presence had become so imposing that not one of the bullies, typically cowards themselves, ever had the nerve to test him. Gabe was a normal, healthy boy who was quickly growing into early manhood. He loved professional wrestling, superheroes and science fiction movies. He didn't like violence in the real world, but he was rapidly coming to understand that it was a constant, often very dangerous, force in society throughout history. Gabe came to believe that failing to prepare for violence was preparing to fail when faced with violence. Had any of the young bullies actually stood up to him, they would have discovered he was something of a prodigy in martial arts.

Jimmy, along with his and Gabe's brother Justin and the older of their two sisters, Felicia, studied several different disciplines and various styles of self-defense.

Jimmy and Justin, the brother between himself and Gabe in order of birth, actually went a step further and became exceedingly proficient with weapons as well, long guns, handguns, the bow and even close-in knife fighting. The two boys had a natural aptitude for anything from a slingshot to a machine gun. Gabe went with them to the firing range on one occasion, and recalled it was one of the few times he had ever seen Jimmy truly happy and smiling. The two boys developed a good-natured rivalry and constantly tried to outdo each other.

Their father encouraged his sons and would directly supervise whenever he had the time. A combat veteran himself, Richard Adams was both extremely proud and thoroughly impressed by the boys' superior abilities.

Although Cindy didn't like guns herself, she was all too aware that in today's world, it didn't pay to be defenseless, even at home. In contrast to her husband, Mrs. Adams was barely over five feet tall. She had been highly sought after in her school years because she was not only smart but very pretty, and she had a curvaceous, attractive body.

She turned away all potential suitors until Richard came along. They met in church, and from the beginning, she knew there would be no one else for her. After bearing six children, Cindy's pear-shaped body, despite her best efforts, stubbornly refused to return to its former curvy yet fit state. She was still a lovely woman, nevertheless. She and Richard were untiring and diligent with the education and spiritual guidance of all of their children. They went to church regularly, had weekly Bible study in the home, and encouraged the kids to be engaged with the community, whether it be volunteering in some capacity or participating in community events.

Although their kids, mainly the younger ones, were growing up as the technological age exploded into an integral part of modern culture, the two devoted parents limited the use of such things to a bare minimum. Cindy, specifically, encouraged her children to read, actual paper books, though she would allow the use of tablets or laptops as well since a large part of the school's curriculum was quickly becoming computer based. It was expressly forbidden to bring any electronic device to the dinner table, and after ten o'clock at night, all tech was powered down.

She and Richard considered themselves extremely fortunate that none of the children ever expressed more than a passing interest in the video games rapidly becoming more and more popular and that was mainly when visiting the homes of friends or classmates.

The kids all had cell phones, but they were to be used for practical purposes or emergencies only. Both parents, Cindy in particular, felt it was vitally important to socialize with friends and family in person or to actually talk to them on the phone rather than texting. An exceptionally intelligent woman herself, Cindy felt the world was becoming much less intelligent due to a growing dependence on the wealth of information instantly available on the rapidly evolving internet.

Advances in technology were truly amazing. In some ways they shrank our world, making it easier to keep in touch. They could also bring abject terror and paralyzing fear into your home. Online predators, pedophiles and serial killers seemed to be materializing out of thin air in droves.

 The Adams's were forced to discuss sensitive topics with their children, even the youngest ones, that their parents would never have considered. The world was a more openly hostile and casually violent place than ever. At the same time, society was demanding more effort to understand alternative lifestyles and gender identification. No matter what Cindy and Richard felt personally, they instilled in their children the deep respect and non-judgmental tolerance and love for others taught by Christ.

The greatest fear the two parents had was that their children would become hardened and distant from the desperate struggle many people wage every day simply to survive, to put food on the table and provide comfort and protection for their families. Because it was in this growing callousness, this cold, utter lack of concern for the sanctity of human life, the worried mother knew, lay the path to final destruction.

Societal pressures reduced the value of life to a point where a difference in opinion was more and more frequently a life-or-death situation. Cindy and Richard fervently prayed that the children growing into young men and women under their guidance, would somehow be able to make a difference, even if only in the life of one person.

SECOND CHAPTER

Jason Summers knew he was a hopeless drug addict. His drug of choice was heroin which could be bought cheaply and provided a euphoric high that could not be matched. Jason had originally found the drug as a young man at a party with friends, or at least he'd thought they were his friends. He became instantly hooked and began a downward spiral that eventually showed him that he truly had no friends.

He lost his job, his home and family, his car, and even his health all in a matter of months. All that concerned him was getting to the next high. What he did to obtain that high didn't matter. His dignity and self-respect quickly evaporated in the more important concern of scoring.

Now, he was desperate. It had been nearly 12 hours since his last fix, and he had no idea how he would get straightened out. His regular dealer had made it very clear that there was no more credit to be had. The message was delivered with a brutal beating that would have put him in the hospital if he had insurance. As it was, he lay in an alley behind a dumpster, shivering in the cold. Every part of his body was racked with excruciating pain, either from withdrawal or from the savage beating.

His stomach was twisted in knots, had there been anything in his stomach, he would have thrown up. As it was, dry heaves kept coming and going. It was mid-December in Cleveland, Ohio, and so far, it had been a harsh winter. Lying in a soggy hollow in the filthy snow piled up beside the foul-smelling dumpster, Jason clutched his torn, threadbare coat closer to his painfully thin, nearly emaciated body trying to ignore the searing pain in his ribs and back caused by repeated kicks from the dealer and his laughing cronies. His arms were bruised and sore because he had held them over his head for protection, and he knew his trembling legs wouldn't support him if he tried to stand. So, he lay there on the frigid ground, suffering, alone and uncared for.

A sudden noise at the entrance to the dirty alley, maybe twenty feet away, cut through the thick haze of his numbing pain and nausea. Jason managed to peek around the bottom edge of the foul, rusting dumpster and saw three men roughly dragging a girl into the alley from a door that opened into the kitchen of a Chinese restaurant.

The terrified girl was obviously young, maybe fifteen, and scantily dressed, now shivering in the sudden bitter cold. Her plain, teenage face was covered with heavy makeup, streaked with the pale tracks of recent tears.

Jason could almost feel the stark horror in her quivering voice as she desperately pleaded with the hard-faced men.

Apparently, she was one of many young prostitutes in the employ of their boss and had been unable to pay what was expected of her for his protection. One of the men told her that she had to be made an example. After all, what if other girls began thinking it was acceptable to come up short.

One of the cruel looking men told her that he had a daughter her age, and it would give him no pleasure to hurt her, but orders were orders. The menacing glint in his eyes as he spoke failed to match the intended comfort of his words. One of his associates, a short, heavy-set man with a nasty smile on his pockmarked face with dark beady eyes, looked as if he had no such reservations. It was clear he was going to enjoy every minute of what was about to happen.

The girl became all but hysterical, frantically offering to service all three of them, right there, if they would just let her go afterwards. The third guy, a tall thin scarecrow of a man with an ugly scar over his left eye dealt her a solid, backhanded slap that knocked her to the filthy asphalt of the alley.

He then snatched her up by the front of her cheap, flimsy dress, ripping it open, exposing her pale young breasts to the bitterly cold night air. The heavyset man chuckled with malicious glee. The thin man wrapped a large, thickly calloused hand, around her soft pale neck and held her two feet off the ground against the crumbling brick wall of the old building. With both of her tiny delicate hands, the girl frantically clawed at his unyielding wrist and desperately fought for precious air as she kicked and squirmed in a pitifully ineffective attempt to free herself. The heavyset man leered obscenely at her bared skin and reached in to grope at her, roughly squeezing the tender flesh of the struggling girl's chest.

The man who had spoken earlier stood silently watching, then casually lit a cigarette. He drew in a deep lungful, then blew the acrid smoke upward as the playful brutality went on.

Jason, afraid to attract attention, heard the girl straining to speak what might be her last words, "Please God, help me," past the unrelenting pressure of the tall man's implacable grip. In his entire sad life Jason, the junkie, had never thought of anyone other than himself, but something in the teenage girl's tearful plea for help touched a long-buried part of his soul. With all the strength he could muster, Jason pulled his battered body from the mush of clutter trash in the grimy alley. Leaning against the greasy, foul-smelling dumpster for support, he croaked through swollen lips and broken teeth.

"Hey," he said, intending to shout, though it came out as more of a hoarse stage whisper. "Leave her alone!" All three men turned, startled by the sudden interruption, and for the first time, saw him. The first guy, obviously in charge, took a few slow steps toward Jason. It was clear that he had at one time been heavily muscled but had allowed the lesser physical demands of his more supervisory role to flesh him out a bit. Just above average height, the brute had a large, hawkish nose that clearly had been broken more than once. His dark, close-set eyes narrowed beneath bushy salt and pepper eyebrows. Thin, cruel lips and a shiny bald head completed the picture. He jerked a thick thumb towards the street at the other end of the alley and deciding the shaky junkie presented no threat, dismissively said, "Take a hike Dirtbag."

Even though his sense of self-preservation screamed inside him to mind his own business, Jason took a couple of wobbly steps towards the man. "Come on, Man. She's just a kid!" he said, trying to appeal to their humanity.

The lead thug pointed an index finger sporting a gaudy gold, diamond encrusted ring and spoke in a tone that clearly indicated there would be no other warning, "You better get your little dope fiend ass outta here or you're gonna be next!"

Using all of what was left of his meager strength and against every instinct telling him to run as fast as he could, Jason picked up what was left of an old, half rotten two by four from the ground near the smelly dumpster.

Broken off at about the length of a yardstick it was jagged on one end and Jason held the ragged end out in front of him like a sword. It shook in his unsteady hands, trembling from the cold and withdrawal, but in stubborn defiance of good sense, the pathetic Samaritan stood his ground and repeated in a voice not much stronger, "I said, let her go!" He brandished the improvised weapon for emphasis.

During this almost comical exchange, the punishing grip of the tall man's hand eased a bit on the young streetwalker's throat. The still suspended girl managed to look in the new arrival's direction with a potent mixture of deep gratitude and profound disappointment at her woefully inadequate would-be rescuer.

The leader turned, walking away and in a perfunctory manner said, "Bobby get rid of this little prick." The heavy-set guy, apparently named Bobby, approached Jason with not the slightest concern for the totally impotent weapon the young man kept aimed in his direction.

Jason drew the board back over his shoulder, preparing to swing when Bobby abruptly closed the distance between them with surprising speed for a man of his ample girth. He quickly snatched the piece of wood from Jason's weak grasp leaving behind painful splinters in the palms of the young man's hands.

There was no time for the sudden pain to register before Bobby laid into Jason with the commandeered plank, knocking the weaker man back down into the filthy wet slush of the alley. Jason reflexively covered his head with a profound sense of Deja vu, and as blow after numbing blow landed, he retreated deeper into himself and not having the slightest idea why, did something he'd hadn't done even through long months of crippling drug abuse, he prayed. "God, please...I don't want to die. I know I'm a piece of shit, and I don't deserve your help and I don't even know her but please don't let me and this little girl die!"

Propelled by the heavy thug's strong right arm the board slammed into Jason's left side where at least two ribs were already cracked, and as fresh white-hot pain shot through him something happened. Bobby suddenly stopped and turned around, aware that someone else was suddenly there in the alley.

Through a bright crimson veil of pain, Jason saw a man of well above average height, standing in the mouth of the alley. He stood probably six feet eight inches tall, maybe even a little more. He had a powerfully muscled but trim build with wavy dark, almost black hair and a neatly trimmed beard and mustache of the same color. Jason couldn't determine his race, and he looked to be possibly biracial. He seemed to radiate great power and calm authority that made him seem much bigger than he actually was. Bobby took a step toward the new guy, still holding the wooden plank, and the leader appeared ready to join Bobby in attacking the new arrival when the man spoke just one word.

His voice was incredibly deep and clear, resonating in the tight confines of the grimy alley like the low roll of thunder before a storm. He said, simply, "Stop!"

Jason fully expected the clearly insane man to be lying in pain, beside him in the alley in the next moment, but surprisingly, all three men froze in their tracks. It was then that Jason noticed the man's clothes.

He was wearing a snugly fitting, deep red, almost burgundy colored shirt, clinging to his muscular frame like a second skin. It was unadorned save a symbol on the left side of his deep chest; a crucifix centered on a shield like something out of the crusades. His pants were black, held up by a thick leather belt, fastened with a heavy buckle made of a shiny silverish metal. In the center of the buckle was the same emblem that emblazoned on his shirt.

He was wearing heavy rugged, black leather boots with a thick tread like work boots. But the most notable part of his attire was his coat, or more of a cloak Jason thought. It looked a lot like the pastoral robes worn by the priests in the Catholic church Jason's mom dragged him to every Sunday. Only it was open in the front, more like a cape. It draped over the man's broad shoulders hanging almost to the ground. Black as the night, it looked heavy with a silky lining the same color as the shirt.

There were two large silvery discs which appeared to be attached to the shirt at either end of his collarbone at each shoulder and connected by a sturdy looking chain, also of silver. The cloak or robe or whatever it was, was attached underneath the discs in some way Jason couldn't discern. The guy had to be some kind of geeky nut who thought he was a superhero or something. If Jason hadn't been in total agony, he might have laughed though there was absolutely nothing funny about what was happening. The booming voice filled the space in the filthy alley once again. The cloaked man turned his intense gaze to the thin thug holding the girl then back to the group leader and said, "Leave them alone."

His face going slack as if in a hypnotic trance, the thin knee breaker gently lowered the trembling girl to the ground and released his grip. Desperately gasping for air, the girl pulled the ragged ruins of her tattered dress together as best she could and stood gaping in wonder at the scene in front of her. Except for letting the girl go, the three men hadn't moved a muscle since the big man had first spoken. As a group they looked utterly confused, as if they had no idea why they weren't collectively stomping the dogshit out of the moron with a death wish. In a still deep, but much softer tone, the big guy squatted down and spoke gently to the girl. Tenderly, he asked, "Are you alright?"

Wiping blood from her nose and mouth with the back of one tiny hand she stifled a sob, and answered in a shaky voice, "I think so."

"Would you like to go home now?" he asked, smiling at her with a genuine kindness she was unaccustomed to, and she abruptly began to cry like the innocent little girl she really was.

"Yeah," she replied, "I ran away because my dad was always on my case. Be home by nine, no boys, do your homework, do your chores. I could never do anything right." The words seemed to spill out of her of their own volition. "I thought I was all grown up, so I got out of there. When I first got here, those guys were at the bus station," she said, nodding toward the still motionless group of thugs, "promised me a job working for their boss, but he's so disgusting!" She practically spat the last word. "I was supposed to be a secretary or something, but instead he made me do awful nasty things with a bunch of creepy old guys."

The tears flowed freely now, making fresh streaks down her reddened cheeks and she couldn't seem to get the painful words out fast enough. As if the words themselves tasted bad. "He takes almost all of the money they pay him and keeps me locked up in my room until they want me." Burying her face in her hands, she leaned against his chest sobbing with bitter shame.

"Don't cry." the big man said. "Go to the street. There's a cab waiting. The driver will take you to get your things. On the back seat of the cab, you'll find a bag with clean clothes and some money, enough to get you back to Hershey."

She looked up at the big man in complete shock. "How do you know...." her voice trailing off.

"Don't worry Sandy." he said with sincere compassion. "Learn from your mistakes and share your pain with others." He said gently. "You can prevent someone else from living through the horror you've been through. Will you do that?" With a huge lump in her throat she answered, "Yes. Thank you!" After a final brief hug, she ran swiftly to the street where Jason could see the promised taxi waiting, the back door open. Marveling at the three still seemingly frozen goons, Jason watched in awe as the unexpected rescuer moved toward him.

Jason had absolutely no idea what was about to happen, but he definitely couldn't have predicted what did. The big man bent down, his heavy cloak settling around him as he once again, squatted in the damp, dirty alley. He held out a powerful hand and helped Jason to stand on unsteady legs. His frail body wracked with terrible pain; Jason gratefully accepted the much-needed assistance.

 In the same kind, gentle voice he'd used with the tearful girl, the man spoke to him. "You risked your life for a total stranger." he said. Not a question, a statement of fact. Nodding his head, which brought on a fresh wave of dizziness and nausea, Jason replied, "Yeah, pretty stupid huh?"

"No Jason." Like the girl, Jason wondered how the guy could possibly know his name. He was certain he had never seen his unexpected savior before. The big man's deep, somehow supremely comforting voice seemed to come from both the alley and inside the troubled young man's head. "No greater love has any man than he lay down his life for another." the stranger said.

Jason remembered the familiar words from his days in church as a kid. He coughed suddenly, blood spattering the front of his already filthy clothes. The big man reached out, toward Jason's dirty face and the young man surprised himself by not reflexively avoiding the sudden contact.

The man's warm dry palm settled on Jason's sweat-soaked feverish forehead, and dry soothing heat radiated from it, spreading throughout the junkie's drug ravaged body, making the young man feel like he was in a sauna.

Closing his bloodshot eyes, Jason let the deeply comforting wave of engulfing warmth wash over and throughout his tortured body. It felt like an hour passed, but Jason somehow realized it was in reality just a few seconds. When the man withdrew his hand, the crippling pain had miraculously vanished. Not just the pain from the beatings, but the feverish ever-present craving for heroin was gone. Jason was somehow instantly clean and sober. It had been so very long since he'd felt this way that it was like a powerful high in itself. "Who are you?" Jason asked the man, in profound wonder with renewed strength and a sharp clarity that totally surprised him.

Through clear hazel eyes that sparkled like stars in the night sky, the man regarded him and the corners of his mouth turning up with a slight smile answered, "My name is Gabriel."

Jason stood in a deep state of profound awe and utter confusion. What had happened? He felt better than he had in years. His mind was now completely clear, blissfully free of the relentless pressure for a fix. It was impossible but true! This man had healed Jason with no more than a touch of his hand. Somewhere in the back of his once again lucid mind, Jason recalled the three thugs, standing stock still like wax figures in a museum display. He looked toward them wondering what would happen next as Gabriel stood, turned, and stepped over to face them. His powerful voice changed once again, to a timbre somewhere between the thunderous commanding tone he first used and the kind infinitely compassionate tone he used with Jason and Sandy. "You all have a choice," he said. "You can choose to change your ways and find a way to help the people around you instead of preying on the innocent and victimizing the weak. I'm going to release you now and whatever choice you make will determine what happens then."

Jason was unable to see the three goons' faces due to the size and breadth of Gabriel's imposing form, but the young man had a pretty good idea what was coming. With a slight gesture of his right hand hanging relaxed at his side, his rescuer apparently undid whatever Jedi mind trick he had used on the career felons, and the easily predictable results were immediate. Bobby and the thin guy quickly pulled handguns from concealment, and their leader started talking as if he had been interrupted mid-sentence. "Look Asshole," he began, "I don't know what the hell you did to us, but the only choice I'm making is to have my guys put a bunch of fuckin holes in your crazy ass!"

The lead thug's face was red with red hot rage, total frustration, as he clenched and unclenched his fists. "But first we're gonna beat the livin' shit out of you, and then you're gonna tell me who the hell sent you to stick your nose in our business!" The furious con started toward the taller man, assuming the shuffling posture of a boxer, his fistes held up in front of him in preparation.

Jason didn't know why, but he was truly afraid for the big man. Gabriel, however, stood ready, completely unafraid as what promised to be a severe beating approached. The lead thug launched a lightning swift punch up towards Gabriel's unmoving face and Jason closed his eyes dreading the unavoidable impact.

Jason heard the loud, telltale smack of flesh on flesh and the loud, brittle crack of bones breaking. A loud shriek of sudden agony followed, and the young former junkie opened his eyes, fully expecting to see his erstwhile savior laid out in the filthy alley. Instead, he saw that Gabriel had only moved to bring his right hand up in front of his face. Now, the hand was holding the thug's apparently broken hand in an iron grip. The mob enforcer grasped the wrist of the injured limb with his other hand, his face tightened in misery as he frantically jerked and pulled in a futile attempt to free his damaged hand. With less effort than it would take an average man to toss a wadded ball of paper, Gabriel casually shoved the man away, releasing his crippled hand.

Jason couldn't believe his eyes as the guy shot across the alley like a human cannonball crashing into the heavy, garbage filled dumpster with enough force to lift it off of two of its wheels and send it skidding down the grimy alley for at least 10 feet. The chief goon crumpled to the ground against the displaced trash container and lay groaning in pain on the ground. The man's two armed cronies then started shooting their deafening weapons, filling the cramped alley with acrid smoke as they emptied the magazines. Squinting through the haze of gun smoke, the men searched for the bloody corpse of their unwelcome adversary, but as the smoke quickly cleared, they saw.......nothing. The big interloper had disappeared! They spun around to find themselves looking up at the big man who was now, somehow standing behind them. They two goons frantically tried to reload their weapons, but before either could manage it, Gabriel grabbed them by their jackets and lifted them both off the ground with astonishing ease.

He slammed them together, hard, their colliding heads making an almost comical thud, then he easily tossed them into the walls, on either side of the alley, like two bags of garbage. They both slumped to the ground unconscious. At that point Jason heard the sirens. Someone must've heard the barrage of gunshots and called the cops. Before Jason could beat a hasty retreat, Gabriel said, "Don't worry Jason. They're not here for you." All of Jason's instincts and his unenviable history with the law told him to get the heck out of there as fast as humanly possible, but something about Gabriel instilled in him an instant trust. He instinctively knew that this man, whom he had never met, would not allow him to come to harm. Four cruisers screeched to a stop, two at either end of the alley and officers jumped out, entering the alley, guns drawn and ready for action.

Amazingly, they cautiously stalked past Jason and Gabriel without so much as a glance in the two men's direction. While one officer kept watch, his weapon unwaveringly trained on the down crooks, the rest of the wary officers holstered their weapons and approached the prone thugs, quickly applying handcuffs and taking the villainous trio into custody. One officer radioed dispatch requesting ambulances as it was obvious the suspects were in need of medical attention. A few moments later, with the three men in cuffs and barely able to walk, the cops escorted them to the parked squad cars. Jason looked at Gabriel, eyes wide with wonder and said, "They didn't even ask us any questions!" Gabriel looked down at him and answered, "That's because they don't know we're here."

"But they walked right by us! They were so close I could smell the oil on their guns!!" stated Jason, dumbstruck.

"They can't see us because they don't need to." answered Gabriel.

That only confused Jason more, and he said as much. "It isn't important," Gabriel said in response. "What IS important is what do you want your life to mean Jason? Do you want to be of use? Or do you want to waste all that you have been given?"

This question surprisingly irked Jason. Given? What the hell had he been given? He had wasted most of his life on drugs and alcohol. He'd never had more than a minimum wage job, and then only for long enough to collect a paycheck or two to fund his addictions and get high. Although he hadn't spoken aloud, Gabriel somehow knew what he was thinking.

"That isn't all you are." he said. "You have many skills you are as yet unaware of. Do you want to use them to help others like you tried to help Sandy?" the big man asked.

Jason thought about that for several moments while he watched the thugs being loaded into the police cars to await the arrival of EMS crews.

He tried to help the girl out of instinct and against his better judgement. It hadn't really been a conscious choice, but as he thought about it, he realized that even as he was being savagely beaten, he still felt good about himself for not just standing or rather lying by and watching it happen. After a few minutes, as Gabriel patiently waited, he answered, "Yes, I do." he said, surprising himself. "I want to be more than just a worthless junkie. I want to help."

Jason became more and more sure of himself as the unexpected words came out.

Gabriel reached out his powerful hand, and Jason shook it, his grip firm and steady for the first time in years. "Good my friend. Come with me." Gabriel said with a warm smile. Feeling as if his life mattered for the very first time in his life, Jason held his head high and confidently stepped out of the dark dirty alley alongside the first person he felt he could call a friend since he had been a teenager.

THIRD CHAPTER

Nearly six months had passed since Jason's life dramatically changed. There had been a complete turnaround in every aspect of the young man's world. He gained almost forty pounds, most of which was healthy muscle due to a membership at a local gym and eating healthy at Gabriel's insistence. He now had a job working as a freelance writer for an inspirational magazine called Living Fully.

Since his fortuitus acquaintance with Gabe, as he now called him, Jason discovered he had a prodigious, natural affinity for computers and technology in general. He enrolled in a technical school and quickly outpaced his fellow students and even surpassed a few of his instructors.

It was almost as if he fluently spoke the programming language that the operating systems used and was able to work through a completely unfamiliar program within minutes. If only he had been aware of this ability years ago. "Oh well," he thought, "everything happens for a reason." At first, he didn't know how his new association with his mysterious new friend Gabriel would play out. Basically, the big man just kind of showed up when he needed to. Initially it was much more often, since he was helping Jason get established in his new life.

Gabe would suddenly pop up at the boarding house for recovering addicts where Jason had been staying with information about jobs or money for clothes and such. The first time he showed up Jason almost didn't recognize him. He was wearing jeans, a plain blue t-shirt and white sneakers. He looked like any other guy, albeit a tall one. After just a couple of weeks, he located a modest apartment and gave Jason enough money for his moving expenses.

The two new acquaintances had a lot of conversations, and Jason began to feel like he'd known the man for years. Although Gabe was maybe 10 years older than Jason, the pair seemed to have a lot of common interests. Gabriel never demanded anything in return for his help and somehow was always one step ahead when it came to things Jason might need.

To his knowledge, Jason never actually asked his big friend for anything. Gabe just always seemed to know. Jason met a guy at his tech school who knew a guy who knew another guy that was considered something of a mad genius in computer geek circles. He was on his way to meet the guy now and pick his brain some more. Jason hoped he would be ready when Gabriel needed his assistance. He wanted more than anything to be able to help someone else like the big man had helped him.

Gabriel felt great! Ever since he began his mission he knew, without a doubt, he'd found the true purpose he was born for. He had been able to help countless people over the years and in his mind, there was no greater purpose for a life than to make the burden of life easier for others. He knew many people struggled through their entire lives never knowing that connection to something greater than themselves. As he sat in his small meticulously clean apartment eating breakfast, he reflected on the tragedy of so many wasted lives.

Science had tried, for as long as there had been such a thing, to disprove the existence of the supreme being that created humanity. One of history's most passionate debates was if man was created, as was described in the Bible, or had man evolved from prehistoric sea creatures that evolved to crawl up on land and continually adapted to their environment? Gabriel didn't see the two theories as mutually exclusive. God had spoken to man in terms that he could understand. One wouldn't try to explain nuclear physics to a toddler, because they didn't have the ability to comprehend the complex enormity of the information. The Bible states that the earth was created in six days. Six twenty-four-hour days?? Gabe thought not. If you were an eternal being how long would one day last, a thousand years, a million years? Evolution might simply be the process that God used to bring about the creation of the human race. The big bang theory states that a super dense particle of celestial matter spontaneously exploded and rapidly expanded outward creating the universe.

Well, to Gabriel that sounded a lot like it had been dark, and then there was light. There was even a prominent scientist who spent many years doggedly trying to prove that God doesn't exist. However, the more he researched, the more he realized he could not explain many things.

Gabe thought that if mankind would only stop for a minute, opening their hearts and minds, they would feel God's presence in their lives. God never left man and woman; it was the other way around. Gabe felt that the flaw in humanity's thinking was that God was a physical being. After all, the Bible stated man had been created in God's image.

What Gabe realized, however, was that God was an infinitely powerful being composed of pure energy. The human spirit or soul was like one living cell of that vast body of energy. The question of life after death wasn't a mystery at all to Gabe. Science proved that energy can never be destroyed, only changed in its form. A person's soul was energy, so after the death of the physical shell that had contained it, that energy had to go somewhere, be transformed into a different form. That was why all men and women were a part of the larger being that was God. Due to that fact, every person was capable of the miraculous abilities of God, their father.

The stumbling block was humanity's doubt in the glorious power of the Lord. The solution was for every man and woman to accept that simple truth with absolute certainty. God is within all of us and we are all part of God.

Gabe finished his simple breakfast of fresh fruit, nuts and cheese, then took a hot shower and said his morning prayers. Never having taken for granted the things he could do through the power of the Father; he began and ended every day in prayer. His day normally began early. He enjoyed watching the sun come up as he listened to several newscasts on both radio and television.

Although he knew of the inherent manipulation of the media by the wealthiest and most powerful people, he could still glean enough information from the broadcasts to aid him in his tasks. The way his day-to-day assignments came to him was very simple. During his prayers, he would ask the Lord to lead him to the place where he was most sorely needed. These decisions were not his, but God's alone.

Gabriel would leave his apartment secure and confident in the knowledge that all would go as God wanted it to. Then, Gabe would go wherever he was needed. Sometimes he would drive his car, a ten-year-old Crown Victoria, which he meticulously maintained in pristine condition. Other times when the distance was great or the need was more pressing, he had only to close his eyes, clear his mind, and wait. When he opened his eyes, he would be at his intended destination. Gabe never gave conscious thought to the actual process by which he was transported. He just knew God would take care of it, and He always did. Gabe never felt any sensation of movement or disorientation. He was simply in one place one minute and somewhere else the next. Six months ago, he had a revealing vision. He entered a waking, dreamlike state in which he saw a new development unfold for his holy mission. The time had come for him to have a witness to his everlasting campaign.

He had the testimony of the countless people he had helped, and they spread the word to whomever would listen. But, often, their tales of a mysterious man with what could only be described as superhuman powers, were often discounted as the vivid imagination of people under great stress and frequently dismissed out of hand.

The firsthand accounts that Jason could provide would stand up better now that his mind was clear, and he could serve as a scribe of sorts. Gabriel was both greatly gratified to have a companion and yet deeply concerned for the bright young man. Many of the challenges that the Holy Warrior, as he had come to think of himself, faced were extremely dangerous, both in situations and violent individuals.

Jason knew the things he'd seen Gabriel accomplish were real, but the enemy and his chosen minions, would sow the poison seeds of doubt at every opportunity. Doubt was the nemesis of power in Gabriel's sacred work, and it would take time for Jason to be able to fortify his spirit against it.

As Gabe thought on these things, his task for the day came to him. There was no need to change out of the clothes he was wearing. Having put on worn but comfortable jeans and an old faded blue t-shirt, he was in something of a standby mode. He had nothing pressing to take care of at the moment, and typically, these times were spent reviewing news feeds or reading literature on any of a dozen subjects that he felt he needed to stay current on. The attire most appropriate for 'work' would be what he was wearing when he arrived at his destination. It was one of the things that he really liked about this calling. God had an incredible sense of efficiency! With a slight smile curling his full lips, Gabe closed his eyes and mentally prepared himself to profoundly change someone's life.

FOURTH CHAPTER

Camella Bishop had what she considered to be a good life. At thirty-eight years of age she was entirely self-sufficient. She had a much sought-after, white-collar position at a prominent St. Louis advertising agency. Her salary was commensurate with ability and productivity, and Camella was very good at her job. With incentive bonuses that she routinely earned; she was easily the highest paid account rep in her company. She wasn't very well thought of if you were to ask any of her coworkers, and in truth, she didn't care one bit. Life was a fierce competition, and she hated losing. She was small in stature, standing only a fraction above five feet in heels. She studiously maintained her weight at just over one hundred pounds and was extremely diligent about fitness almost to the point of obsession. She began every day at the gym with a punishing workout routine followed by a five-kilometer run. Camella was a stunningly attractive woman with clear, olive skin and thick, lustrous hair, black as a moonless night which she usually wore pulled back in a tight, efficient ponytail. Even so, her raven tresses fell to a point between her shoulder blades. Her eyes were a deep piercing blue that she knew had the capacity to freeze a person's blood at her command. Her petite, hourglass body was well toned and trim with only enough body fat to maintain a healthy balance. She never drove a car more than two years old, preferring to lease as opposed to buying. She lived in a gated, upscale housing community that had a waiting list of nearly two years for a purchase.

Although she dated occasionally, she had never felt a strong enough bond with anyone that made her want to share a committed situation. Her longest relationship to date lasted just over three months and ended the way all her others typically did. Inevitably, the guy would want more of an emotional commitment from her, becoming possessive and demanding, and that would be the end of it. Her career was her life, and there was simply no room for anything or anyone else. She didn't even have a pet, too much responsibility. She hated being tied down in any way and lived her life in avoidance of true connection. She told herself that the emptiness she frequently felt was because she was still waiting for that signature account that would make her a legend and put her in line for a top executive position.

To her shocked surprise, she recently found out that she had actually been passed over for a key promotion a month ago, the first time her name had come up for consideration. When she angrily asked why, the V.P. in charge of personnel told her it was due to her complete lack of people skills. That caught her completely off guard since, in her opinion, her people skills were the reason she was consistently number one in new accounts and customer retention every quarter.

The arrogant little man then explained that he meant people within the company. She didn't socialize with any of her peers, not even so far as a drink after work. In fact, her nickname in the office was The Little Bitch. She was aware of the unflattering appellation but could not have been less concerned. She chalked it up to jealousy over her obvious beauty and unparalleled success. She saw other reps as obstacles to her ultimate goals not potential friends. What really bothered her were the zealous morons that stupidly worshipped an imaginary deity. Camella could never understand how any thinking person could believe in the laughable existence of some all-powerful being who somehow had nothing better to do than voyeuristically watch the everyday lives of mere human beings. The entire concept was totally ludicrous to her, and she wondered how these people, who seemed to have at least average intelligence, could be taken in by such superstitious nonsense.

Any guy she dated who said the first thing to her about being a Christian or wanting her to go to church with him, was dropped from her lengthy list of people who deserve to share air with her.

Today had been a good day so far, Camella thought as she power walked through the long, marble tiled corridor that led from the elevator to the office building's lobby. The distinct click clacks of her Jimmy Choo pumps announced her approach. Although the security guard at the desk waved and gave her his obligatory smile, she passed by him with hardly a glance.

When she first started working at the agency, the misguided buffoon had made a doomed attempt to strike up a conversation with her as an overture to asking her out. Little did the peon know, Camella wouldn't be caught dead on a date with a man on an hourly wage. The very thought made a shudder of revulsion ripple through her.

Stepping out into the bright afternoon sunshine, the humid heat of the Missouri air engulfed her like a hot wet blanket. She reached into her expensive designer handbag and pulled out a pair of sunglasses quickly settling them on her face. She took a moment to adjust from the crisp cool atmosphere inside the building to the nearly stifling heat of the air outside.

Once this adjustment was complete, she struck out toward the paid parking lot, six blocks away where her car was parked. Although there was a private lot at the office building, Camella preferred to keep her Mercedes-Benz CLA250 at a distance to avoid any accidental door dings and where an extra fifty bucks, regularly slipped to the attendant insured no one would get near her vehicle. An added benefit to the walk was that it kept her from being waylaid in the parking garage by any of the annoying drones in the office.

As Camella made her way along the crowded sidewalk, she passed three scruffy looking young men on the corner, a block from her chosen lot and pointedly ignored the vulgar comments and the hungry looks in their eyes as the undesirables stared at the rolling motion of her floral print skirt. She paid them no mind as they began to follow her at a distance. There were two blacks and a white kid with dirty blond dreadlocks. The blacks had flat billed caps cocked to the side, and all three had their baggy jeans belted just below the curve of their behinds, leaving their boxer shorts exposed to their waists.

One of the blacks and the white guy were shirtless, leaving their wiry torsos exposed nearly to the pubis. The remaining black who at least wore a basketball tank top, sported a glittering gold dental overlay, referred to in street slang as a grille.

It was inlaid with diamonds, and one of his front teeth had skull and crossbones cut into it. They all had the strong, sour smell of perspiration wafting from them like the inside of a gym locker room.

Their lean sculpted muscles glistened with sweat in the hot Missouri sun. For some reason Camella's senses went on high alert about halfway down the block from the paid parking lot. Stopping at a newspaper machine at the curb, she bought a paper and took the opportunity to casually check the sidewalk behind her. There was no one there. Chiding herself for allowing a moment of fear, she closed the machine and quickly walked the rest of the way to her car.

Opening the door which unlocked with a beep at her approach, she slid into the rich leather driver's seat and let out an involuntary yelp at the heat of the surface.

As Camella reached out to pull her door shut, there was a sudden loud thud on the passenger side of her vehicle. She turned, startled at the sound and saw the black kid with the basketball shirt grinning at her with his face pressed against the glass. His tongue slid out and traced a line across the window.

In that moment of distraction, she failed to notice the white kid with the dreadlocks on her side of the car until he slid in beside her forcing her to sit in his lap as his partner slipped into the passenger seat. "Wassup Baby?" the white kid said. "We goin for a lil' ride." The smile on his deeply tanned face sent a powerful wave of revulsion and sudden panic through her, and all of her self-confidence rapidly drained out of her like water through a sieve. Dreadlocks started up the expensive car and slowly pulled out of the lot. Once clear of any potential witnesses, he pressed the accelerator pedal, and the powerful German built machine surged forward. Both of her unwanted guests hooped and hollered at the smooth rush of acceleration. Camella wanted to say something, but her vocal cords were maddeningly paralyzed. She desperately searched her mind for some way out of this dreadful situation. Her phone was in her purse which the punk in the passenger seat was now carelessly rummaging through.

The aggressive way Dreadlocks was driving was made her stomach lurch as he erratically weaved between other cars on the road like a race car driver. She hoped someone would call and report them, or better yet, that they would pass a police car.

The young punk gleefully sped through the surface streets then made a couple of sharp turns to test the vehicle's handling. When he had a satisfactory feel for the steering, he took the on ramp to the interstate. Once on the highway he tromped on the accelerator pedal and the german road machine took off, pressing them all back in the seats with the surge of speed.

The two young men hadn't really spoken to her since jacking the car and she began to hold out hope this would simply be a joy ride and a maybe a robbery. Both were things she could easily recover from, but when the driver abruptly took the offramp for an upcoming rest area, a renewed wave of terror washed over her.

There was only one other car in the parking lot of the deserted rest area and it was unoccupied, its owner apparently making use of the facilities. Dreadlocks slowed to a stop in a space located in the area reserved for trucks. Since there were none present at the time, it was an even more secluded spot.

He shut off the ignition and pocketed the keys. That worried her because her house keys were on the ring as well.

Then, the guy in the passenger seat spoke up. "Alright Shorty," he said. It sounded like A'ight Shawty. "This what's gon' happen. We gon' run some errands. We goin to the bank and you gon' take us out some........um..capital." This brought a low chuckle from Dreadlocks, and the guy in the tank top, Grille as she came to think of him, smiled. As Grille spoke, an older model dark green SUV, with huge chrome rims, pulled up beside Camella's car and stopped. She could see the missing member of the trio at the wheel. "After the bank, we gon' run by yo crib and have us a lil party." Grille said.

At that, a lascivious grin appeared on his dark face, exposing his jewel encrusted dental work. The expression chilled her to her bones, and she felt goosebumps break out on her skin. Finally finding her voice, Camella said," Look, you don't have to do this. Just take my purse, you can even take the car. Just let me go. I won't call the cops or anything, I swear. Please!" Her voice was surprisingly steady, and she even managed not to cry.

Her plea didn't have the effect she hoped for. Instead of defusing the situation and giving the young punks a way to avoid more serious charges, Grille suddenly became enraged. He opened the door on his side and got out, quickly stepping around to the driver's side where Dreadlocks was already getting out of his way. Grille reached in and grabbed her by the ponytail. He roughly dragged her small body out of the car, not giving her time to even put her feet on the ground. Her knees painfully struck the hot asphalt, and she felt her skin scraping against it.

Snatching the woman to her feet, Grille struck her with a backhanded slap that slammed her back to the hot pavement. One of the heavy rings on his right hand opened an ugly gash on her right cheek, warm blood running down to stain her expensive white linen blouse. Camella's vision swam crazily, and for a moment she thought she was going to vomit. Now that he felt he had the proper attention from her, Grille clarified her position, "Bitch, you ain't runnin shit roun' heah!!!" His dark face was flushed with barely restrained rage. He leaned down close to her, spit flying from his mouth as he spoke.

She felt the droplets hit her forehead, but she was too busy holding in the contents of her stomach to react. The two men picked her up easily and threw her into the back seat of the SUV. There was a popular rap song playing on the radio, and once her captors were inside the SUV, the driver turned up the volume to a deafening level.

Dreadlocks sat beside her in the back seat, and as her vision slowly returned to something close to normal, she saw the way he was now looking at her.

Her white top was ruined with blood all over her shoulder and the right side of her chest. Looking behind the seat where huge speakers filled what would've been the cargo area, Dreadlocks grabbed something from the top of them. With a look that she could only think of as creepy, he grabbed the front of her ruined blouse. Camella reached up but before she could stop him, the punk yanked downward, HARD!

The expensive fabric tore apart and in one move, he roughly snatched the entire garment from her upper body. "Whoohoo Man!" he whooped. "Look at those little titties!" Embarrassed, her cheeks flushed red, Camella vainly tried to cover herself, but Dreadlocks swatted her hands away. Resigned, she turned her head and endured the humiliation as the men gawked at her breasts, covered only by her sheer bra. Grille turned around in the passenger seat for a better view, and even the driver had to sneak a look. "Yeah, dis party gon' be the shit!" Grille said as he ran his tongue over his bejeweled teeth, and hot, involuntary tears of shame sprang from Camella's eyes.

Dreadlocks handed her a sweat stained t-shirt and said, "Put this on. Can't go in the bank like that. Too much attention." he said with a cruel laugh. When they reached the bank, they decided it would be better to go through the drive through lane since their captive was now wearing the rapidly swelling evidence of Grille's former anger on her lovely face. Dreadlocks produced a small gun and kept it poked into her side. Camella withdrew five thousand dollars from her checking account as she was instructed.

Her captors all agreed they didn't want to attract undue attention by being too greedy. Once they had the cash, they headed back to the rest area to retrieve their hostage's car since an abandoned vehicle of such value would also arouse suspicion. They allowed her to drive with Dreadlocks keeping the little gun aimed at her the whole way. The others followed the Mercedes to her house, having noted the address on her driver's license in case she tried to lead them astray.

A large pair of dark sunglasses hid her badly swollen cheek as she passed through the security gate. The on-duty guard looked skeptical but passed them through as Camella assured him the men in the SUV were her guests. Her panic was almost unbearable. The thought of their filthy hands on her body was positively terrifying. Once inside her home, Dreadlocks kept the gun pointed at her as the other two hoods took in the swanky decor of the upscale dwelling. Returning to the foyer, they all three agreed that it was time to start the next phase of the party. Camella had now lost all hope. She was resigned to the acceptance of her fate, suddenly questioning everything she thought she knew. She had the feeling that there should be some way out of this. She knew the stats on situations like this were not in her favor, but it just didn't seem right that she was now destined to die. She decided on a desperate strategy, knowing it could be her only hope. With all the considerable strength in her well-toned leg, she abruptly stomped the four-inch heel of her shoe into the bridge of Dreadlocks' left foot. The man shrieked in agony, momentarily forgetting about the weapon in his hand, and Camella darted to her right and ran full tilt through the well-appointed kitchen.

One of the things she loved about the three-level house was that the staircase had two entry points. One off the foyer and another that came off the rear of the kitchen. At the moment, it could be a lifesaving feature as she sprinted up the stairs taking them two at a time. She could hear the thugs scrambling in hot pursuit behind her, but she made it to her master bedroom ahead of them and quickly slammed the heavy oak door behind her. She locked the door, and she grabbed the cordless phone from the bedside table and punched 911 on the keypad. A sigh of relief escaped her as the operator answered, "911, what is your emergency?" Camella opened her mouth to speak, but before she could there was a click on the line, then nothing, no static, no tone just dead air. The thugs had cut the phone line! The dispatcher was gone.

In utter frustration Camella threw the phone across the room. It crashed against the wall shattering into pieces. Gathering her wits, Camella held onto a faint ray of hope that the dispatcher might still be able to follow up on the call. She had read somewhere that it was now a policy to follow up on interrupted calls and her location would have appeared on the computer screen's caller ID.

She couldn't count on the cops arriving before the thugs managed to get into her room, so she furiously tried to come up with a new plan. She heard them banging on the heavy door, but she knew it would hold for at least a few minutes. She quickly changed into jeans and threw off the filthy t-shirt, replacing it with a dark blue pullover workout shirt and traded her heels for sneakers.

The loud banging on the bedroom door had stopped, and she knew her would be rapists were trying to pick the lock or find something to ram the solid door with. Her time was quickly running out, so she went to the double hung window that overlooked the thickly wooded property behind her house. The highway was only a couple of miles through the woods, and if she could lose her unwelcome guests in the woods, she might be able to reach it and flag down some help. Maybe even a state trooper if she was lucky. Camella raised the bottom sash of the window and quickly scrambled out onto the roof. The drop to the small backyard was only about ten feet or so, and she only hesitated for a moment. Lying down on her belly, she eased herself feet first over the edge then dropped to the little flagstone patio.

The patio was composed of large irregular stones, and as luck would have it, she turned her ankle on one when she landed.

An involuntary yelp of pain escaped her, and she clapped a hand over her mouth to stifle any more noise. Tears sprang from her eyes joining with rivulets of sweat running down her cheeks. Camella fought against the pain, struggled to her feet and boldly struck out towards the tree line less than fifty yards away. She almost made it to concealment in the trees when she heard an angry shout behind her. She looked back and could see Dreadlocks pointing in her direction from the bedroom window. Wasting no more time, she darted into the thick woods.

Camella bravely made her way through the dense woods, her injured ankle screaming at every step. She was grateful for the pullover even though she was now sweating profusely. The long-sleeved garment partially protected her skin from being torn by brush as well as providing some defense against the ravenous insects that were everywhere. She figured she had covered maybe a half mile, and despite her injury she was making decent progress.

So far, she had managed to evade her pursuers, but she could still hear them cursing in the distance behind her as they awkwardly stumbled through the woods after her. In spite of her dire circumstances, Camella smiled to herself thinking of the two thugs that were shirtless. Even Grille's basketball jersey would be little defense in this environment. Wooded areas in Missouri, particularly around St. Louis were largely swampland. Often referred to as a hunter's paradise, along with neighboring Georgia, it was home to many different species of game. Wild boar, deer, alligators and armadillos were plentiful. There were many species of snakes, a diverse variety of fish, even flying squirrels.

None of these creatures were high on Camella's list of things she wanted to encounter, so she kept her eyes open for any evidence of them. She made it to what she figured was the halfway point to the highway and had actually begun to have fleeting hope she would be able to escape her attackers when she gingerly stepped over a fallen tree and let out a shriek as her uninjured foot sank into a deep, muddy hole.

Unable to stop herself, she toppled into what amounted to a small marsh. Camella frantically struggled to right herself, both arms submerged to her elbows and began to panic as she could get no purchase in the thick mud. She was only in about three feet of water at the edge of an area maybe forty feet in circumference, but she could barely keep her head out of the muddy water as her hands, knees and feet kept sinking into the sucking ooze. In desperation, Camella frantically searched through the clinging muck and finally found a stout tree root, using it to pull herself upright. With the back of a forearm, she wiped the slimy goo from her face as best she could. Her feet were still mired in the cloying mud, but at least now she was mostly standing upright.

Her eyes were stinging from the muddy water, and she spat the filthy stuff from her mouth. She was no longer sinking, but she could hear the three relentless men closing in on her location having heard her scream when she fell. She was trapped and exhausted, her hopes of escape now blown away like dandelion seeds in the wind.

An overpowering sense of despair overcame her, and she wanted to just give up. The larcenous thugs would find her, and then her real nightmare would begin. The thought of enduring what the street thugs obviously had in mind was overwhelming.

Camella found herself wishing she had a gun or even a sharp knife so she could end it all before she was debased, humiliated, and finally murdered. In the depths of her despair, she instinctively looked up. Piercing the canopy of magnolia, oak and spruce trees a shaft of sunlight cut through the trees like a beacon. In it she could see particles of dust, pollen and insects swimming in the moist haze of the Missouri swamp. With fresh tears rolling from her weary eyes, she sent up a silent plea. God, if you really are there, I really need some help here, please.

Unwilling to give the vicious urban animals that rapidly approached any added satisfaction, she once again used her forearm to wipe away her tears. Now could hear them, loudly crashing through underbrush toward her. They were very close.

Then she heard a deep voice say, "Give me your hand Camella. I'll get you out of there." She was so startled she let out another short scream. What startled her more than the voice was where it came from, behind her. That would put the speaker farther into the marsh than she was. Turning slowly, she saw a tall, powerfully built man wearing white slacks and a collarless shirt of the same color that hugging his muscled frame like a second skin. He was also wearing a long white cloak, trimmed in dark red and attached to the shirt somehow, secured with two golden discs of metal connected by a heavy chain. There was a symbol of some sort on the right breast of his shirt and the same emblem on the large belt buckle at his waist. There were too many things to process at once, and Camella felt a wave of disorientation roll over her and her vision began to narrow like a tunnel, the darkening edges crowding her view.

Shaking her head, the young woman fought to stay conscious. The big man, with the inexplicably clean clothes, reached down offering his extended hand to her. That's when she saw that he was standing on dry, solid ground. How could that be?? She was sure the filthy mud hole was at least the size of half a basketball court. She reached up, gratefully and took his rock steady hand. It was refreshingly cool to the touch, and all at once the disorientation evaporated like a glass of water spilled on hot concrete.

An incredible sense of peace and wellbeing filled Camella as if she were a dry sponge dropped in a bucket of water. She was immediately certain that this man would absolutely not allow her to be harmed. She also realized that her injuries were instantly healed. She was still soaking wet, sweaty and covered with foul smelling mud, but all of the dozens of cuts and abrasions she picked up on her mad dash through the woods were gone. Her injured ankle felt perfectly normal. Then, the pressing urgency of her desperate situation resurfaced when all three of her pursuers suddenly broke through the brush and pulled up short of the mud hole. Spotting the woman's sudden rescuer, Dreadlocks and the third guy who had been the driver, aimed their guns at him and pulled the triggers without hesitation. Nothing happened. Almost in unison, the two punks attempted to pull the slides on the semi-automatic handguns in order to clear the jam, to no avail. The weapons were evidently fused solid, like toy pistols and rendered completely useless.

A stress relieving giggle nearly escaped Camella's lips as the perplexed thugs comically stared at the now worthless weapons. Not willing to allow the sudden lack of lethal hardware to alter his authority, Grille spoke up. In his most intimidating voice, he addressed the unwelcome newcomer, "Yo my man, I don't know where you came from, but you best take yo ass back theah fo mah boys get dem guns fixed!" At this, he shot a withering look at his two struggling henchmen, both of whom immediately resumed their futile efforts to free up the hopelessly jammed weapons.

Gabriel met the evil glare of the misguided young man with an expression the punk was totally unprepared for. It took a long moment for Camella's attacker to identify the unfamiliar facial expression. It was genuine compassion. "You guys know that what you have done today, what you have put this innocent young woman through, is wrong," he said. "But it's not too late for you to turn this around. You can be forgiven and make up for the selfish things you have done. All you have to do is ask for God's mercy and give this lady her money back."

Grille, his face and upper body dripping with sweat, looked at his two companions, and as one, they all broke into a fit of hysterical laughter, slapping each other on the back and holding their sides. "You crazy Man!" Grille said when he could finally catch his breath. "We ain't asking God fuh nothin!" he said, his cruel face once again ominously serious. "We take what we want, Dog! And right now, we want that little bitch beside you. Step off and maybe you won't get fucked up!" Pulling a switchblade from his pocket he pressed a stud on the side of the handle and the deadly, eight-inch blade snapped in place with a loud click. Following suit, the others produced blades of their own waiting for direction from their leader. They tossed the now worthless handguns to the soggy ground of the swamp.

They stood ready to move, showing no concern for the other man's distinct size advantage over them.

Gabriel looked at them as if they were no more than disobedient toddlers. "Is this the way ALL of you feel?" he asked. He calmly directed his sympathetic gaze, in turn, to each one of the homicidal young thugs. The young man Camella thought of as Dreadlocks, whose real name was Chris, hesitated, his mind obviously conflicted. Something in the big man's calm, deep voice and his honest, forgiving manner made the young man feel safe somehow.

He felt the searing hot stares of his two cohorts on him, but he ignored them.

Chris had always been more of a follower than a leader. He had grown up with a single mom, in a predominantly black neighborhood, located in a section of St. Louis that traditionally populated by the poorest people in the city. He did what he had to in order to survive. It was either be a part of the criminal element or be a victim of it.

Away from the others though, he was known to have a good heart. He helped his overworked mother take care of his younger sister who had been born with cerebral palsy. Almost every dime of any money he hustled for, he gave to his mom to help with the staggering bills and crucial medication for his fifteen-year-old sibling. In school, he purposely shaved his grades, keeping a consistent C average so as not to stick out. Though he could easily have made straight A's, Chris didn't need the hassle of being cast a nerd in addition to being in the white minority.

All his life the underachieving youth had knowingly made the wrong choices, all due to peer pressure, but this time, here in this hot humid swamp among the incessantly buzzing insects and the hostile warning glares of his cohorts, Chris sensed this might be his last chance to make the right choice. Candidly meeting the stranger's gaze, he slowly shook his head no, indicating he was ready to change his path. Grille gave him a look intended to freeze the white boy's soul. The young black man's intense glare promised certain retribution.

But before the young caucasian's former leader could say a word, Gabriel spoke, "Then come join us, Chris."

Camella drew in a sharp breath of surprise as Chris stepped over the same fallen tree, she knew marked the edge of the swamp and onto now firmly solid ground. She did a double take and saw that the muddy pit was now gone, replaced by solid earth, fallen leaves and thick undergrowth.

Grille reached out suddenly, in an attempt to grab Chris's arm, but even though he was well within easy reach, his hand somehow missed. It was as if it passed through Chris's arm which had no more substance than a morning fog.

Now off balance the thug leader nearly fell forward on his face. Awkwardly regaining his footing and realizing his control of the situation was slipping away like the last vestiges of a good high, Grille found his voice,"Boy you betta git yo ass back hea NOW!!" His voice cracked with impotent rage.

Chris totally ignored him, reaching out to grasp Gabriel's outstretched hand. The moment he felt the man in white's powerful grip, a profoundly deep tranquility filled the young man.

He felt truly loved, completely accepted and unquestionably safe like a small child lovingly cradled its father's arms. Chris turned and faced his former companions, suddenly seeing them from a totally new perspective. To him, they now looked like newborn puppies, lost and thoroughly confused, somehow separated from the protection of their mother.

Gabriel again addressed the now two visibly furious thugs Chris had left behind. The big man's deep, rich voice took on a different quality that would have been extremely difficult to explain. It was hollow and echoing, as if he spoke from the depths of a deserted concert hall. It filled the wooded area like as if amplified by ten bullhorns, coming from seemingly everywhere at once. "You two have made your choice." His voice boomed. Grille and the remaining lackey nervously scanned the area, growing wild eyed with panic. "Now the consequences of that choice are waiting for you." Fully expecting squads of police to suddenly jump out from behind the concealment of the dozens of large old trees, both men hastily dropped to the ground, frantically searching for the previously discarded weapons. Their frenzied search finally turned up the guns, and both men quickly racked the slides, amazed and pleased to find the dangerous weapons now back in perfect working order.

As both scrambled back to their feet, Grille turning to point the weapon at the weird ass dude in white. *"Imma blow a big ass hole in that muthafucka's face. Then Imma shoot Chris's bitch ass in the nuts and rape dat damn little bitch right in front of bof of em."* But as he turned around to the spot his intended victims had been standing in just a few seconds ago, the now flustered thug found that he and the other remaining member of his crew, named Cleo, were standing all alone in the muggy woods. Only the sounds of chirping birds, the annoying whine of tiny insects and the occasional distant croak of a bullfrog could be heard.

There were no telltale sounds of three people crashing through the trees and hanging vines in a frantic attempt to escape. No yelling cops ordering them to get down on the ground. He could detect no sounds of any kind of vehicle carrying his intended victims to safety, absolutely nothing.

Cleo looked at his equally confused leader, whose given name was Curtis, and with an undisguised look of complete bewilderment asked, "Where dey go, Man?"

Curtis slowly turned in a complete 360-degree circle. He saw not one thing that hadn't originated right there in the miserable Missouri swamp. "I don' know Bruh," he answered, "Les git the fuck outta heah Dog!" He said, turning to head back the way they had come. With Cleo trailing close behind him, Curtis struck out back in the direction of the white girl's house. After only a short distance however, he became maddeningly disoriented. Nothing looked the least bit familiar. They passed trees, even a small creek that he couldn't remember seeing before. Now he could hear the comforting drone of traffic very close. Somehow, they were much closer to the highway than Curtis had guessed. Figuring it had to be because they were so intent on catching the fleeing woman that they didn't notice it before, he gratefully turned toward the bustling sounds of cars and trucks on the roadway. After only a quarter mile or so, the heavy concentration of trees began to thin, and within a few minutes, they broke through the tree line and found themselves in a deep ravine off the shoulder of the road. Tall cattails and thick briar bushes lined the deep crevice, and there was about three inches of stagnant water at the bottom. The two bone-weary and totally unhappy men slogged through the shallow, slimy water. Briars tore unmercifully at their exposed skin and clung to their sweat-soaked clothes.

The pair of frustrated and angry thugs slipped and struggled up the bank, thick with weeds and finally made it to the shoulder of the road where they both collapsed, breathing heavily. Their sweat slicked chests heaved with effort as the now unimpeded rays of the Missouri sun beat down on their exhausted bodies.

 The filthy men closed their eyes, holding up arms across their faces to shield them from the relentless rays of the blazing sun. They lay that way for a time catching their breath, quietly rehearsing what they would say if the cops came looking for them. It wasn't the first time the two delinquents were forced to hide out for a while.

There had been an elderly couple the two of them, along with four other guys, were forced to kill during a home invasion. The old couple had a son who got a glimpse of the murderous bunch leaving the scene and had gotten the cops all fired up. The cops furiously tried to put the pieces of the vicious crime together, but the street savvy thugs managed to stay ahead of them until it all blew over due to a lack of physical evidence. Dumb ass cops couldn't find they own asses with both hands without help, Curtis thought. No big thing.

Finally, unable to bear any more of the blistering heat, Curtis was just opening his tired eyes when a hostile, distinctly female voice shouted, "Don't move!"

Already certain of what he would see, Curtis blinked his eyes against the glare to find himself staring at the business end of a Smith & Wesson .40 caliber semiautomatic handgun. The dark hole of the barrel looked big enough to swallow his head. Swallowing hard, Curtis saw the female Sheriff's deputy's finger locked firmly on the trigger of her weapon. The moment was so clear and detailed, the violent thug could clearly see the red polish on the fingernail of her trigger finger. The deputy was clearly waiting and fully prepared for him to furnish her with a reason to pull the trigger.

Her thick southern accent and relatively soft voice did nothing to dull the grave severity of her words as she spoke again. "Both of you, turn over on your bellies and cross your hands behind your backs!" she said. Her no nonsense tone made it abundantly clear that any resistance would turn out badly for the two suspects.

Curtis obediently did as he was ordered, and as he rolled over, he could see the idea of making a break for it evident in Cleo's eyes. At that precise moment, another black and yellow cruiser slid to a stop, its tires throwing up gravel, at the shoulder of the road maybe fifteen feet away. Gritty dust and small stones peppered the two prone thugs a burly deputy rapidly jumped out of the car almost before it stopped moving and immediately drew his weapon. Aiming it at Cleo's head, he barked out orders nearly identical to those of his fellow deputy.

His tiny window of opportunity slammed shut and Cleo wisely complied. A few moments later both men were cuffed and stuffed, sitting uncomfortably in the back seats of the idling cruisers as several more law enforcement and even some news vans arrived. There were even three black unmarked sedans immediately identifiable as FBI.

Apparently, their female captive's abruptly terminated, 911 call started the legal wheels in motion, and a second call from an anonymous source gave the St. Louis County Sheriff's office almost the exact location where they would find the two, newly designated armed kidnappers. Curtis sat, silently fuming, behind the Plexiglas divider separating the front of the squad car from the back. If they could have just been able to make it back to the city, he knew they could have eluded capture until the heat died down. How the hell did they find us so damn fast, he wondered. As he watched the prisoner transport van pull up, Curtis abruptly realized that with kidnapping, assault, attempted rape and armed robbery charges just to start with, he and Cleo would have a long, long time to think about it all.

Gabriel made sure Camella was in good hands at St. Alexius Hospital in St. Louis. Although her physical injuries were healed, Gabriel wanted a detailed record of her terrifying ordeal so that the human predators who victimized her would not slip through the cracks of an overworked and grossly understaffed justice system. To that end, the doctors and nurses who examined Camella saw her as she had been before Gabriel's touch healed her. Every cut, scrape and bruise was plainly visible during her examination. Even her severely sprained ankle appeared to be red, badly swollen and painful. At first, Camella was puzzled as to why the hospital staff were all being so overly cautious and apologetic every time, they touched her. Then, she accidentally caught a look at her chart when one of the nurses laid it down on a small instrument stand near her bed. Her eyes opened wide as saucers in surprise, but she instinctively held her tongue. She made direct eye contact with Gabriel as he peered through the glass door of the exam room. He was turning to leave, and with powerful emotion welling up in her throat, she mouthed the words thank you, a single tear slipping from her left eye.

He smiled, holding his large palm against the glass and then just like that, he was gone. Her timely rescuer had made no demands or requests of her. She had offered to pay him, but he staunchly declined. The big man had literally saved her life and wanted absolutely nothing in return.

Camella found she could no longer deny what she had held for so long as a ridiculous notion. God WAS real, after all. She made a silent, solemn vow to herself and to God that she would show Him, from now on, just how truly grateful she was. Furthermore, if her unforeseen rescuer ever needed anything she could provide, she would not hesitate for one second to assist him with whatever he might need.

FIFTH CHAPTER

Jason was just getting out of the shower. Wrapped in a thick cotton towel, he used a smaller one to briskly dry his short, sandy blonde hair. He sported a neatly trimmed mustache, a shade darker than the hair on his head and a triangular growth of hair beneath his lower lip, commonly called a "soul patch". His eyes were light green, and he now had a smooth, healthy complexion deeply bronzed from extensive time spent outdoors in the warm sun during his recent rehabilitation. Looking in the mirror, he reflected on the radical changes he'd undergone in the past six months. He had put on so much weight and increased muscle mass that he sometimes still didn't recognize the face looking back at him in the mirror. As he finished brushing his teeth, there was a knock at his apartment door. He wiped his mouth with his damp washcloth, then tossed it in a laundry hamper in the corner of the bathroom.

He opened the door and found Gabe smiling down at him. He just couldn't get used to the guy's height. He actually seemed taller than six feet eight inches. Jason finally understood what the phrase "Larger than life" actually meant.

"We have work to do my friend, are you ready?" Gabe said. Jason's heart began beating faster and a rush of adrenaline surged through his frame at the chance to help the man who had literally rescued him from himself as much as from the three goons in the alley. "I am soooo ready." Jason said, returning the smile. "Just give me a few minutes to get dressed and get my stuff together." Jason felt like a kid on Christmas morning. God was actually going to use him. He didn't worry or even ask what the work would entail because it really didn't matter. There was nothing that could be asked of him that he would refuse. He simply wanted to be of use. With practiced efficiency, he quickly got dressed and stuffed a prepared list of tools and equipment that he might need in a large canvas backpack. He was ready to leave in just under five minutes.

Gabe waited in the kitchen, helping himself to a glass of orange juice. He was placing it, washed and rinsed, in a dish rack on the counter next to the sink as Jason emerged from his bedroom. His young friend was ready for work in well-worn jeans, comfortable boots, and a dark blue, short sleeved t-shirt. There was a light jacket in his backpack as well, just in case. Gabriel had informed him there was often no predicting where they might be needed. It was best to be prepared.

Jason opened his eyes when Gabriel told him it was ok. For a second, he was completely disoriented. One moment, the two of them were standing in Jason's apartment. Gabriel told him to close his eyes and recite The Lord's Prayer to himself, repeating it, if necessary. Gabe said it was very important for him to focus solely on the prayer and nothing else.

Jason did as he was instructed and had only finished the first mental recital when Gabe told him to open his eyes. Taking a moment to get his bearings, Jason noticed several things simultaneously.

First, he noticed several powerful, conflicting odors. He and Gabe were standing in a littered alley, in what Jason instinctively felt was a downtown area. The sounds of pedestrian and vehicle traffic blending together. In addition to the typical smells of an alley, decomposing garbage in commercial dumpsters, the sour smell of urine, he could smell the almost overpowering, unmistakable odor of a nearby paper mill. It was a smell he remembered from living near one as a child. There was also the fishy, muddy smell of a large body of water, like a nearby lake or river.

As he assimilated the more unpleasant odors, he began picking out the distinct, enticing smell of several different varieties of cuisine. He smelled fresh seafood, the smoky sweet tang of barbecue and the mouthwatering aroma of pizza, among others. On cue, Jason's stomach growled loudly, and he realized he hadn't eaten breakfast before Gabe arrived. As he stood there, he abruptly realized that he knew they were in Savannah, Georgia. He couldn't have explained *how* he knew; he just knew.

After a few seconds Gabe's deep, clear voice pulled him from his reflections. "You'll get used to it." He said, a wry smile on his face.

"Ok," Jason said. "Why are we here?"

"Very soon, a good man will need our help. He doesn't know it yet, but his faith is about to be tested," the big man answered. Since Gabe was still in his "civvies" Jason figured nothing was about to happen right away so…..

"Ok, then do we have time to get a little something to eat?" Jason asked, his best Oliver Twist expression displayed on his face.

Gabriel looked down at his friend with a grin and said, "I know the perfect place."

Twenty minutes later, Gabe sat across from Jason on the other side of a small, neatly decorated table, situated beneath a large bay window, in a middle of the road eatery. The restaurant was located on the famous River Street in the Southern coastal city of Savannah.

Jason and Gabe had a clear, panoramic view of the harbor and the comings and goings of various freighters and support craft. Named The Prime Catch, the scrupulously clean restaurant's theme was typical of many coastal cities in its nautical motif. The walls were festooned with canoes, old wooden paddles and fishing nets littered with shells and starfish. There were lanterns affixed, in various methods, to the walls and ceiling of the rustic, wood framed, structure.

There was even an authentic, Atlantic seagull, skillfully immortalized by a popular, local taxidermist. It appeared to stare at them, with its beady black artificial eyes. The stuffed aquatic bird perched on a white, freshly painted wooden post, at the head of a short flight of stairs leading from the entrance, at ground level, to the upstairs dining area overlooking the murky river outside.

Swinging his gaze from the intense scrutiny of the mummified avian scavenger, Gabe reflected on his younger companion, currently wolfing down his second plate of sausage, eggs over medium and rye toast with blackberry jam along with a side of grits.

Gabe smiled and reflected on how much the affable young man had changed in the short-time they had been associated. When they first met, without God's intervention, Gabe wouldn't have given the man favorable odds of seeing the new year come in. But now, Jason was healthy, happy and chomping at the bit to help someone else the way God had helped him. At first, Jason had tried to give his gratitude and credit for his rescue to Gabe, but the big man quickly corrected him. Gabe told Jason, who at the time, was still painfully thin, that all the credit and praise for the changes in his life were to be given to God and God alone. "The things you see me do," he'd said, "are not of me. They are nothing that you, yourself can't do, if you will just have faith and KNOW, to the core of your soul, that God will make it so." Jason had given him a look that was both confused, and full of wonder. That God was real, had heard his cry, and sent an agent to rescue him was an incredibly powerful and nearly overwhelming revelation. Tears flowed from the tortured young man's eyes like a salty river as he poured forth all of the reasons, he hadn't been worth saving to Gabriel's willing and sympathetic ears. It all came out in a shame filled torrent of self-hatred and selfishness. When he was finally spent, torn down and utterly humble, Gabriel began lifting him up. "That's why He sent me Jason," he said. "Those are His children who can be of greatest use. Those who have reached the bottom and found themselves with nowhere to turn. Because it is at that time, when your soul is empty, that He can come in and fill it to overflowing. You can't pour water into a full cup. The water just flows over the rim and runs off to be wasted. When you're hungry, starving for grace, that's when He can truly feed you with the holy word of God.

Once you have dined from that table and keep yourself true to Him, you will never be hungry again."

Jason took to the word like mother's milk, and promptly began reviewing and studying, not only the Bible, but as many arguments against Christianity as he could find. Gabriel had been amazed at Jason's keen mind. A mind long obscured and clouded by the poisonous drugs he had so willingly flooded it with. In no time at all, Jason proved to be more than just another reclaimed soul. He was now a fellow soldier in the crucial war Gabriel was fighting. The war that was entering a new phase in the history of man. Lucifer was stepping up his influence on Earth to the point that chaos was more the rule than the exception. In the United States, gun violence was at an all-time high. Men and women were increasingly using the deadly weapons to cry out for attention, even if it was their final act. Innocent lives were being lost, including children, which were most precious to God. There were so many atrocities being committed in His name, they defied counting and there were now more displaced refugees than at the end of World War II. Humanity had given up on God in all but a honorific sense.

So, The Lord decided to refresh their memory before He would be forced to wipe the slate clean once again. Gabriel's mission in life was to remind mankind of their unique and precious spiritual connection with God. The immense power that originated with the creator was present in each and every man, woman, and child who accepted him and believed in him with all their hearts. Gabriel would show them God's unmatched power, channeled through a human being, just like them. He would tell them that nothing he did was impossible for them, if they would only believe it. And now, it was not just him anymore. It was at that point that Jason looked up from his once again empty plate and noticed Gabe watching him. With a blackberry jam laced grin, Jason said, "What?"

"I hope you at least tasted that." Gabe said, smiling.

"I did," Jason answered, wiping his mouth with a napkin. "It was yummy!" Jason answered, closing his eyes and contentedly patting his full belly.

"I'm glad." Gabe said. Even when he spoke quietly there was a deep, powerful quality to his voice. "You're going to need your strength, it's time to get to work." With that, he stood. Jason followed his tall companion after leaving money on the table to pay for their meals with a nice gratuity for their server. He was excited and a little nervous, but ready to enter the fray.

SIXTH CHAPTER

In the coastal Georgia city of Savannah, there was a great deal of history and atmosphere. Spanish moss hung like draperies from trees lining the long boulevards of the city. As with any city of decent size, however, the inner city was rife with criminals, always intent on gleaning all the cash possible from the abundant tourist crowds, either voluntarily or by force. The Russian mob was an expert at exploiting both tourists and merchants to shake any available cash loose. Vitaly Gorsky was the Russian mob's man responsible for a vast region which encompassed Georgia, South Carolina, and Northern Florida. His assignment was to establish and develop illicit markets in these areas and manage the men set in place to maintain those enterprises. Gorsky was not the stereotypical mobster from the movies. He didn't like fancy suits or flashy jewelry, and more often than not travelled alone, without the cliche of being surrounded by a platoon of inept bodyguards. The main reason was because, although he was of a slight, wiry build, Gorsky was himself, a walking weapon and quite honestly did not need anyone to guard him. His service record before the collapse of the Soviet Union was a state secret. However, if one could view those records, they would learn he was an expert in seven different martial arts, including Sambo, Kung Fu, Jujitsu and Ninjitsu.

The unassuming Russian agent knew literally dozens of ways to kill a man or woman with no more than his bare hands. He was qualified expert with at least fifteen weapons and could drive any vehicle ever built. He was an expert in tactical strategy, demolitions, and he was also scuba certified. However, once the cold war was converted to mostly a digital front, and HUMINT, or Human Intelligence, on the ground became passe, his skills were less and less in demand. Being unmarketable as an assassin, Gorsky needed a way to earn a living.

Although, outwardly, he looked like a working-class citizen, his bank account had once been a point of pride with him. Only a year ago, however, he had been down to the last of his reserves. That was when a former comrade of his recruited him for an opportunity in America. With no ties to hold him in Moscow, Gorsky readily accepted the offer. Walking the picturesque streets of Savannah, he could smell the sea nearby, as well as the fetid odor of the paper mill that seemed inescapable. The odor didn't bother him though. In fact, he had become quite accustomed to it after only a couple of weeks after arriving in the city. Although there were at least fifty men and women assigned under his command, Gorsky preferred to add "new clients" to his roster in person.

The newest acquisition appeared before him as he rounded a corner from Abercorn Street to East Congress Street. Savannah is the oldest city in Georgia and is also the county seat of Chatham County. Established in 1733, on the Savannah River, it had been a British colonial capitol of the Province of Georgia. Gorsky loved the air of conflict and bloody battle that knowledge evoked. He stopped and took stock of the frontage on his new target. Dubbed "The Old Colonial Inn", it boasted an authentic looking Olde English storefront, complete with the scroll and banner type sign. Feeling the mild excitement in anticipation of dominating a new business owner, Gorsky stepped through the heavy wood and glass door.

Several smells competed for dominance within the old building. It was among the oldest buildings in Savannah, so there was the ancient smell of the river soaked into the wood of the structural members. There was also an aroma of newer materials that the owner had used to refurbish the dining area, kitchen and office space.

He also got a variance from the city to build an additional area onto the original building with a well-stocked bar and a dance floor, all with brand new materials. Over these scents was overlaid the smell of wonderful seafood dishes and some traditional American cuisine prepared by the owner's major investment, one of the less than 70 Certified Master Chefs in the United States. This expenditure, although initially a strain on the restaurant's finances, had been well worth the risk.

"Chef Louie", as he preferred to be called, was the major factor in the Inn's meteoric success. In fact, the business might soon have to relocate or build another venue to keep up with it's growing upscale clientele numbers. These numbers are what brought Gorsky to the Inn. Numbers meant money, and money was what the Russian was all about.

****

The owner of The Colonial Inn was Shepherd Andrews. Shep, as he was known to most, was well on his way to being a self-made millionaire. He started as a busboy and part time waiter at one of the better hotel restaurants in Savannah. He worked hard and was almost obsessive in learning every facet of the business. It had always been his dream to own the finest seafood eatery in the south, and so far, he had let nothing stand in his way of achieving that goal.

The driven young businessman willingly sacrificed any sort of a meaningful social life. Both, present and any possible future family was put on the back burner. He didn't worry about material possessions or anything else that could distract him from his ultimate goal. He consistently excelled at any task he was given, no matter how menial or insignificant it might seem. He got to work early every day and was almost always the last to leave at the end of the day.

Shep's supervisors all loved his hard working, positive attitude and were more than happy to teach the pleasant young man everything they knew. Now, at the age of thirty-five, Shep stood on the verge of making his mark in the upper crust social circles of Savannah and the surrounding area. He stood just under average height at five feet, eight inches and was almost unanimously considered by most of the female population to be very handsome, or more colloquially, "Hot". His thick, sandy blond hair was neatly tapered in the back and on the sides but worn longer on the top. He had a medium build, and although not as heavily muscled as a bodybuilder, Shep stayed in good physical shape.

His attire was dress casual on most days with an eye to the persona of a pragmatic yet fashion conscious entrepreneur. The Inn was his whole life and not one to trust all of the many details of running his investment to a general manager, Shep was a "hands on" owner.

He was at the restaurant every day from open to close and many days long after business hours which is the reason, he was standing behind the bar, taking inventory of liquor supplies, when three tough looking men casually strolled through the side door, normally used only for deliveries. Two of the men looked like extras from the set of the movie Rocky IV, massive mountains of thick, solid muscle on pillar-like legs. The men all wore well-tailored, short sleeved, dress shirts and tasteful slacks but the air of imminent danger surrounding them was all but palpable.

Nearly every inch of exposed skin was covered with intricate tattoo art and the uniform look on their craggy faces practically screamed killers. The third man was different, not quite as tall, although still above average height. He was less bulky than his companions, but trim and tautly muscled. However, his face was by far the most frightening of the group. He had the chilling carriage of a man who had been around, seen things, and been in places that most people never even knew existed.

His deep blue eyes, like chips of sapphire, were set in an angular face, smooth except for a scar shaped like a comet above his right eyebrow. Barry, Shep's trusted manager who also doubled as Maitre D', stepped over to address the three as they entered with a professionally pleasant, yet cautious, expression on his bearded face.

"Gentlemen," he said amicably, a touch of his native Georgia accent coloring his speech, "I'm afraid we haven't opened for supper yet. If you would like to come back at four, I'll be sure to get you a wonderful table by the window where you can watch the river as you enjoy your meal." As he spoke, Barry reached out his left arm, attempting to herd the group of men as he gestured with his right for them to exit back through the door they used to enter.

The man mountain on Barry's left reached out his tree branch of an arm and grabbed manager's left wrist in his huge right hand. With almost no effort at all he lifted medium built Maitre'D from the hardwood floor with one arm. The giant easily held the struggling man six inches off the floor, then tightened his steely grip as Barry grimaced in sudden pain and let out a sharp cry.

The nearly empty room echoed with the loud, gruesome crunch as the fragile bones in the Maître D's wrist shattered under the incredible pressure. Barry screamed in agony punching, ineffectually, with his right fist against the man's granite like side. His point now effectively made; the monstrous goon casually tossed Barry aside like a bag of trash. His injured friend slammed into the edge of the bar, and Shep clearly heard the whoosh of air rush from the man's lungs along with a dull crunch. Barry then dropped, bonelessly to the hardwood floor and lay frighteningly still.

"My name is Vitaly Gorsky" the smaller man said, with only the slightest trace of a Slavic accent. The man spoke as if nothing more had happened than someone coughing in the middle of his sentence. "As I am sure you have determined, we are not here for a meal."

As he spoke, all three slowly men walked towards Shep, one of them glancing back, occasionally to be sure the Maitre D' posed no threat. "Where is the owner of this establishment?" Gorsky said.

More angry than scared, Shep answered carefully, "I am the owner." he said, not completely able to hide the subdued rage in his voice.

"Good." Gorsky replied, "That saves us much time, yes?" He gestured toward Barry, lying unconscious on the floor. "As you can see," the Russian continued, "I do not have time for polite conversation. You have opened this business in an area that is under my protection."

"Protection from what?" Shep asked.

"There is much crime in this area." Gorsky replied. "Crackheads and heroin junkies to steal from your patrons, break into your building, vandalize or steal cars, all to finance their particular habits. Prostitutes will solicit your customers and bring unwanted police presence to the area." As Gorsky spoke, Shep waited for the other shoe to drop. He knew exactly where this conversation was headed. How much was this man's "protection" going to cost him?

"So how much do you want to "*protect*" me from these undesirable people?" he asked, cutting right to the chase.

"It is a relative bargain," Gorsky answered. "Only fifty percent of your net profit each week and you will sign over half ownership of the business to me."

Despite himself, Shep laughed out loud. He stopped abruptly when the third goon laid a wicked backhanded slap across his face. It felt like being hit with a baseball bat. Blood flew from Shep's mouth, and his knees buckled. He nearly lost consciousness, but his assailant grabbed him by his shirt with both meaty hands and jerked him up halfway across the bar his feet dangling in the air.

Now situated below them, Gorsky looked up at the beleaguered businessman.

"Not a laughing matter I think," he said. "You will have the papers drawn up when we return tomorrow. If you do not, I think your restaurant will have a very short history with a sad, tragic ending. Do we understand each other?" the mob boss asked.

Shep's eyes refused to focus and his grip on consciousness was shaky at best. Still, Shep knew he needed to buy time. Not trusting his ability to speak without vomiting, he simply nodded his understanding.

"I'm sure I don't need to tell you that this matter is between us businessmen, not the police, yes?" Shep nodded, once again indicating he understood. "Good, then I will see you at this time tomorrow." The big goon let go of him, and Shep had all he could do to stay on his feet, both hands tightly gripping the edge of the polished wood bar. As the three men went out the door, Gorsky turned back and added, "Partner."

SIXTH CHAPTER

Two hours later, Shep sat beside Barry's bed in the emergency room of Candler Memorial hospital. The on-call doctor told him that Barry would need surgery to repair his injured wrist. The doctor appeared skeptical that a man had broken the limb with nothing more than his bare hand. He told Shep that both bones in Barry's forearm had been completely crushed, as if the arm had been squeezed in a vice. Barry also had four broken ribs that had been wrapped and braced. He was extremely lucky not to have punctured a lung, according to the doctor. Barry had been Shep's best friend since they met in his early days of college and was actually a silent partner in Shep's business. As he watched his only true friend sleep, seriously injured and loaded with painkillers, Shep knew he couldn't risk anyone else getting hurt, or worse, but fifty percent? It was ridiculous!
He wouldn't even be able to clear a profit, he would basically be working just to pay Gorsky. But what could he do? Almost all of his hard-earned money had gone into extensively refurbishing the inn. He had no available reserves to pay for additional security, and he had no idea how big the apparently ruthless Russian's operation might be. He couldn't just give up though, there had to be some way out of this, there just had to be!

Wearily leaning over in his chair, Shep put his elbows on the edge of the hospital bed and clasped his hands together. He put his head down on top of them, closed his eyes and silently began to pray. Having been brought up in a devoutly Southern Baptist home with a strong staunchly religious mother, Shep was taught early on who to ask for help when no one else could do anything about your situation. There, in the hospital, at the end of his wits and with Barry as a silent witness, Shep earnestly laid his petition before the Lord.

SEVENTH CHAPTER

Gabriel sat quietly at prayer, in the guest bedroom of a large historic colonial home, not far from downtown Savannah. Jason was out familiarizing himself with the area. Gabe had assured him they wouldn't begin their assignment for a bit yet, and they both agreed it would be a good practice for the younger man to quickly acclimate himself to a new area. It was also something of a shopping excursion to acquire some of the computer equipment that Jason would need to assist Gabe when the time came. As was his habit, the big man sat cross legged on the hardwood floor, his powerful hands clasped in his lap, eyes closed. The pleasant aroma of the authentic cedar chest at the foot of his bed filled his nostrils, along with the equally comforting smell of sage and citrus from a candle warmer down the hall.

The spacious home where he and Jason found lodging belonged to a wonderfully friendly couple, both native to Savannah. The elderly pair Ezra Gibson and his charming wife of 61 years, Ruth. Gabe and Jason met the old couple while walking in the area near River Street, getting a feel for the place. Of course, Ezra and his wife had no idea that they were part of any plan in befriending the two nice young men from out of town.

Offering their vacant spare bedrooms just seemed the right thing to do when they discovered the two men had no place to stay at the moment. The Gibson's children had long since grown up and moved away, starting families of their own and the big house was quiet and empty except for holidays and special occasions. The two men being white never even factored into the couple's gracious decision. Having been devoted, active members of their church for most of their adult lives, they didn't see people as colors, just as people. Ezra was a short man with tightly curled hair cropped short on his head. Although gray as winter snow clouds, it was thick and full. His short legs were prominently bowed as if he'd been born on a horse, and his back was bent with age and a lifetime of hard work. His tough skin was weathered and dark as tanned leather from years outside in the Georgia sun, and he had a sprinkling of moles across his cheeks and neck. But the old man's eyes were bright and clear as purified water. Brown as oak, outlined by the bluish, telltale ring of macular degeneration, his irises stood out starkly against the untarnished whites of eyes that had never known drug or drink. When he spoke, the rich timbre of his deep voice sounded like it would be more suited to singing rather than something as ordinary and mundane as talking.

Ezra's loving wife, Ruth, was also short in stature, but there most of the similarity to her long-time spouse ended. Ruth was what was widely described in the south as a "Red Bone". Her extremely light brown skin was flawless and smooth, belying her advanced age with a near complete absence of wrinkles. Her eyes were hazel green, and like her husband's, had the bluish ring around the iris, and looked to be perpetually on the verge of twinkling with laughter. Solidly built and still very strong, Ruth was a truly lovely woman with an abundance of true class and an air of genuine dignity about her that could never be removed.

A true southern belle, Gabe and Jason's attentive hostess dutifully saw to her guest's comfort with elegance and poise, never showing the slightest hint of discourtesy. Her hair was, amazingly, still almost completely black as polished ebony with only thin streaks of white just above either temple. It was silky, very long, and customarily worn in an immaculate french braid that ended just above her lower back. Eschewing a flashy appearance, the only jewelry she wore was her wedding rings and a small gold crucifix on a delicate chain of the same metal around her neck.

It had been given to her by the couple's oldest granddaughter years ago when the now grown woman was just a child. Ruth had not taken it off since that day. As Gabe communed with God, he offered sincere thanks for the exceedingly kind couple and their generous hospitality. Although any and all of his needs were provided, without exception, Gabe never failed to take time and thank the Lord for his blessings or took anything for granted.

When in prayer, Gabe concentrated on totally opening his mind to God and becoming a willing receiver for whatever instructions were forthcoming. This quite often was relayed to him in the form of images or symbols which were then deciphered in his mind by a means Gabe could not explain. He thought of the process as God translating the language of heaven into English. Like deep meditation, this holy trance would often carry him to a different plane of existence.

He could often see himself, as if from above and frequently he would begin to see images of unfamiliar people and new places he had never encountered. He learned quickly, in the beginning, that these were details and instructions concerning what he was supposed to do, where he should go, and who he needed to help.

The images were deeply layered with information, like code or encryption, embedded within them. Times, locations, weather, potential hazards and locations of resources all were available to him within each viewed image. More often than not, the Holy Warrior would find himself swept along as if riding in a boat on a fast-moving river, watching as events unfolded before him like a feature film. When he emerged from prayer, he would possess all the knowledge he needed to fulfill his mission.

Finishing his prayers for now, Gabe gracefully rose from the floor beside the large four poster bed in his room. As he stood, there was a soft knock on the door. He opened it and found his hostess standing in the hallway.

Wearing a long bright yellow sundress with blue and white flowers along the bottom hem, she looked for all the world like she'd stepped out of a *Good Housekeeping* magazine. Her twinkling eyes looked up at her guest, and Gabe saw she was carrying a steaming cup of tea and a small assortment of cookies on an ornate silver tray.

He could tell the tray was very old, but it was spotlessly clean and polished to perfection, probably only used for company. "I thought you might like a little something to hold you over until supper" Ruth said, craning her neck to look up into Gabe's face.

Her voice was soft and delicate with a cultured, demure quality rarely passed down to most women of younger generations.

"Thank you very much, Mrs. Gibson." he replied with a warm smile.

"Oh please, young man," she said, as he stepped aside making room for her to enter, "Call me Ruth."

"Yes Ma'am," he said, "I mean Ruth." She chuckled softly as she set the tray down on the coffee table in front of an old-style divan beneath the bedroom window. Outside the window was a large cypress tree draped with the ever-present Spanish moss common in the region.

As she turned to leave the room, Ruth looked up at the big man and said, "Now if there's anything else you need you just let us know Sugar." She pronounced it "Shugah".

"Yes Ma'am." Gabe answered.

After Ruth left, he thought to himself, it was unlikely that he or Jason would require anything further from the kindly old couple tonight. His prayers had showed him that they would both be busy this evening.

****

It was nearing eight o'clock as Gabe and Jason walked along, soaking up the historic atmosphere that permeated downtown Savannah. The lively buzz of the city's robust tourism industry was clearly evident as the two men approached the newly refurbished Colonial Inn. With still nearly two hours of sunlight left to the day, a gentle evening breeze swept through the canopy of moss-covered trees keeping the summer temperature more bearable and the stifling humidity at bay. As Jason and Gabe neared the restaurant, they judged by the number of cars parked in the adjacent lot and along the street that the place was opening to the prospect of very good business. As they got closer to the entrance, a heavy set of wooden double doors with polished nickel handles, and both men noticed several inadequately dressed women on the sidewalk in front of the restaurant. They all wore lots of cheap, heavy makeup and their various outfits had obviously been selected to showcase as much flesh as was permissible by law.

The women didn't appear to be waiting to dine at the establishment, and as Gabe and Jason got close enough to hear their conversation, they discovered why. A well-heeled, middle aged couple had just stepped out of a sleek silver Mercedes, and as the valet carefully eased away from the curb to park it, the two men could see the look of profound distaste on the clean shaven face of the man. He shook his head dismissively as he hurriedly attempted to shepherd his wife past the crude women.

One of the hookers, a thin blond woman with a large tattoo of a dragon across her nearly bare, surgically enhanced chest was aggressively making her pitch. The man was trying to be polite and maneuver around the woman, but she quickly stepped in front of the embarrassed pair and persisted. The man's wife dressed casually, but stylish in a business suit, shot a withering look of barely veiled disgust at the uncouth prostitute.

The blond, who was *almost* wearing an extremely inadequate halter top and red leather short shorts, so tight it was amazing she could breathe, stuck her tongue out at the woman through the thick red paint on her collagen filled lips. Her spiked high heels adorned with blue glitter, made her tower over both the visibly angry woman and her increasingly uncomfortable husband. As Gabe and Jason passed nearby, they heard the blond woman say, in her gravelly cigarette induced alto, "Come on Baby, you don't know what you're missing! I'll take good care of **both** of you." She was trying hard and failing miserably to cover her thick Slavic accent.

Both men could smell the potent reek of alcohol on her breath, even out in the open. At this final insult to her senses the wife had clearly reached the limit of tolerance. "Charles!" she said, through tightly gritted teeth, insistently tugging at her nonplussed husband's arm. Her tone left no room for argument, and she was evidently ready to body check the blond if necessary.

The disgusted couple nearly ran over Gabe and Jason in their rush to escape the lewdly aggressive streetwalker. The jilted working girl bellowed scathing obscenities in at least two languages at the couple's retreating backs, graphically gesturing to show her displeasure at the rejection. Gabe and Jason shared a knowing look, noting the incident and mentally filing it away for later consideration. Finally making it inside, The Colonial Inn's rich tastefully appointed atmosphere took over. The wonderfully cool air and solid stone walls soothed away the moist heat and excess noise from the street.

As Jason confirmed their reservation, Gabe heard the wife of
the couple from outside giving the acting Maitre D' an earful
at the disgrace of being accosted by such gutter trash. The
poor man looked exactly like a school kid being reprimanded
by an angry teacher. The last-minute stand-in for the Maitre
D' worked for a temp service and was only filling in due to an
accident involving the regular guy.

He effusively assured the furious woman that he would take
care of the situation immediately and guaranteed her that for
the inconvenience, their drinks and appetizers would be on
the house. Seemingly mollified, the couple followed the man
to their table.

After being seated by an expansive window overlooking the
river, Gabe and Jason were treated to the gorgeous tapestry of
breathtaking colors as the dwindling sun sank lower in the
evening sky. Dinner progressed smoothly and the two men
talked about their lives as they enjoyed their meals. Gabe
filled Jason in on some of the particulars concerning the
members of his large family. Jason was filled with empathy as
Gabe described the unexpected death of his beloved mother
about five years ago. He had been home for the funeral as
were all his siblings except one. His younger brother, Jimmy
who had only recently returned home from combat in
Afghanistan, simply couldn't bring himself to come to the
funeral.

Jason could tell there was a lot more to the story, but the gist
was that Jimmy, a solitary man by nature, had met a girl in the
service and she had been"the one". She was a fellow soldier, a
combat medic in the young soldier's unit. He had fallen in
love with the bright, funny young woman and fallen hard.
The girl was everything Jimmy could have ever dreamed of.

The two spent every second they could together and planned to get married in a few months when their tour of duty was over. Details were a little sketchy about the next part, but apparently, Jimmy's fiancé had been trapped behind enemy lines and captured. Jimmy's unit sent in a rescue team, and against his supervisor's advice, Jimmy went along on the mission. The mission failed, and Amanda, Jimmy's fiancé, was brutally murdered, evidently right before the young soldier's eyes. It was horrible, and Gabe, after taking a moment to collect his thoughts, apologized to Jason for bringing up such a sad subject.

After that, the two men deliberately spoke about more cheerful things and allowed themselves to fully enjoy the moment. The cuisine at the Colonial Inn was excellent and the service top notch. Obviously, the chef Shep had retained was among the elite. Every course of their respective meals was perfectly prepared, fresh, and delicious, with just the right amount of seasonings and generous portions. Jason was beginning to think maybe they weren't in the right place when the evening suddenly took a turn for the worse.

EIGHTH CHAPTER

Shep was making his rounds through the dining room, attentively checking to make sure every customer was satisfied and enjoying their meals. He made mental notes to himself about this or that person on his wait staff as well as which entrees seemed to be the most popular. These were things he needed to know in order to keep enough of the more in demand items on hand while avoiding things that might end up being wasted, costing him much needed revenue. Just as he was heading in to check on the kitchen staff, there was a loud crash, a woman's startled shriek, and a sudden loud commotion from that area. Linda, manager of his service team, abruptly came barreling through the swinging door leading to the back, a shrill scream still bursting from her throat. A petite, handsome woman, she had a slim, athletic build. Her long, salt and pepper-streaked hair worn in a flawlessly tight French braid, Linda was normally the picture of southern grace and composure. For anything to get such a drastically out of character reaction from her, Shep knew it had to be serious. He started to grab the obviously terrified woman by the shoulders to find out what was going on when he heard more crashing and the distinct smacking sound of flesh striking flesh. Then a male voice cried out in sheer agony, and Shep hurried into the abnormally chaotic kitchen. Pots, pans, and various other cookware was strewn across the floor of the entire space.

The pair of huge, hulking Russians were back and were apparently doing their level best to destroy everything and everyone in the kitchen. One assistant cook lay prone and unconscious, face down on the tile floor. The chef, Lou, a short rotund, perpetually cheerful man with a thick red beard and a head full of untamed curls the same color was down on his knees on the floor between the prep island and the line of stoves.

One of the big Russians held the front of the chef's apron wrapped in his heavily scarred fist, repeatedly bashing Lou's already bloody face even though the plump defenseless man was clearly unconscious. The other half of the twin towers had the remaining chef's apprentice, a tall, rail thin young man named Chad, pinned against the door of the walk-in cooler. He was holding the squirming young man nearly three feet off the floor with his left hand dangling by his long thick ponytail and was gleefully hammering his other fist into the young man's abdomen.

Shep heard a loud sharp crack of a bone breaking and realized the harrowing scream he'd heard earlier had come from him as the horrifying sound was repeated. Shep shouted to be heard over the din. "Hey!" he yelled, "Stop! What are you guys doing? Please, you're killing them!"

The nearest thug, the one holding the nearly insensate chef, turned to Shep. "This kind of thing happens a lot when you have no protection." He said, with a chillingly casual air.

As far as the two slavic monsters were concerned, they could just as well have been stomping cockroaches or trapping mice. The other mob goon chimed in, "It can be really hard to make profit with no staff." He said, his accent much more pronounced.

Shep was grief stricken and torn. This business was his dream, but how could he justify allowing his employees to be subjected to this kind of needless torture and pain? How many patrons would come to a place with lewd prostitutes and foul-smelling bums panhandling on the sidewalk? With a final, silent plea to God for help, the defeated man resigned himself to bitter failure, forced to capitulate, when a deep, powerful voice filled the room from the doorway behind him. "Gentlemen'" the voice said. "The best thing for you to do is to let go of those men, right now, and leave quietly the same way you came in." Shep's head snapped around, startled at the unexpected sound. He found himself looking up at an incredibly tall, powerfully built man accompanied by another less massive man just behind him. The second man was very muscular and obviously fit as well, though several inches shorter and not nearly as imposing. What struck Shep, immediately however, was the fact that neither man had the nervous, adrenaline-fueled look of fight or flight, one would expect for the situation. Both looked as calm and totally relaxed as if they just stepped into a barbershop for a haircut. The mountainous Russians looked perplexed, as if not knowing whether to attack or laugh. After a second's pause, the one with the less pronounced accent took charge of the situation. "I don't know who you are," he said, "but you should mind your own business and leave now while you can still use your legs to do it."

As the brute spoke the last few words his thick black eyebrows drew together, and a dark dangerous tone colored his suggestion. When neither of the two intruders showed any signs of backing out of the conflict, the Russian goons dropped their previous victims who both fell unconscious to the floor. The two slavic bruisers turned ready and willing to face this new, unanticipated threat, and Shep, cautiously stepping back from between the four men, could see the huge thugs sizing up the new arrivals. The totally confused but grateful restaurant owner then began to slowly make his way to see to his seriously injured employees.

Truthfully, Shep expected his would-be rescuers to suddenly think better of their rash decision to intervene and beat a hasty retreat. However, on the contrary, both men moved further into the kitchen to meet the challenge the violent Russian gangsters. Then, the larger of the two, who had initially spoken, said something so unexpected, Shep wondered if he had heard him correctly. "The choice is yours to make my friend."

His utterly calm tone genuinely sounded patient and kind, not at all like someone about to engage in a fight, possibly for his life. "If you leave this life of crime and violence you are living, right now, tonight, there can be true redemption and tender mercy. If you don't, the consequences of that choice will be swift and just." A second later, the wrecked kitchen was filled with the incredulous laughter of the two Russian mobsters.

After a moment, the more talkative of the two wiped a tear from his eye with the back of his bloody hand, then pointed a thick finger at his unexpected opponent.   "You?" he said, "*You* are giving *us* choices? I tell you what, my funny friend.

I will give you a choice. Walk out of here, right now, or be carried out later." As he uttered the last words of his threat, his cruel face darkened and his voice took on a deadly timbre, leaving no doubt that this was no idle threat. The entire room, now ominously quiet, fairly crackled with dangerous tension as the inevitable confrontation between the two opposing forces reached critical mass.

After a few seconds, as it became obvious that the verbal threat hadn't sent the two, clearly suicidal, intruders running for the exit, the lead Russian made his move. There was a large meat cleaver laying on a wooden cutting board near one end of the prep island. Snatching the blade up, the big Russian lunged at Gabe with impressive speed for such a big man. With a roar of contempt, he swung the razor-sharp cleaver in a wicked downward arc with the intention of burying it in the tall intruder's skull. Gabe stood, unflinching and motionless as impending doom swiftly approached.

At the last possible second, in a lightning swift move, Gabe reached up with his left hand. He grasped the charging behemoth's descending wrist so quickly the man hadn't even realized his arm was no longer moving before Gabriel's hard right fist crashed into his thick, square jaw with devastating force. The three hundred plus pound thug suddenly shot backwards, airborne, crashing through pots and pans hanging, suspended on a rack above the central island. The assorted cookware sounded like unorthodox wind chimes the beast's giant frame smashed through them. The Russian mobster sailed nearly twenty feet across the room, where he crashed, headlong, into the polished steel door of the walk-in freezer.

His shiny bald head left a sizable dent as the big man slid unconscious to the floor. The other thug heard the clatter in his periphery, but his attention was primarily focused on the smaller of the two unwelcome intruders.

When his associate made his move for the meat cleaver, the other half of the bald duo rushed Jason. He reached out his thickly muscled arms toward the smaller man, intending to grab him by the throat and lift him from the floor thereby eliminating his presumably more agile opponent's mobility. But as his powerful hands reached his target, they encountered only empty space. Jason skillfully ducked under the big man's grasping paws, launching an astonishingly rapid series of short brutal punches into the right side of his larger attacker's exposed rib cage. The vicious kidney punches suddenly robbed the thug of air as he dropped to one knee. Before the man could catch his breath, Jason launched a spinning back kick that connected solidly to the side of his smooth head, dropping him to the floor like a sack of wet cement.

Shep stood, his jaw hanging slack in awe as he realized what had just happened. The two unstoppable behemoths, who had effortlessly decimated his staff had themselves, just been easily taken down in a matter of seconds. Now that the immediate danger had passed, the restauranter's first, overriding concern was for his injured employees. With no further obstacles in his path, Shep rushed quickly to the fallen men and began checking on them. After confirming, with great relief, that all three men were still breathing, Shep turned to thank his timely rescuers and found himself alone with the three unconscious members of his staff.

He heard the high-pitched warbling of police sirens approaching and assumed that Linda must have had called 911 after she fled the sudden violence in the kitchen.

To Shep's huge surprise, he realized only a few minutes had passed since he nearly collided with the flustered woman in her panicked escape from the kitchen. It seemed as if hours had passed while he stood, helplessly watching his employees being brutalized. There was a surreal, dreamlike quality to the entire experience. If not for the very real devastation in the kitchen and his three bloody staff members, he might've believed he imagined the whole thing. His worried examination of the three men revealed they all were badly beaten, but all three were breathing and their pulses were steady and strong, thank God. Shep heard the police entering the building, the somehow comforting sounds of traffic on their two-way radios filling the nearly empty dining room and now he could hear the familiar high/low wail of an ambulance siren. A heavy sigh escaped him as Shep faced the grim prospect of another long night in the hospital.

Deciding to stop and check on Barry, the first casualty of this business fiasco, before heading to the emergency room, Shep made his way to his friend's room on the fifth floor. As he neared the room, he spotted a nurse and a man he presumed to be a doctor, leaving his friend's room. They two of them were looking at charts on a clipboard and holding up x-rays to the ceiling lights, shaking their heads in obvious disbelief. A sense of dread filled Shep, and he feared the worst. Quickening his pace, Shep hurried into the room, only to find his dear friend standing, wide awake beside the bed, placing his belongings from the hospital into a plastic bag. "Barry?" Shep said, in a greatly surprised voice. Barry turned around to greet his old friend and Shep then saw that there was no cast on his badly broken arm. In fact, he was now moving that arm with all his usual dexterity. "Hey Boss!" Barry said, with a bright, seemingly pain free smile, and held his arms out wide in welcome. Unable to disguise his total shock, Shep gladly accepted the warm bear hug of affection his oldest friend gave him.

"What happened?" Shep asked. "The last time I was here, you looked like roadkill!" Barry chuckled at his boss' colorful description of his formerly grave condition and shook his head in response.

"I can't explain it Boss. Late last night, I was just laying here, kinda in and out because of all the pain meds, ya know? But in one of the more awake times, I could suddenly feel someone else in the room. At first, I was terrified, because I didn't hear the door open, which is weird because it squeaks. Anyway, I look up and see this huge guy standing beside my bed. Well, I tell you, I was scared shitless, figured one of those mob bastards was back to finish me off. Then the fear passed, as if I somehow knew the guy wasn't here to hurt me. He was wearing what looked like white robes and all white clothes. To tell you the truth, Shep, I thought he was an angel." As he told the story, Barry's grey eyes seemed to momentarily lose focus, as if he were seeing the strange figure all over again. "Anyway, he reached down and put his hand on my forehead," he continued. "I remember feeling really warm and comfortable, like curling up in my flannel onesie when I was little. And the warmth seemed to start in my arm and my side and spread "out to the rest of my body."

Shep was intrigued, having his own unbelievable tale to relay. "Did he say anything to you?" he asked.

Barry nodded his head and, placing his hand on Shep's forehead to demonstrate, he answered, "he said one word, rest. Then I fell asleep, and I'm telling you Shep, I honestly haven't slept that good in years. When I woke up this morning, all the pain was just…. gone, even the bruises!" Barry held up his arm, pulling back the sleeve of his shirt so his friend could see. "The nurse couldn't believe it when she came in to give me my morning pain medication. She ran out and called the doc, and they did some more x-rays right away. That was two hours ago. They were just here a minute ago and told me everything is normal now! Even the scar on my forearm, from when I burned my arm on an iron when I was a kid, is gone. They can't figure it out! They're saying it's some kind of a miracle."

Shep listened to Barry's incredible story and his mind immediately returned to the two defenders from last night. After the paramedics had left to take his injured employees to the hospital, the mystified restaurant owner searched the dining room, the parking lot and even the surrounding streets, wanting to sincerely thank the two timely Samaritans but they were nowhere to be found. Barry's voice snapped his mind back to the here and now.

"So how did the night go without your right-hand man, Chief?" Barry asked. Not wishing to spoil his friend's jovial mood, Shep simply told him everything was fine and no one even noticed he wasn't there. The two good friends shared a good-natured laugh of longtime friendship, then Shep hugged his friend, once again and told him how glad he was that Barry was ok, even if it defied explanation. After agreeing to see each other at work later, Shep headed down to the emergency room to check on his three most recent casualties of war. Twenty minutes later, he left the hospital in a state of befuddlement. He'd expected to find one or all three men in the intensive care unit but was told by the staff that all of them had been treated and released from the emergency room shortly after their arrival.

Shep was at a total loss to explain it. He had mentally steeled himself for the tragic news that one of them might even have died as a result of such grievous injuries.

As he left the hospital, on the way back to his car, Shep called all the men, in succession, on his mobile phone, getting three more stories almost identical to Barry's. Standing in the relatively cool shade of a moss-covered elm tree near the parking lot, Shep wondered what in the world was going on? How could all three men be perfectly healthy so soon after such savage beatings. Deciding not to look a gift horse in the mouth, Shep allowed the smile he had been subconsciously suppressing, to spread across his tanned face.

His spirits high from all the good news, Shep whistled cheerfully as he drove deciding to head home and catch a quick nap before he had to go in to work and clean up the wreckage of The Inn's kitchen before his staff came in to work. He had no plausible explanation for the undeniably miraculous recovery of his employees, but it was most definitely welcome news.

NINTH CHAPTER

Two days later Gorsky, the mob boss, was absolutely furious. This morning one of his men had, very hesitantly, informed him that not only was the new restaurant not closed, but had apparently done a very profitable night's business last evening. The two enforcers tasked with delivering an abject lesson to the owner of the place were now in police custody and, so far, all attempts to have them released had met with unaccustomed failure.

This was a grievous affront that the Russian mobster could not and would not tolerate. If word got around in the street that his organization could be defied with such impunity, his extremely lucrative, extralegal businesses would rapidly unravel like a moldy old rug. He had to correct this situation and correct it fast. It would call for extremely harsh measures that would cost a small fortune in the short term but would pay much greater dividends in the end.

Unfortunately for this unlucky restaurant owner, it meant the destruction of his restaurant in a loud and very public manner, and more than likely his very tragic but necessarily brutal death.

****

Shep was uncertain of how he should be feeling. It was early, the time of day he most enjoyed. The rich aroma drifting up to his nose from the steaming mug of coffee in his hand, blended with the salty tang of the sea and the familiar fragrance of a large magnolia tree in his backyard. He was sitting on an old wooden bench on his back porch. The aged piece of furniture held many wonderful memories of his life, learning how to whittle with his grandfather, his mother cleaning and bandaging his skinned knee when he fell out of the Magnolia tree, and dozens of others. He was only half concentrating on reading the daily newspaper in front of him wondering what this day would bring. Despite the strong-arm tactics of the persistent Russian thugs, the restaurant had a very successful evening the previous day. A phone call to the police department in addition to the violence of a few nights ago, managed to clear undesirable individuals from his property. And in this morning's paper there was even a glowing endorsement of singularly delicious food and stellar service of The Colonial Inn, from one of the city's most respected critics. Shep knew full well he should be on top of the world. However, he absolutely could not shake the nagging fear that the violent gang of criminals were far from finished with him. He didn't know who the two heroic strangers who stepped in to save his bacon a few days ago, and he knew he couldn't count on lightning striking twice in that regard.

He also had as yet, no explanation for the inexplicably miraculous recovery of his staff, but once again, he couldn't depend on such an unlikely occurrence happening again.

This restaurant was his dream, his life, and he would do whatever he had to in order to make the dream a reality, but how could he, in good conscience, willingly expose his friends and employees to the whims of such dangerous people? He was quite literally, at a loss as to what he should do. Laying the all but forgotten newspaper on the bench beside him, Shep clasped his hands tightly together and leaning his elbows on his knees, bowed his head and prayed to God for guidance and strength. He asked for wisdom and clarity of what to do, what course should he take in order to protect his people above any consideration of his own goals. Earnestly laying his petition before the Lord, Shep finished his prayers and found salty tears running down his cheeks. He got up from the old bench and headed out to start his day. There were several errands he had to run and a few details that must be attended to before he went to The Inn.

****

Gabe finished the morning round of prayer for the day, and as the wonderful aroma of Ruth's cooking teased his nose, he found his mind travelling back to morning breakfasts with his family before his mission had been revealed to him. His parents fervently believed that meals should be shared together, as a family. Everyone was encouraged to talk about whatever topic they wanted, and any question or concern was given an honest and informed answer or response.

Gabe and his siblings were taught to back up their opinions with facts, either from independent news sources or from scripture rather than just spouting off in an emotional manner just to get their way. In this regard, Gabe felt blessed and much more fortunate than most of his classmates. He knew a lot of kids who almost never shared a meal with their family. Many of them had only one parent at home and often ate alone because that parent, more often than not, worked more than one job just to make ends meet. Gabe's mother and father were uncommonly loving and dutifully involved all aspects of their children's lives. The devoutly Christian couple strongly impressed on them all that it was supremely important to be truly grateful for the things they had that others may not have been blessed with. Richard and Cynthia Adams were unfailingly frugal and very shrewd with money, using the Bible's teachings to guide them, and due to that shared philosophy, had been able to provide a very stable though not glamorous life for their children.

More than that, they emphatically stressed the children should never consider themselves better than those less fortunate, because all of what had been given to them could just as easily be taken away. Gabe and his siblings were taught that to unselfishly help and humbly serve others was the basic mission of each and every Christian.

Christ, they taught, spent his entire adult life, not elevating himself above others, but humbling himself and untiringly teaching love for one another, even as he prepared himself to take on the collective sins of all mankind and selflessly pay the highest price in his own precious blood for our salvation.

His sharp mind returning to the present, Gabe silently asked God, as he did every day, to use him for the glory of His name. Rising from his cross-legged position, Gabe headed downstairs to share breakfast with his gracious hosts and his closest friend and ally. He knew that today would be very important for their current mission and he mentally prepared himself for what was to come.

TENTH CHAPTER

The morning began very differently for Vitaly Ivanovich Gorsky. His mood was profoundly dark and dangerously foul. Someone would have to pay a very high price to purge the steely grey, angrily billowing storm clouds from the Russian mobster's vengeful soul. Defiance was something that absolutely could not be tolerated. Additionally, his people all had to know that failure on any level was not an option, and that it carried dire consequences. If these basic truths were not strictly enforced, without exception, his leadership position would become completely untenable.

That was something he would not allow. To that end, two things were on his short list of things to be accomplished today. Gorsky strolled calmly and slowly into the, normally busy, loading dock of the expansive, single-story warehouse that served as his headquarters. The historic old building was situated near the waterfront and was totally saturated with what Gorsky considered the foul, fishy stench of the filthy brown Savannah River. Wooden crates, both large and small, were stacked on a sea of pallets filling almost all the available space of the interior of the cavernous building. Most of the remaining area was crowded with forklifts, hand jacks, and other equipment used for loading and unloading freight.

At the center of the warehouse floor, all of Gorsky's people were gathered in a large circle, awaiting their unhappy employer. They all knew the intense man as one who always moved swiftly, both figuratively and literally.

The fact that his current pace was slow and measured was a sure sign that something very bad was about to take place. The nervous tension in the air was as heavy as a foggy Savannah morning. Men and women quickly stepped aside, giving him room to take his place in the center of the circle. Gorsky, though small in stature, did not suffer from the all-too-common insecurity about his below average height.

If anything, the ruthless gang leader used that difference in size to augment his already formidable presence. In order to be clearly seen by everyone, a less confident man might utilize a crate or a step stool as a way of overcoming this disparity, but not Vasily Gorsky. He stood in the center of the circle, slowly turning to stare each man and woman in the eye before he spoke.

Each and every person knew that to not meet his intense gaze would indicate to him that they had something to hide. THAT would be a certain death sentence. Gorsky accepted nothing short of absolute loyalty from all of his people, and there were a few vacant spots in his organization which bore that out. His voice, low and dangerous yet somehow still loud, filled the area. "Recently," he began, letting his native accent come through. "We appear to have lost sight of what we are all here to accomplish. To allow anyone to defy, openly or in private, and impede progress toward our goals is tantamount to destruction."

As he spoke, the intensity in his eyes actually increased. It was a frightening sight to behold. "If we are not completely feared and unquestionably obeyed, we will eventually be driven out like gypsies in the night. That is something I cannot and will not allow."

Suddenly raising his voice, Gorsky called out. "Bogdan, Ivan!" he shouted.

"Come"

The two huge, bald hulks, who had been sent to secure the restaurant owner's submission, stepped quickly into the center of the circle to face their master. They stood before him expressionless, knowing without a doubt, what was about to happen.

Without another word, Gorsky smoothly pulled a deadly looking .45 caliber semi-automatic handgun from a shoulder holster under his left arm. With two quick single shots, he fired upward through the chin of each man, and a grisly shower of blood, fragments of bone, and wet chunks of brain tissue rained down on the men and women behind the doomed giants.

Not one of them showed the slightest reaction as the two huge lifeless corpses dropped unceremoniously to the warehouse floor. The sharp smell of gunpowder and the coppery tang of blood filled the cavernous space. Gorsky stood in silence as he slowly returned his weapon to its holster. Once again, meeting each man and woman's gaze, he turned and left the circle knowing that the two bodies would be quickly disposed of and that any evidence of what had occurred would be painstakingly removed as if it had never taken place. Now moving at his more customary pace, the determined crime boss headed out to make arrangements for the second order of the day.

Though Shep began his day with mixed emotions, he was still amazed at the incredible healing of his employees and profoundly thankful. But he couldn't escape the feeling that they were all far from out of the woods.

An incessant apprehension stubbornly refused to leave his busy mind. As he went about his tasks overseeing operations for the day in preparation for opening, he caught himself jumping nervously at every unexpected sound and looking at every unfamiliar person he encountered through a new lens of suspicion.

It was keenly stressful, and it was beginning to show. More than once he had to apologize to one employee or another for snapping at them or for overly curt responses to innocent questions. At about 10:30 in the morning, Barry approached him. Laying a firm hand on his old friend's shoulder, the older man spoke softly. "Can I speak with you for a second, Boss?" he asked. Shep could see the undisguised concern in Barry's grey eyes.

"Sure." he answered. The two men climbed the narrow staircase at the back of the kitchen area and entered Shep's small second floor office. The smell of old wood and good leather filled the cramped space. Shep had an old leather office chair that had previously belonged to his father sitting in front of an old-fashioned roll top desk. The desk was also very old, but it had been carefully maintained over the years. The desk originally belonged to Shep's grandfather, the very same man who taught young Shep to whittle. It was first used by his grandfather on an old Merchant Marine freighter. There were two large bookcases on one side of the room stuffed with business manuals and generations of cookbooks. Situated in one corner, an old wooden file cabinet with four drawers stood. It contained personnel files, tax paperwork, and other various business documents. To the right of the doorway, against the wall, was a small table and two folding chairs which

Shep used for interviews. On top of the filing cabinet sat a well-used coffee maker.

The carafe was filled with hot water, because while at work, Shep preferred tea to the stronger dark beverage. Barry placed a few tea leaves from a tin next to the coffee maker in a heavy mug then filled it with the steaming liquid. He set the mug on the small table to steep then turned to his old friend. "Are you okay?" he asked. There was no scorn or judgement in his tone, only true concern and genuine affection. Shep stopped himself before the automatic yes could leave his mouth. His true friend and his business partner deserved nothing less than the naked truth.

"I'm worried, Old Buddy." he said. Reflexively running one hand through his sandy hair, he continued. "Those thugs aren't going to just go away because things haven't gone the way they wanted them to. I'm absolutely terrified they'll just take things to the next level. What do I do if or *when* someone gets crippled, or worse, killed? How will I live with that?" Barry could see how badly this situation was hungrily eating at his friend's troubled soul. Shep wasn't worried about the restaurant, his reputation or his dreams. There was no trace of anxiety over his family name, his standing in the community, or even being held liable in civil court. He was plain and simply horrified at the idea that someone could be seriously hurt because of him. That was just the kind of decent man he was. Shep was perfectly willing to do whatever he had to when it came to working hard, long hours or sacrificing his personal life for his dream but the thought of someone else suffering for his sake was positively stifling.

Barry took his time carefully composing his thoughts before answering his old friend. "Shep, we are all here of our own accord. We're all grown adults, and we know what we are willing to risk, not just for you but for ourselves. No matter what happens, it will not be your fault. We are all trying to create something good here, together. What happens to you happens to all of us, and believe me when I say, we wouldn't have it any other way."

Shep looked into Barry's lively grey eyes and found nothing but earnest total loyalty in them. He counted himself incredibly lucky to have such good unselfish people on this journey with him. He reached out his hand, and the two men shared a firm heartfelt handshake. As if that was the end of the matter, they began preparations for the day.

****

The waterfront in Savannah was typical of many around the world. Hard faced men and women with scarred calloused hands and hard muscled bodies, performed back breaking Labor Day in and day out in order to feed their families. They worked side by side with others who were little more than petty criminals always on the lookout for a quick buck or a shady payoff.

The latter were the type Gorsky often turned to in order to keep his hands relatively clean when there was a particularly nasty task to carry out that he didn't want traced back to his organization.

One of the worst of these unscrupulous goons was a tall heavyset man with a long greasy ponytail of thick, dark hair. In his mid-thirties, the knee breaker had built a considerable reputation for himself as muscle for hire. He had no boundaries or limits to what he was willing to do as long as the money was good.

Gorsky casually leaned against a tie off post on the dock outside the freight company where the guy, Bill McNabb, earned the legitimate portion of his living. A loud steam whistle blew from somewhere causing a small flock of seagulls to take flight, wings fluttering, screeching in protest at the sudden disruption. Nearby, from a pair of huge double doors, scores of tired men and women began filtering out of the big storage building. Visible toward the middle of the throng, Gorsky spotted McNabb.

It wasn't difficult since he stood nearly head and shoulders above most everyone around him. Catching the big man's eye, Gorsky made a slight nodding gesture indicating McNabb should join him. The odd pair spoke quietly for several minutes after which Gorsky handed the larger man a thick envelope which immediately disappeared into a pocket of the man's coveralls. With their business now concluded, the two men parted company. Gorsky was supremely confident that his temporary defiance problem would very soon be a thing of the past.

****

Jason was fast becoming increasingly comfortable in his new element. He had been able to acquire an impressive amount of both hardware and software to create an operation center for his and Gabe's use.

The Gibsons had a dear old friend who just happened to own some commercial property on which there was a modest sized, empty building, that formerly served as a television and VCR repair shop. In today's high-tech world of WIFI and HD streaming, there was very little or nothing for him to do so he sold most of his diagnostic equipment, save a few tools he chose not to part with and padlocked the shop. The building was located near an abandoned middle school, scheduled to be demolished in the near future. The concrete block building sat back off the street with a one lane access road leading to the rear of the old man's home.

Nearly hidden by large mature trees, it was partially covered with the ever-present Spanish moss. Jason couldn't have chosen a better location. Better yet, there was a large, powerful generator that provided more than enough power to the entire building to keep it separated from the city's electric line to his residence.

The long-time repairman was a stickler for maintaining his property and equipment, thus the generator was in tip top operating condition and the interior of the shop was immaculately tidy. Jason was currently in the process of creating a PowerPoint presentation for Gabe. The young man had been able to uncover a wealth of information on Gorsky's illicit operation, but specific details on the man himself had been a great deal harder to find.

As near as Gabe's partner could tell, Gorsky dropped off the map in the early nineties following his mandatory two-year stint in the Soviet army. It appeared that he was then drafted into the FSB, a largely covert police force that stepped in to fill the void left by the KGB after the breakup of the Soviet Union. He had received extensive training in a large number of areas including combat strategy, weapons and tactics, computer technology, logistics, and several other fields that had been redacted from his accessible files.

He spoke at least four languages fluently and had a working grasp of nearly a dozen more. He was initially sent to the U.S. to cultivate and manage sources of human intel or HUMINT, at many military installations across the United States. Roughly ten years ago he arrived in Savannah. and after that, the paper trail went completely cold.

Jason was unable to determine if the former government agent had been sent to the coastal city on official orders or of his own accord. Prying deep into Gorsky's financials over the past five years, Jason discovered incredibly vast amounts of cash tucked away in a large number of offshore accounts around the globe. The man's personal net worth looked to be measured in hundreds of millions of dollars.

Just as Jason was finishing up the final pages of his presentation, Gabe came in. His young associate chuckled as the big man had to stoop to get through the door of the makeshift tactical operations center. Gabe turned a nearby chair around and sat backwards on it as his friend briefed him on everything he had uncovered.

Gabe rapidly absorbed the huge amount of information like a dry sponge. Jason marveled, for perhaps the one hundredth time, at the big man's uncanny ability to comprehend and fully retain vast amounts of information without taking notes or recordings of any kind. The young apprentice reflected on the time not long after their first fateful encounter when he had asked Gabriel how he got his powers.

Gabe then explained that he didn't have any powers, that he was absolutely no different than anyone else other than perhaps the depth of his faith in God. The way Gabe explained it was radically different than Jason had ever heard. Jason's experience with church specifically and religion in general had been that it was professed by a bunch of judgmental, self-righteous, hypocritical people who liked nothing better than to look down their noses at others from their own perceived superiority.

Gabe was totally different. He made absolutely no pretense of being perfect. Quite the opposite in fact, the big man candidly admitted he had flaws, many of them. However, the spiritual essence of God, which abides within every man, woman and child and which Gabe fed daily, kept him from giving in to his baser thoughts and worldly temptations. He explained the mistake Jason had made was common. Gabe explained that he had no power whatsoever. Instead, it was the awesome, limitless power of God, channeled through him that accomplished such amazing feats.

All Gabe, or anyone, had to do was to have absolute undeniable faith that God was able to do anything, absolutely anything those who believed asked of him.

"You see," the big man explained, "most people totally have the wrong concept of the being we know as The Lord. When He told us that man was created in His own image, He wasn't referring to the actual physical form, how could he be? We're all uniquely different. What He was actually referring to was the undying spiritual essence of mankind, the incredible, eternal energy that comprises the individual soul of every human being. That boundless energy IS God! We are all part of Him, created in His image because that indestructible energy, within each one of us, is but one tiny particle of an infinitely larger, non-corporeal being. We are all connected to Him and to each other through Him. That's why what you and I do, along with others we'll gather on our journey, is so vitally important. Think of us as antibodies attacking a deadly, rapidly growing body of cancerous cells. That poisonous mass is humanity's dwindling belief and crippling lack of true faith in God, our Father. We surgically remove or nourish and heal diseased cells so the rest of the body can become more robust, happy, and fully prepared to join him when our physical shell expires". Jason had been truly amazed and enlightened. Nothing he had ever heard even came close to such a completely understandable description. It made the young man feel both incredibly tiny and remarkably powerful at the same time, to know that within him, existed one tiny piece of an all-powerful, eternal celestial being was strangely uplifting and refreshingly liberating. Every man, woman, and child on the face of the planet had the innate capacity and the natural ability to do the incomparable things Jason had witnessed Gabriel perform. All that was required was to believe with absolute certainty that God would make it so.

Jason recalled his Sunday school lesson about Jesus's walking on water, remembering that Peter was actually walking on water himself until his own doubt caused him to sink. The knowledge had been overwhelming and difficult to process. Throughout his life, Jason had consistently been told by virtually every person in authority over him, what he should not, could not and would never be able to do. Then, this remarkable man calmly informed him that practically anything he could conceive was, not only possible, but absolutely certain, as long as it was done for the benefit of others and not for self-gratification.

Everything Jason had learned from his experiences, up to that point, was that the pinnacle of society to which a person could aspire was the acquisition of money and material possessions, find someone to share those possessions with, and reproduce in order to have someone to leave those acquired possessions to. Gabriel told him that those things were just that, **things**. They could not pass from this life with you, so you never truly owned anything. Everything under heaven belonged to God to give or take as He saw fit, and only what you did for the sake of Him and His children, your brothers and sisters, would actually matter in the end. His mind returning to the present, Jason waited as Gabriel thoughtfully considered the large volume of highly detailed information Jason turned up. It was abundantly clear that Gorsky would let no level of resistance to demands of his criminal organization stand. There had to be a reckoning. If he let the stark insult stand, momentum would build and soon others would adopt the dangerous, suicidal urge to defy the crime lord's patently non-negotiable demands.

Gabe abruptly closed his eyes, allowed his face to go slack in relaxation, and entered a deep trance. Jason knew, from experience, not to question his friend when he was in this state. It was an indication that Gabe was in a more direct communication with the Holy Spirit. After a few moments, Gabe's hazel eyes popped open, clear and determined. He stood suddenly and said with an edge of urgency in his deep voice, "We have to go." Without another word, the two Christian soldiers left the makeshift command center and quickly headed out on the day's mission.

ELEVENTH CHAPTER

Shep was just finishing up the last of several errands he had to run before heading to the inn. This last stop was at his preferred seafood vendor to pick up fresh lobster, shrimp, clams and a few other select items for the menu. He had a large panel van he used to pick up supplies for the restaurant. It had been painted with the logo of The Colonial Inn by an old acquaintance that owned a collision repair shop. The middle-aged lady had been a friend of his mother and would not accept a penny for the job.

Presently, the van sat with the rear loading door open, backed up to the loading dock of the vendor's building. The dock was located at the rear of the building, in an alley that ran parallel to the river only two blocks away.

As Shep was storing the last box of seafood packed in ice into the van, he failed to notice six dangerous looking men approaching from one end of the alley which was paved with red brick. With a few minor changes of clothing and accessories, the men could easily have passed for a roving band of pirates straight out of a previous time period. The predatory look of men who got whatever they wanted simply by taking it was evident on each hardened face.

Their unwary chosen victim pulled the rollup cargo door of the van down, secured the latch in place, then turned to walk to the front of the vehicle.

As he turned around, he suddenly found himself face to face, or rather face to chest, with the large greasy looking man standing at the front of the lethal looking group.

Shep's stomach seemed to drop to the brick surface of the abruptly crowded alleyway. There was no awkward moment of confusion in which he assumed he was just standing in their way as the motley crew, all thoroughly filthy and reeking of sweat and alcohol. He also had positively no doubt that his days were done. Shep reflexively brought his hands up in defense just a fraction too late as the big guy with the ponytail, apparently the leader of the group, reached out with startling quickness, wrapping his rough dirty hands around the smaller man's throat. Shep desperately struggled to breathe, his face turning red in his attacker's viselike grip. In panic, Shep pulled and slapped at the big thug's rock-hard forearms with absolutely no effect as the brawler shoved him against the wall of the seafood store hard enough to make his vision blurry and sprinkled with bright spots. Still firmly holding his frantically squirming victim with his right hand, the attacker drew back his left arm, and the huge hand balled into a sledgehammer of a fist. Shep was not at all sure that it would take more than one blow from that ugly weapon to render him senseless, especially since he could see even more bright sparkles of light dancing in his peripheral vision as his brain was starved of vital oxygen.

Just as the pulverizing blow was launched, Shep's frantic eyes saw a few knives appear in a couple of the men's hands and one of them was now holding a gun. Still defiantly clawing at his assailant's implacable grip, Shep felt his strength failing.

His struggles were weakening, and the young man began making peace in anticipation of the brutal end, only seconds away. In a flash, he thought of the many things he had yet to do. He pictured all of the many people he intended to help through his success. His soul wept at the horrible senseless act that would ultimately be what he was remembered by. Time slowed to a crawl, and he saw only the wicked deadly looking fist hurtling with unavoidable force toward his doomed face. Seemingly magnified, the brutal image dominated his field of vision, practically allowing him to count the many scars crisscrossing the weathered knuckles. Shep's eyes squeezed tightly shut and waited for the devastating impact, but it never came.

For Jason, keeping pace with his long-legged partner was no small task. The big man's powerfully muscled legs carried him along at a distance eating pace that would tire even the most experienced cross-country runners. It had taken Jason weeks of grueling cardio work before he could keep up with Gabe. The two of them were downtown near a row of buildings adjacent to the pier. As they neared the rear of a shop supplying fresh seafood for various restaurants and stores, they spotted a group of a half dozen burly men.

It was obvious from the look on those weathered faces that they were not meeting to get the group discount for lunch. The two men slowed their pace and held back a bit as the suspicious looking group entered an alley. When they reached one of the many historic buildings bordering the narrow passage, they cautiously peered around the corner into the dank alleyway. They saw Shep Andrews closing the door of his company panel van, then turning to be confronted by the unfamiliar group of men.

Before the man could say a word, the apparent leader of the group reached out and grabbed Shep by the throat almost immediately. As Shep struggled, the bigger man drew back his arm preparing to deliver a crushing blow.

At that moment Gabriel and Jason sprang into action. With blinding speed, Gabe crossed the thirty odd feet of space between them and Shep's attackers in less time than a single heartbeat. The designated leader of the group of hired muscle suddenly found his left wrist immobilized in a punishing grip that brought involuntary tears to his own eyes. Finding himself suddenly cast as prey rather than predator, he let go of his nearly passed out victim. Dumped unceremoniously to the moldy bricks of the alley, Shep lay greedily gasping for air like a fish suddenly pulled into a boat. Before he could mount any effective defense, McNabb, as if bouncing off a trampoline, collided with two of the men behind him with numbing impact.

The veteran dockyard bully somehow managed to stay on his feet, unlike his less fortunate companions who stumbled off balance and crashed to the ground. Fiercely shaking his wrist in an attempt to restore sensation, McNabb faced off with this new arrival. The guy was maybe a couple inches taller than himself, but McNabb figured he probably had at least fifty pounds of advantage in weight against his new opponent. There was another guy standing next to this unanticipated intruder, smaller but fit and muscular as well. "I don't know who you are Bubba," McNabb said measuring his words, "But you're sticking your nose in some business that ain't got shit to do with you!"

Even though McNabb's tone fairly dripped with menace, neither of the two newcomers seemed appropriately impressed. "So, the best thing you can do," McNabb continued, "is to turn your nosy asses around and leave while you still can." Being accustomed to intimidating people always getting his way, McNabb was both sorely frustrated and more than a little irritated by the complete absence of fear or even the slightest degree of concern on the two stranger's faces.

Then the big guy who had grabbed his arm with a grip like a hydraulic press spoke, his deep, resonating voice sounded as if it came from everywhere at once. "You're making a very big mistake William. The man who gave you this assignment has made an even bigger one. If anyone should turn and leave, it's you and your friends here." He said nodding in the direction of McNabb's crew.

McNabb's eyes widened while the man spoke until they looked ready to jump from their sockets. The hired leg breaker paused for several seconds, totally nonplussed by this unprecedented behavior. The balls on this guy had to be carried in a separate pair of pants they were so big. He stood there, empty handed, calm as you please, and not even standing in any kind of defensive stance or anything. Judging by his manner, they could just as well have been discussing the current weather or last night's football scores. Then, one of McNabb's men, a brutal serial rapist called Crank Wilson, took it upon himself to make a surprise move on the smaller of the two men. He had been given the nickname "Crank" allegedly due to prodigious size of his anatomical weapon of choice.

Although charged multiple times, he had so far been able to avoid imprisonment for more than a dozen vicious attacks on women both young and more mature in and around the coastal city. Brandishing a large, razor-sharp hunting knife in his right hand, he abruptly lunged toward Jason's left side hoping to puncture a lung or kidney. Expecting this unexpected interruption to be short lived, McNabb was visibly stunned to see Wilson go flying across the alley as the other guy grabbed his wrist and used some kind of Judo move to redirect his sudden attacker. As sudden as the attack was, the guy moved swiftly and smoothly, deftly twisting Wilson's arm, taking control of his elbow.

Bending low, he turned in a tight circle, pushing up and forward as he came to the end of the rotation. The deceptively simple looking move launched his knife wielding opponent into the air with no more effort than it might take to toss a dirty shirt across a room into an open hamper. Wilson performed an involuntary somersault, making a complete rotation, then brutally crashed into a wooden telephone pole on the other side of the alley. His arms wrapped around it in a sudden awkward embrace, the knife clattered to the ground, and Wilson briefly sagged against the pole like a deflating balloon, then slumped unconscious to the ground. What came next was a frenzied flurry of frantic activity that was nearly impossible to follow. The group of thugs attempted to rally and regain the upper hand in the quickly deteriorating situation. McNabb and two other guys rushed the bigger intruder as the smaller one faced off with the remaining pair of thugs. McNabb dove headfirst into a fast tackle and braced for the contact, aiming at the guy's midsection.

Having worked together numerous times before, his companions instinctively went high and low, one grabbing for Gabe's arms, the other diving for his legs. The man to McNabb's left was a thick, barrel chested man named Crockett. Although, at first glance he looked bulky and fat, anyone who knew him knew that beneath his "winter coat", as he called it, was a stout frame layered with rock hard muscle. Crockett's preferred method of persuasion was breaking bones. He often bragged about truly loving the sound of bones cracking. Music to his ears, as he was known to say.

The bruiser on his right was taller than Crockett but shorter than McNabb. Tom Weathers was his name, and he rarely spoke. His nickname was The Weatherman because when his normally bland expression grew dark, watch out, because a vicious storm was coming. His past included a once promising career as a golden gloves boxer, until his natural bloodlust began to reveal itself in the ring. The tipping point came during a championship bout when he trapped his less skilled opponent in a corner and mercilessly pummeled the man, even after the official called for the break. Weathers actually held the defenseless man up with his gloved left hand under his opponent's right armpit and broke nearly every bone in the man's face with devastating punches. Weathers had the sculpted, well-defined muscles of a bodybuilder with minimal body fat. He had a scar across his brow from the tip of his right eyebrow to just above his right ear, evidence of one of his father's frequent, alcohol fueled rages. Banned for life from competition, Weathers migrated to working at the docks and eventually to moonlighting as an enforcer with McNabb and company.

The three men employed a tactic that, in the past, never failed. Taking a moment to size up their larger opponent, they wordlessly agreed via hand signals to employ a rapid three on one attack. The tried-and-true strategy was designed to have the first man occupy the victim's full attention with defending himself as the others followed in quick succession to overwhelm him. This insured the mark would only be able to engage one man before the others took him down. No matter how big a guy was, once he was on the ground, it was all over. Weathers had the most formal fight training, so he was first to attack. Assuming a boxing stance, he moved in quickly to face off with his target. To his surprise, the guy just stood there, waiting. He didn't take up any kind of defensive posture, and judging by his facial expression, he might as well have been looking at paint samples.

The Weatherman tested the waters with a stiff, snappy left jab. It failed to connect as the big guy moved his head to the side, almost faster than Weathers could track. Closing the distance, a little more, the former boxer feinted with another lightning fast jab, preparing to catch his challenger with a right cross as he was forced to move to his left to avoid the jab. McNabb and Crockett waited for their opening.

As soon as The Weatherman connected with that right, they would swarm in as the big guy was stunned. Instead, Gabe easily avoided the jab, and rather than leave himself open for the brutal right cross, caught Weathers' fist in his left hand.

The startled former boxer's eyes went wide in shock, and as the other two men charged, their surprisingly unpredictable adversary leapt straight up into the air. Still holding Weathers' trapped fist securely, he jumped over him, landing behind the charging pair. Weathers arm was painfully wrenched 180 degrees, and he suddenly found himself facing the other two men as they closed the short distance between them. His arm was now stretched between his two fellow thugs, and before he could do a thing about it, the shockingly agile guy used it like a club striking both men on the sides of their heads in a move so fast it defied belief. Both men dropped, bonelessly to the ground as if poleaxed. Before another heartbeat passed, Weathers was propelled backwards by a hard flat handed strike to his chest that felt like being kicked by a horse. He slammed hard against the brick wall of the building behind him, and for the first time in his life, The Weatherman was down for the count. As their three cohorts faced off with the bigger intruder, the remaining members of the hit squad, Jackson Lindow and Zach Tracy squared off with the shorter guy. They figured this momentary distraction would be dealt with swiftly, and then they would have three bodies to get rid of instead of just the restaurant guy. What they couldn't account for was the total absence of fear, even normal concern, in this guy's eyes. Either he didn't know he was about to die, or he was just plain stupid. Lindow was a product of a gang culture, growing up in one of the poorest areas in Atlanta. He was only in Savannah while he evaded the cops who were after him on suspicion of double murder. His cousin lived in the coastal city and got him hired on with McNabb's crew so he could make a little cash while he was flying under the radar. With no formal training, he had come by all his considerable fighting skills in actual practice in life-or-death situations throughout childhood and his early manhood.

He knew every dirty trick and treacherous tactic there was in street fighting and had absolutely no compunction against using them. Zach Tracy was an import from Australia. He travelled to America by stowing away on various cargo ships across the globe and discovered a place on the docks where he finally felt like he belonged. Having grown up in the foster care system in Sydney, the Aussie was in and out of juvenile detention centers. The violent young man then graduated to the real deal of federal prison following convictions for drug trafficking, manslaughter, and his personal favorite, rape. A man of few words, he preferred to do his talking with his fists. Unlike the other more diverse members of the group, Tracy and Lindow resembled each other enough they were often mistaken for brothers. Both were just over six feet tall, lean and muscular, with dark hair and brown eyes. Tracy carried a short length of thick chain wrapped around his right fist with a tail about two feet in length dangling free. Lindow carried a heavy wrought iron crowbar in the same hand.

The pair approached Jason rapidly, trying to force him into retreat and get him off his guard. Tracy went to Jason's left while Lindow angled to his right. Jason calmly stood his ground as the two leg breakers rushed in. Tracy drew back his arm swinging the tail of the heavy chain in a lethal arc towards Jason's head. At the same time, Lindow squatted and struck out in an attempt to sweep Jason's right ankle with the curved end of the crowbar. Once both men were committed in their chosen courses of action, Jason launched into motion. To an onlooker, it would have looked like an impossible move as Jason lifted his right leg to avoid the crowbar and simultaneously leaned backward as the chain whistled past his forehead.

At the same time, Jason grabbed Tracy's right forearm and rolling to his right, deftly changed its trajectory. Completely caught off guard, Tracy was unable to stop his forward momentum and crashed face first into the grimy brick surface of the alley. Lindow couldn't fully register what happened before Jason reversed direction again rolling to his left. He bowled into Lindow's shins causing the man to stumble forward, attempting to keep his balance. While Lindow struggled to keep from falling, Jason locked his right arm around Lindow's left leg applying leverage to bend the knee forward. Lindow, suddenly unable to remain standing, crashed backward to the ground. His skull made a dull thud as it contacted the pavement.

Tracey had scrambled back to his feet charged at Jason as he nimbly rose from the ground. Swinging the chain back and forth in front of him, he taunted Jason and advanced toward his opponent. When he was within striking range, he faked a slashing move to Jason's legs changing at the last second to bring the chain whistling toward the young man's face in a backhanded swing. Tracy figured Jason would lean backwards to avoid the chain enabling him to stomp the guy's foot and push him off balance. However, Jason unexpectedly leaned forward ducking under the chain and springing toward his attacker. He hooked Tracy's waist with both arms and in a twisting, rotating move, spun the man around and launched him face first into the nearest wall.

The chain wielding thug appeared to melt to the ground, unconscious. Lindow was shaking his head to clear the cobwebs. He saw Tracy go down and knew he'd be next if he didn't act quickly. In desperation, he threw the crowbar with all the strength he could muster, and as it spun toward his foe, he charged in following the projectile.

There was only about twelve feet of space between the two men, but time seemed to crawl at a snail's pace as Lindow moved to close with the troublemaking intruder. In slow motion, he saw the young guy roll forward beneath the rapidly spinning crowbar. Unable to stop himself in time, he felt the painful contact as the guy crashed into his right leg. Lindow's vision filled with bright light followed by sudden darkness and pinpoints of light like stars as he once again slammed to the surface of the alley.

Before the paid enforcer could react, Jason dropped an elbow onto the back of his skull, and suddenly the impromptu battle was over.

The entire battle transpired over just a couple of minutes, and during the brief fight, Shep stood frozen unsure of what to do. Before he could decide on a course of action, his assistance was shown to be completely unnecessary. He looked around the dank alley at the battered now harmless thugs in amazement. It looked like the aftermath of a scene in a Hollywood martial arts movie, and Shep couldn't help but smile at the thought. He turned to thank his timely rescuers only to find he was once again standing all alone in the alley. There was no sign of either man, and he had no idea how they could possibly have left without him noticing. There was at least thirty feet of space to cover to reach either end of the alley. For the second time in the past few days, Shep felt an undeniable sense of divine intervention.

He heard sirens approaching, and unsure of what to do next, Shep stood stock still amid the carnage in the alley with the groans of the injured thugs the only sounds.

Within less than a minute, police cars bracketed both ends of the narrow passageway.

As the officers rushed into the alley guns drawn, Shep was sure they were going to find at least one of the sprawled goons dead. However, as the cops began securing the scene and checking the men on the ground, Shep was thoroughly shocked to see not one of the violent thugs had so much as a bruise on them. Two of the officers isolated Shep cautiously checking him for weapons, then finding him unarmed, began asking what happened. Shep began explaining to the best of his ability, but before he could get very far into his account of the incident, one of the cops came out of the warehouse and interrupted. She had reviewed footage from two security cameras, one mounted on either side the warehouse loading dock.

It clearly showed that Shep had been accosted by six men, and two other unidentified men appeared suddenly, quickly, and efficiently to dispatch his attackers. Although clearing Shep of any culpability, she said the weird thing was that neither of his rescuers could be identified from the footage. Their faces were blurry and distorted from any angle, almost as if the recording had been doctored. Of course, that was unlikely in the extreme since the fight had ended only moments ago. Shep stood flabbergasted, as he realized he couldn't recall the details of either man's appearance himself. He could describe all six of the thugs with detailed precision, but when he tried to remember the two good Samaritans his mind was a total blank. He thought once again *what in the world was going on*?

TWELFTH CHAPTER

Gorsky flung a chair through the large glass window of his office. Heads turned at the sudden loud crash of shattering glass, then quickly looked for ways to ignore the commotion. It was totally out of character for their boss to lose control, and no one wanted to be seen noticing the telling break in character. Gorsky stood at his desk, staring angrily at his phone, making a supreme effort to regain control of his seething emotions. He couldn't believe the amount of trouble this one little restaurant owner was causing him. The call he just received was from one of his contacts in the Savannah Police Department. The men he sent to put a stop to the problem were now an even bigger part of it. They were in jail, and what was worse, they implicated him in the failed hit. Gorsky knew that even payoffs were going to be out of the question now.

  The Chatham County prosecutor was on a very public and high-profile quest to clean up the coastal city, and this would be a major feather in her cap. He was going to have to close up shop temporarily and return to his home country before he could be detained. As the warm humid night approached, Gorsky made a decision. He stabbed the intercom button on his phone with a thick scarred index finger and spoke in a no-nonsense tone to the thirty or more men and women still in the building.

"Everyone arm yourselves." he said. "The police will be here as soon as they can get a judge to sign off on a warrant. I want everything loaded and taken to the ship, **now**!" If he could manage to make it out of Savannah's territorial waters, he would be home free. "No one gets into this building, and I mean **NO ONE!!**"

The warehouse then erupted into a hive of frenzied activity as his people carried out his orders. There were enough weapons and ammunition in the building to hold off a full tactical response for several days. Hopefully, he would only need a few hours. But one thing was for sure, he would kill that damn glorified short order cook before he left if it was the last thing he ever did.

Two hours later, the warehouse was ready. All possibly incriminating evidence was safely aboard Gorsky's trawler. The little Russian was ready to leave for the ship. As he grabbed his go bag, stuffed with passports, money and weapons hidden under the clothes, a P.A. system pierced the quiet night.

"Gorsky." a somewhat high-pitched male voice called out. The accent was heavy but the man seemed calm and confident. "We know you're in there, and we know about the weapons. You and anyone else in the building need to come out with your hands in the air. Nobody needs to get hurt here. We have a warrant to search the building and a warrant for your arrest. You have 30 seconds to comply, Sir, or we will have to use force." This was the final straw; those traitors had actually informed the police about his defenses!

"выжженная земля!" Gorsky shouted. Translation;
Scorched Earth!

****

Jason sat in his room at the boarding house running over a mental checklist. His equipment and clothes were all packed up waiting by the door. He had made all the preparations Gabe had given him. He had to admit that he had no idea what those preparations were actually for, but he had learned not to question his partner unnecessarily. Whatever Gabe requested always had a purpose, and that purpose would become clear when the time came. Gabe told Jason Gorsky found out where they were staying through his extensive network of street informants.

Their gracious hosts were away from the house having been required to travel to a store on the other side of town for some items Gabe hinted at needing. The inseparable couple would not hear of their guests having to find their own way to pick up the items. With typical grace, they set out to fill Gabe's list of items. The large, three-story home, actually listed on the registry of historical buildings in Savannah, was empty and uncharacteristically quiet. Jason missed the wonderful aroma of Ruth's cooking that seemed to perpetually fill the comfortable home. On this particular precaution, Jason was completely cognizant of Gabe's intentions. Not wanting to take the very real chance of the elderly couple being hurt or worse, Gabe made sure they were safely removed from the scene of imminent danger. Ordinarily, criminals tended to carry out violent acts of retribution during the wee hours of the night or early morning in order to use the concealing darkness as a passive aid in their escape.

However, Gorsky's illicit operation was rapidly crumbling around him, and he needed to get out of Savannah as soon as possible to avoid his impending apprehension. This necessitated avenging himself on the two unwanted obstacles to his plans immediately and permanently. His frustration with his organization's inability to rid him of the pair was maddening in its intensity. It was as if the pair was protected by some invisible shield that somehow prevented Gorsky's rightful vengeance. The determined Russian vowed to himself that the shield was about to be penetrated in the most brutal fashion.

Jason closed his eyes praying silently and mentally preparing himself for the coming conflict. The sudden screech of overstressed tires abruptly stopping on the bricks of the street outside, heralded the official commencement of hostilities. Jason was ready, as he knew Gabriel was.

Now dressed in what he liked to refer to as his "action wear", he stood, waiting for the assault to come. The outfit consisted of a form fitting long sleeved shirt made of a Kevlar mesh the same dark red color as the lining of Gabe's night robe. Black jeans, of the same fabric were secured with a thick black leather belt and a brushed nickel buckle with their mission insignia embossed on it. Sturdy lightweight black boots with steel toes and dark gloves with Kevlar forearm guards attached to them completed the outfit.

Jason heard the assault crew shuffling toward the house, even though they were using nonverbal forms of communication to coordinate their efforts and no one spoke.

They knew Gorsky would have the hide, literally, of anyone who spooked the prey and allowed them to escape again. Since the boss himself was leading this charge, there was extra care being taken to follow his orders to the letter.

Gorsky signalled his lieutenants to surround the big house with firepower while he sent two scouts to confirm the intended targets were actually inside. Nearly forty men and women ringed the three-story structure covering every possible avenue of escape with scopes and laser sights. There were all varieties of weaponry evident, handguns, rifles, shotguns, machine pistols, there were even two rocket launchers and most of the assault force had flash bang and fragmentation grenades. There was no possible escape this time. After a couple of minutes, the scouts returned and informed Gorsky that the two men were indeed inside and going about their evening in a most casual way, although they were strangely dressed. *I'll show them casual*, Gorsky thought. This was going to be very, very satisfying. At the Russian's silent command, two men lobbed flash bang grenades through the windows of the two separate rooms in which the men were located. Even with their ears protected by foam earplugs, the heavy vibrations could be felt through the ground.

Thick grey smoke billowed from the two shattered windows, and the sounds of glassware and other fragile objects breaking briefly filled the air. On command, the forward element of the assault, consisting of half a dozen stone faced killers, smashed through the front, rear, and side doors of the house in teams of two.

They rolled into the building on the floor to avoid possible return fire as they opened up spraying the rooms with fusillade of bullets from their machine pistols. Not taking an inch of space for granted, they filled everything in sight with high velocity lead projectiles. Cabinets, closets and any piece of furniture large enough to hide behind was riddled with enough ammunition to kill an adult elephant. Not even the refrigerator was spared in the relentless barrage. After the initial penetration, the lead force reloaded and deployed through the home, methodically aerating any possible hiding place.

Gorsky was running the numbers in his head, anticipating the response time of police, who would have been notified after the first shots. They would be delayed due to some well-placed distractions Gorsky had set up across the city, but that didn't mean his crew had all night.

After 3 minutes, Gorsky broke radio silence, and using a small handheld two-way radio, requested status updates from all crews. There were eight more sweeping through the house room by room following the lead assault team. So far, no one had seen any sign of the two meddlesome men. Suddenly, Gorsky felt a drastic change in air pressure inside the building. Having joined the crews sweeping room to room, he felt his ears pop, and there was a loud bang like a heavy door slamming and several muffled yells.

"Report!" he snapped into his radio. "What happened?" Gorsky demanded. One of the sweep teams failed to answer up. "Talk to me, someone! What the hell happened?" the mob boss hissed.

One of the other team leaders answered him. "Vajna's crew is gone Sir!"

Gorsky could feel the heat rising from his neck, suffusing his face and ears with redness. "What do you mean, gone?" he barked.

"They were in the room behind us. When we heard the noise, we all took cover. Then we turned around to investigate, and they were just gone!" the voice carried a hint of shocked fear that infuriated Gorsky.

"Get a hold of yourself and find out where they are, or you are going to wish you had disappeared along with them! Do you understand?" The dangerous tone of his voice threatened to cause icicles to form on the ceiling. "The rest of you spread out and find them, NOW! I don't want to have to fight our way out of here through a wall of cops!! Join the other teams and stay together."

Gorsky, along with two more men he called in from outside, moved swiftly and quietly through the wrecked interior of the house. Since the other teams had formed one large crew and proceeded down the stairs into the basement, he took his team up the staircase to the third floor intending to work his way down from there. The thick haze from the grenades had dissipated, and they could see everything inside clearly now.

With all of the potential exits covered there should have been no way for the men to escape. Gorsky and the others fanned out and began to sweep the converted attic space on the third floor. Stopping only to fire into closets and other rooms.

Gorsky himself was searching a small room converted into a storage area, when he felt a sudden rush of air in the larger bedroom adjacent to the storage area, like a powerful vacuum. "Sergei?" he called. "Anton? What happened?" Quickly finishing his search of the small room, Gorsky backtracked to the room where he had left the other men. It was empty. "Sergei! Anton! Report!" he called. No answer.

Clicking over to a different channel on his radio, he spoke into it feeling a sudden creeping sense of alarm. "Natasha!" he called. No answer. Natasha Rusoff was the leader of the team searching the basement. In all his career, Gorsky had never known a tougher more capable and vicious fighter than the hard-faced brunette. If there was anyone, he could count on to face down incredible odds, it was her.

There was no answer. Gorsky realized he was suddenly all alone. He raced down the stairs, unaccustomed panic beginning to set in. He switched to the channel reserved for the crew outside covering the exits. "Kruseff!" he shouted into the radio, loud enough that the man heard him without having to listen to the radio.

"Da Tovarish." The man answered.

"Has anyone come back outside?"

"Nyet." was the answer.

Gorsky was baffled. Where could they be? Surely the men could not have wiped out the entire interior team without a sound.

Getting some small semblance of control back, Gorsky struggled to sound more sure of himself as he issued new orders. "Kill anyone you don't recognize who comes out," he said.

After the acknowledgement, Gorsky turned heading back into the house to find himself facing the man who he assumed to be the leader of the two outsiders from the description of his people. Incredibly tall, the man towered over Gorsky's diminutive frame. The Russian felt his confidence returning. Many men had underestimated him because of his size. They were all dead or hopelessly crippled now. "So", he said, a smile creeping across his cruel features. "You are done hiding now, yes?"

Gabe looked down at him with an expression Gorsky, at first didn't recognize, compassion. "Vitaly," the man said calmly, "This doesn't have to be an ending for you. You do have a choice."

With a sarcastic sneer, Gorsky responded, "Ending? You think you have ended something, eh? This is only a minor setback, easily overcome. By this time a month from now, it will be as if nothing has happened." Gorsky blinked his eyes, because even though he could clearly see the man and every detail of his ridiculous outfit, he was completely unable to focus on his face. It was like looking through frosted glass. "And if you think that because you are larger than I, you will be able to easily defeat me, you are very wrong. And I assure you that will be a fatal mistake, my misguided friend."

Gorsky expected the man to assume a fighting stance as he was subtly doing himself, preparing to launch a swift attack that would overwhelm the man with its sheer ferocity. Instead, the man continued talking in his deep, calm voice, almost as if speaking to a child.

"You don't understand, Vitaly." he said.

"I don't need to defeat you; you have defeated yourself with the choices you have made. You choose to terrorize, victimize, and murder those you see as weaker than you. What you fail to see is that all men and women are children of almighty God. We are all his creations, and we all have his protection."

Gorsky snorted a rude laugh. "God? Hah!" you are even more of a fool than I thought! There is no god, you idiot! There is only the weak and the strong. I thought you were one of the latter, but now I see you are nothing but a soft-headed simpleton. The powerful always subjugate the weak. It is the way of the world."

"Man's world perhaps." Gabe answered calmly. "But there is no power unless it is given by God."

With that, Gorsky saw two small white orbs beginning to glow, right where he imagined the man's eyes to be. Squinting as the glow intensified, he shook his head, thinking maybe the guy had somehow managed to drug him. The points of light continued to grow in intensity, eventually forcing Gorsky to look at the man's chest to avoid being blinded.

"So, you think you are powerful, do you?" Gorsky said. As he finished the sentence, he launched a devastatingly fast spinning kick at the man's midsection. He knew there was enough power in that kick to break a man's neck because he had done it on more than one occasion. This time was different. Fully committed to the move, Gorsky was totally off balance when it didn't connect. He abruptly found himself lying flat on his back on the floor, dumbfounded that he could have missed. Scrambling quickly to his feet, he squared off again, preparing for a different strategy.

Perhaps whatever the guy had dosed him with had thrown off his depth perception. He resolved to grapple with the larger man and bring his sambo training into play. The Russian variation of judo was perfectly suited for the size and mass difference between him and his opponent.

"Vitaly, you are wasting time." the man said.

"The police will be here soon. Nothing you can do will harm me, and I don't want to hurt you. I want to save you." he actually seemed in earnest to Gorsky.

"Save me?" Gorsky replied incredulous. "Save me from who?" the sarcastic smile on his face revealed his true feelings.

"From yourself, my friend." Gabe answered.

"I can't hurt you, eh?" the smaller man said, and suddenly rushed forward with impressive speed, aiming his shoulders at the larger man's knees.

Gorsky braced himself for the impact, preparing for the ground assault once the man was knocked off his feet, and so was completely unprepared for what happened next. His arms closed around empty air instead of the man's legs. He skidded to a painful stop on the hardwood floor. His face burned hot from a combination of deep embarrassment, and the effects of a friction burn filled with wood splinters from the destroyed woodwork on the floor of the bullet riddled room.

To add insult to injury, the big man reached down offering his hand in assistance. Gorsky could not understand how he had again missed his intended target. He had one last card to play in his bag of tricks. Adopting a defeated air, he reached up for the proffered hand.

****

The team leader of the outside crew was a huge beast of a man who put most people in mind of a missing link or some kind of freakish throwback. He had thick, cruel features and a large hawkish nose that had been broken too many times to resemble its original shape. His hair was black as pitch, cut close to his scalp revealing the crisscross of scars across his scalp that formed a roadmap of the many injuries it had survived.

Almost like a cartoon character, his huge cranium came almost to a point at the crown, like a bony oversized egg. Small, feral eyes hid beneath a jutting brow with a coarse unbroken cord of coarse black hair serving as eyebrows. A thick square jaw bristled with several days of stubble over a face once ravaged by acne that had left the skin full of pockmarks and scar tissue. Massive shoulders and a heavily muscled barrel chest sat atop legs thick as tree stumps. The machine pistol in his meaty fist looked like a child's toy. But despite his brutish appearance, Kruseff was the most skilled weapons technician and close combat specialist Gorsky had ever known. The man was an accomplished expert with more weapons than Gorsky could name, guns, knives, hell, even a bullwhip. He was a walking mountain of destructive force. Which is probably why, when he saw Jason open the side door and begin walking, apparently unafraid, directly toward him, he smiled.

It was a horrible sight to see for anyone who didn't know him and still uncomfortable for those who did, because there was no real amusement in it, just the welcome anticipation of breaking bones and rending flesh. The small man was obviously unarmed, easy enough to see for someone with Kruseff's training. A person carrying a weapon moved differently than one who was unarmed. There was a swagger, an arrogance that carrying lethal force brought with it. So Kruseff made a show of bending down to place his weapon on the ground and cracked his scarred knuckles with a loud crackle like firecrackers popping.

The huge Russian moved slowly across the grass of the empty lot that separated the Gibson's home from the next structure. Only about twenty feet remained between the two men when the hulking monstrosity spoke in broken English. "You want die, eh little man?" he growled. His voice sounded like a cross between a long-time radio DJ named after a werewolf and a psychopathic movie madman with knives for hands. Incredibly, the much smaller man just kept walking towards impending doom like he was out for a Sunday stroll. He might just as well have been whistling. This infuriated Kruseff, and he decided to show this little American punk the real meaning of pain. With just a few swift strides, the man mountain crossed the last few feet of space between himself and the cocky American.

He pulled his right arm back and launched a straight punch that had once been used to smash through a solid oak door. This time, however, that door was able to move and the American easily avoided the potentially lethal blow. That wouldn't have been so bad except that what he did after that should have been impossible.

Jason slipped under the tree branch the monster called an arm and grabbing the man's wrist as it passed over his head with his left hand, he then pushed upward with unbelievable force, locking Kruseff's right elbow in place. Jason pivoted to his left and pushed with what looked like ridiculous ease and sent the wide-eyed giant sailing through the air to land fifteen feet away flat on his back.

 As he slammed hard to the ground on a patch of dry red Georgia clay and rocks, the air in his lungs was violently expelled with a great whoosh of air. Pinpoints of light sparkled in front of the big man's eyes as he fought to draw a breath. After what seemed an eternity, he was finally able to turn over onto his belly and get to his hands and knees. Shaking the light show from his eyes like a stunned animal, the big man couldn't believe what he was seeing. The little man was methodically working his way through nearly a dozen battle hardened mercenaries as if he were dancing with children. The frustrated soldiers had been reluctantly forced to abandon their weapons. Because of the close quarters, two of them had been accidentally shot dead by their companions. Their elusive target kept dodging and swerving, almost as if he somehow could sense the deadly shots before they were fired, and the other soldiers unwittingly found themselves in the line of fire.

In close combat, there should have been no way that seasoned veteran fighters would be bested by one man, no matter how skilled, but that was exactly what Kruseff was seeing.

Blind rage helped him shake off the last of the cobwebs in his head, and he rapidly launched himself to his feet, bearing down on the tough little bastard like an unstoppable T-72 tank.

He reached the incredibly elusive man just as he summarily dispatched the last mob fighter with a wicked back elbow to the right side of his jaw. Grabbing the little man by the throat, he easily lifted him high in the air determined to crush his throat and discard him like an old rag doll. Instead, Jason crossed his arms, and with a sharp twisting motion, managed to lock one of the charging Russian's massive wrists between his surprisingly strong hands. With a grip that felt like a hydraulic powered vise, the guy forced Kruseff to open his other huge hand.

Bending himself tight into a ball and turning in the opposite direction, Jason pulled forward yanking the much bigger man off balance and rolling forward to the ground as the huge Russian came down, seemingly on top of him. At the last moment, Jason executed another pivoting change of direction and came up with an arm bar, just as Kruseff slammed to the ground on his back.

Pinning the big man's shoulder between his powerful legs, he applied brutal pressure to the thick stump of Kruseff's practically non-existent neck. Jason then straightened his body, isolating the elbow and pulled with uncanny strength. Kruseff began to fear his arm might actually tear free of its socket. He screamed in impotent rage and searing pain. With one last, herculean effort he rose to his feet, preparing to slam the little man to the ground.

Before he could get enough leverage to make the move, however, Jason bent his left knee, pulled his foot back, and delivered a quick spine shocking kick with the flat of his foot to the big Russian's jaw, and for Kruseff the mighty, out went the lights.

As Gorsky took the offered hand of his hated enemy with his left hand, he craftily concealed the view of his right hand with the motion of his body as he was pulled from the floor. For a few seconds he presented the air of a beaten man who has faced the fact that he has been defeated. He kept his gaze fixed on the floor and let out a huge sigh of grudging acceptance. Then, in an unbelievably quick move, he yanked forward on his foe's hand and jammed the snout of his .45 caliber semiautomatic handgun into the guy's left side and pulled the trigger repeatedly as fast as he could. Gorsky allowed a cruel satisfied smirk to spread across his face as he finally got this man where he wanted him.

He glared with gruesome anticipation into the big man's eyes eager to see the sudden realization of impending death, accompanied by shock and horrific pain. Unfortunately, after a second or two the eyes that held shock and surprise were not his victim's but his own. So consumed by anger and frustration, myopically focused on the sweet final victory over this most surprising and unexpected enemy, Gorsky's senses went on autopilot. The merciless Russian gangster realized two things almost simultaneously. First, his opponent's eyes held nothing more than something Gorsky was completely unfamiliar with, compassion. The second was his brain registering what his ears had been telling it for several seconds. There had been no loud bark from the powerful weapon in his gnarled fist, only the dull click of the hammer slamming against

an empty chamber. It was impossible. Gorsky had been rigorously trained and was exceedingly proficient on more weapons than he could remember, since he was a child.
He could no more walk into battle with an unloaded weapon than he could breathe underwater. As he looked into the dark robed man's hazel green eyes, he began to feel the strangest sensation. He became dizzy and lightheaded but without the sickening nausea that usually accompanied such sensations. The big man's hand was still clasped with his, and Gorsky was certain that if it hadn't been, he might have fallen to the floor like a marionette with its strings suddenly cut. The world began to darken, and Gorsky suddenly understood he was passing out for some unknown reason. But, as he descended from darkness into a bright white haze, he could hear the man's deep voice beside, behind, in front of, and seemingly all around him. "It doesn't have to end this way for you Vasily," he said. With yet another surprise, Gorsky realized the man was speaking fluently in flawless Russian. "What do you mean?" he heard his own voice reply as if spoken by someone else.
"This day can be about change for you, for the better. All your life, you have chased money, power, and respect, but respect given out of fear or threat of violence, not affection and admiration. I know you were raised Catholic. You know the word of God better than many, but you choose to ignore it."
Gorsky felt like he was on some kind of dizzying ride at a travelling carnival. It felt surreal, yet somehow even more real than anything he had ever known. How could this man, whom he knew absolutely nothing about have so much knowledge about him

and his life. He knew that all information about his Catholic upbringing had been purged from any official records when he began working special operations in the soviet military. There were absolutely no traces of it anywhere, yet this man knew as if he had been there himself.

"This is a trick." he heard himself say with no certainty at all. "You have drugged me somehow; this is some elaborate interrogation technique." Even as he spoke the words, Gorsky knew they didn't ring true, even to himself.

Suddenly, the man's inexplicably blurry face filled Gorsky's field of vision like a huge image on the screen of a movie theater. The only things that were clear were the big man's intense hazel eyes. The strange glow, that Gorsky noticed before was back and appeared to light them from behind, like keys on a laptop computer. The eyes grew until they were all Gorsky could see, like sitting in the front row of that theater staring up at the screen as gigantic images scrolled across it.

"You know that is not the case my friend." Gabe said. "This is a turning point for you. We are all given countless opportunities throughout our lives to take one of two paths. One path leads to joy, fulfillment, everlasting life. and peace. The other is the road to ruin and damnation. Many times, every day, He gives us chances to correct our course and follow the right path. But the choice is always ours, He never takes that free will from us. Only if we seek the right direction through our own desire for salvation does He guide and nurture us. The other path is directed by the fallen one."

"You mean the devil?" Gorsky asked.

"Yes, that is one name we know him by, but he has many, whichever suits him at any given time." Gabe replied.

"So, what are you telling me, that I'm going to Hell?" Gorsky asked, suddenly feeling like a small child in religion class.

"What I'm telling you," Gabe said, "is that the choice is yours. God can use you to glorify His kingdom and make a place for you in it. All you have to do is ask. All He wants is our love, Vasily, no tricks, no deceptions. Just love Him as He loves us and love each other as we love ourselves."

At some point during this waking dream, Gorsky dropped his weapon. He reached up feeling a sudden wetness on his face and found hot tears rolling down his cheeks. He didn't remember wanting or starting to cry.

"So, I ask you know, Vasily Gorsky, will you change your direction? Will you follow a different path?" Gabe asked.

"But I have been...." the Russian struggled for the right words, "this way, for so long. I have murdered men, women, even children. What place could I possibly have in the kingdom of God?" he asked, incredulous.

"Vasily, you only have to repent and ask Him for forgiveness." The gigantic eyes seemed to twinkle as the unseen mouth spoke. "Will you?" he asked again.

At that point, something hidden buried deep within what Gorsky thought of as his black wicked soul stirred. It had been gone from him for so long, he almost failed to recognize the sensation. It was hope, pure and clean as the bright eyes of a child on Christmas morning. Emerging as a tiny spark, it rapidly grew and grew until it became a bright, fiercely glowing beacon in the stygian gloom that had been his life for so long. It was then that the little Russian felt himself remade, as if his former body had been thoroughly peeled away like the old, dull, shedding skin of a snake. Without hesitation, with more hot tears spilling down his cheeks, Gorsky answered. "Yes, I will!"

Gorsky's rebirth felt to him as if it had taken hours, but as he once again became aware of his surroundings, he could still hear the echo of the metallic click from the last pull of the trigger on his gun and the dull thud as the weapon dropped to the floor from his limp hand. His other hand was still tightly held in Gabriel's firm grip. The gun lay near his right foot and he quickly kicked it away, as if its proximity would undo the miracle he just felt. He looked at his former bitter enemy in a different light, as a newfound friend with wonder and a profound sense of gratitude. "Thank you." he said sincerely.

Gabriel answered warmly, "You are most welcome, my friend," with a smile, that to Vasily Gorsky felt like family. The next day, Gorsky resolved to begin making amends, as best he could. He drove to the site of last night's attempt to destroy his two mysterious antagonists. Pulling up to the curb at the front of the house, the Russian swallowed the huge lump of shame in his throat and walked to the front door of the historic residence.

His forces had been led by him the night before from the opposite side of the house, so he actually hadn't seen the front of the building. Gorsky rang the bell, surprised that it was still working. In his jacket pocket, the former gangster carried an envelope, containing enough cash to remodel the entire structure two or three times.

When Ruth Gibson opened the door with her ready smile and curious eyes, Gorsky almost turned and ran from porch. He steeled himself, however, and began explaining that he was incredibly sorry and ashamed to have been the cause of the catastrophic damage to her beautiful home.

He hoped that the kind lady would allow him the honor to pay for all of the damage possibly put her and her husband up in a nice hotel while the repairs were being made.

Throughout his confession, Ruth Gibson stood with patience and an odd expression on her face. When the Russian finished his plea, she reached out and clasped his right hand with both of hers. The pure and simple kindness in her eyes made Gorsky's chest tighten with emotion.

The short, plump Georgia peach of a woman looked him straight in the eye and said, "Young man, I have absolutely no idea what you are talking about. She opened the door and stepped back to let the man enter and Gorsky was struck speechless as he plainly could see there was not so much as a figurine out of place in the room, he had seen grenades destroy. His eyes wide as saucers, he looked all around the first floor of the townhouse and could not find the slightest indication of the destructive mayhem from the previous night. Explaining that he must have the wrong address, Ruth accompanied the completely confused man back to the front door. Handing her the thick envelope from his pocket, Gorsky told her she could keep it or she could donate it to her favorite charity. Showing him her angelic smile, once again, Ruth assured him she would find a good use for it. He thanked her and left, confused but relieved as well.

THIRTEENTH CHAPTER

Dayton is a medium sized city situated along the shores of the Great Miami River, in southwestern Ohio. Officially, the greater Dayton area lists a population of just over 143,000. Dubbed the City of Neighbors (by overly optimistic politicians) and the location of one of the U.S. Air Force's most vital bases, Wright Patterson, it is situated in the middle of a western curve between Columbus and Cincinnati. Rich in history, as the home of the Wright brothers and the site of the historic Dayton Accords, it, potentially, has much to offer. However, like any large city, it has more than its share of seedy characters and rampant crime, not all of it in urban areas. One of the most prominent figures in illicit activity in not only Dayton but the entire tri-state area was a man named Raymond Buckingham Taylor. Known in most circles as Buck, Big Buck, or The Buck, he was an exceptionally large man.

Standing six feet six inches, he weighed nearly four hundred pounds. He wore his thick, shoulder-length blond hair in an intricate variation of a French braid, almost like a Viking. Having once been a gifted boxer on the rise to the pro circuit, he still had thick cords of steely muscle that even years of privileged living had been unable to hide.

Buck was built on a thick boned frame that gave him the look of an animated refrigerator with freakishly strong hands the size of frying pans. Due to a rare genetic mutation, his eyes were such a pale shade of blue they almost looked like the milky orbs of a blind man. His skin was tanned year-round to a coppery hue which highlighted the pale irises even more and his expansive belly was strategically concealed by flawlessly tailored suits. Even his leisure wear was cut to present him in the most complimentary manner. Not having been born to wealth, Buck clawed his way up the criminal ladder one violent bloody rung at a time.

An unfortunate injury to his right knee as a young man ended his in-ring hopes, and having no other marketable skills, the young Taylor made ends meet as a leg breaking enforcer for a local drug lord. That was during the height of the crack cocaine epidemic of the late eighties and early nineties.

He cemented his growing reputation as a cruel ruthless gangster by killing his employer with his bare hands and taking over his business. Buck then branched out into prostitution, illegal gambling, extortion, and eventually anything that would turn a profit including the sale of illegal firearms. He was now the head of a criminal empire with an unofficial value estimated by the FBI, ATF and DEA at over a billion dollars a year, completely off the books and extremely difficult to trace.

His many legitimate enterprises were key to hiding vast amounts of cash, property, and other assets. Even the ATF had been frustratingly unable to connect him to any illegal arms deals suspected of supplying domestic terrorists, white supremacists, and government separatists to common armed robbers on the street.

It had now been a number of years since it was actually necessary for Buck to get his hands dirty with 'wet work', since he now employed plenty of people both male and female to handle the grunt work. Every now and then, however, he felt the need to keep his hand in the game, so to speak. Standing in the spacious well-appointed living room of one of several houses he kept for 'business' purposes, Buck watched through the open vertical blinds of a large bay window as wind driven snow blanketed the suburban landscape.

It was a fairly typical day for Ohio in December. The temperature over the past week fluctuated on a swing of up to forty degrees. At this particular time, it was frigid with a bitter wind chill of up to ten degrees below zero. There were only a few inches of accumulated snow on the ground, but the local forecast predicted the snow would end by late evening. Buck liked the winter weather. It made people antsy not being able to frolic in the sun, so they found ways to entertain themselves indoors which usually meant more money for his various business ventures.

One of those businesses that had seen a huge spike recently was the heroin trade. An unidentified genius or complete idiot, depending on who you asked, recently made a game changing discovery. He or she found that by adding powerful pain relievers or tranquilizers to the drug, you could extend the supply by a huge margin. Then you could sell a much more potent product at a very cheap price.

Buck's dealers were selling the powerful drug at five dollars a hit, and he could barely keep up with the demand. There was, however, an unfortunate side effect. Many of the junkies failed to consider, partially because they had not been informed, the greatly increased strength of their preferred recreational substance.

They were snorting and shooting up what they assumed was their normally tolerated amount and were dying from overdoses in increasingly large numbers. The now enhanced heroin resulted in respiratory arrest that unless reversed with a counter agent, led to the heart stopping as well. Many died because they were alone or with other users who either failed or were afraid to call EMS.

Pharmacies were struggling to keep up with the demand for a drug called Narcan which many agencies used to counter the powerful narcotic. Buck really couldn't care less if some of the street junkies kicked the bucket, but the death of some high-profile celebrities had his more upscale customers becoming increasingly reluctant. Some even seeking rehab, and THAT was unacceptable. He had given explicit instructions to his distributors that serviced these high dollar clients to provide them with only "the good stuff", minimally cut and only with one of his pre-approved cutting agents. One of these distributors took it upon himself to blatantly violate this cardinal rule, and the result was a city politician who was in Buck's pocket wound up in the ICU at Good Samaritan hospital on a ventilator.

Now there was even more pressure on the chief of police to crack down on this rapidly growing problem. That translated into a negative impact on Buck's bottom line, and that absolutely could not be tolerated. A message had to be sent, and he was just the messenger for the job.

Some days it just doesn't pay to get out of bed. That was the thought foremost in the mind of Leon 'Lucky' Carver as he stepped out of the customized Cadillac Escalade that delivered him to Buck's little 'motivational' center. The driver, known only as Six, turned off the big SUV and came around to escort Lucky to the house.

Six instinctively gave most people the creeps. No one could ever say exactly why. It was just a gut feeling. He was a physically small man standing only a few inches above five feet. He almost always had a lit cigarette in the corner of his mouth and was never seen without his Ray Ban Aviator sunglasses.

Some people even said he probably slept in them. A white man with a ruddy complexion and numerous scars from horrible acne as a teen, Six wore his wavy, black hair in a style reminiscent of a male fashion model. It was longer on top and tapered on the sides and back until it was hard to tell where the hair stopped, and his florid skin began. He had a wiry muscled frame, and Lucky knew the little man could run most guys into a ditch puking their guts out.

His past was something of a mystery, but one fact that was known was that he had been discharged from the military under less than honorable conditions. Lucky knew that despite his stature, Six was beyond lethal. With the creepy little man trailing just behind him and off to his left side, Lucky approached the cottage style house situated at the rear of a cul-de-sac in a suburb of Dayton, Kettering. Buck had purchased the other four houses that had formerly been there, then had them torn down just so there would be no neighbors.

There was a country club with a sprawling golf course located about a mile away directly behind the property and there was nothing but thick wooded hills between the house and the elitist playground. Lucky's throat was tight, and his pulse quickened as he turned the plain brass knob and stepped inside. The house had only two bedrooms and was ordinary. The furnishings were inexpensive, but tasteful. It was apparent that it had been cozy at one time. Now, it had a bit of a motel feel as there were no personal touches; no smell of food in the kitchen, no family pictures, not even a dish or a coffee cup in the sink to indicate habitation.

Buck stood in the modest living room in front of the small fireplace where there were actually a couple of logs burning to keep the Midwestern chill in the air at bay. The look on the kingpin's face was pleasant enough, but the expression didn't reach his icy, pale eyes. They were as flat and lifeless as those of a waterlogged corpse. Although he would never say it out loud, one of the things Lucky disliked about Buck was that he liked to beat around the bush before he got to business, like a cat toying with his prey.

He would bait little traps in his conversation and try to get them to sell themselves out. "Lucky, my man!" Buck said, moving forward to clap his meaty hand on the smaller man's shoulder. Buck usually reserved handshakes for friends and people who could further his standing not employees.

The raw power in his steely grip was evident as he squeezed slightly. Lucky had to hold back an involuntary grimace as he responded. "What's goin on Boss?" he asked with a weak attempt at a smile.

"Just getting out of the office." Buck answered. "It gets a little claustrophobic in there from time to time." Buck had a smooth mellow voice, just a touch too high pitched to suit a man of his size. As he spoke, Buck guided his associate to the kitchen and waved a hand indicating he should have a seat. There were four high stools situated around a central island where the sink and range were located. As Lucky sat down, the big man went to the fridge and pulled out two beers. It was some sort of imported brown stuff that Lucky never developed a taste for, but he knew better than to refuse the offer. Buck didn't handle rejection well. Producing a bottle opener from a drawer in the island, his employer opened the beer and handed one to him. "Thanks." Lucky managed.
"So tell me about business.....Lucky. How are things going?" The way Buck hesitated before saying his name made Lucky even more nervous. He could feel cold perspiration break out on his forehead and upper lip.

"Everything is going good, Man," he said and took a pull of the beer to cover the tremor in his voice. "Numbers are solid. I got a couple of runners that need to grow some balls, but mostly everything is cool."
"Good. I'm glad to hear that." Buck responded. "There's a lot of heat coming from downtown because of these junkies turning up dead. You having any problems with that in your area?" Lucky thought about that for a minute. His assigned clientele was mostly prominent businessmen and women. He had a few street people that he worked on the side, but they largely had jobs even if they were minimum wage. A couple of them had OD'd, but the medics hit them with that Narcan. They woke up

pissed that their high was blown, but they were at least alive.
"Not that I know of Boss." he said.
"So, you would say everything is firmly under control?" Buck
asked.
 The way the man was looking at him now made Lucky
positive he had just stepped into a trap. He had no idea what
Buck was talking about, but he knew that any attempt to
mislead the former enforcer would end badly. "I would have
to say so Boss, yeah."
His throat was suddenly as dry as the Mojave desert. Lucky
took another pull from the beer and somehow didn't see the
straight, right-handed punch that crashed into his face
knocking him from the stool to land hard on the ceramic tile
floor. The blow shattered the beer bottle and laid Lucky's
nose open down to the cartilage, blood spraying across the
room. The back of his head bounced off the hard tile, and he
felt bile rise in his throat. Desperately choking back, the urge
to vomit, Lucky held his hands up in front of him pleading
with the hulking gangster standing over him with his huge
fists clenched.
"Wait, Man, wait!!" he cried. "What did I do?" He tried to
focus, but his head was swimming. He felt like he was about
to pass out. Involuntary tears sprang from his eyes and ran
down his cheeks, mixing with the blood from his ruined nose.
He tasted the salty tears and the coppery tang of blood in his
mouth and his belly heaved.

"I don't know what pisses me off more." Buck said dangerously. There was a look in his boss's eyes now that Lucky had no trouble identifying. He had seen it before. It was the look of a predator about to move in for the kill. "The fact that you fucked up so monumentally or the idea that you don't even KNOW you fucked up!" Buck said, clenching his huge fists in anger. "I gave you a select clientele because you seemed to have a good grasp on the market. But now I see you're just another dumbass not worthy of the trust I put in you."

Had there been any neighbors, Lucky's hysterical cries, the brutal sounds of fists striking flesh, and the gruesome sound of breaking bones would've made even the most hardened soul cringe. Twenty horrendous minutes passed, the tearful pleas and the cries of agonized pain faded away, and still the wet meaty smack of hard fists on bloody flesh continued.

Ten minutes later, Buck stood breathing heavily, yet feeling amazingly energized and invigorated. He moved to the sink and began washing his blood drenched hands. Having stood silently, smoking his ever-present cigarette near the front door, Six produced a thick plush hand towel from a pocket in his heavy coat. He handed it to Buck and went back to his post by the door, stepping over the quivering ruin of a man that had been Leon Carver. Six looked down at the pitiful wretch, uncaring and amazingly the poor bastard managed to look up with his one still functioning eye. The last thing Lucky saw was the heavy tread on the sole of Buck's size sixteen boot rushing toward his face. The last thing he heard was the loud crack of his own skull as it collapsed under the big man's boot. Lucky Leon Carver died without ever being told what he had done wrong or why his luck had so abruptly run out.

FOURTEENTH CHAPTER

Lucky Leon's replacement was a woman named Ivory, a truly impressive woman, both physically and intellectually. Buck knew the striking woman's last name. Six probably knew as well, but Ivory never told anyone else what it was. She was one of the few females in a true power position within Buck's organization, and she got there by being absolutely ruthless. She didn't accept excuses, and more than one hole had been dug for both men and women who made the critical mistake of underestimating her.

She was a tall, striking woman with what most people referred to as a full-figured body. She had clear, very pale skin and silky hair as white as summer clouds. Her eyes were a clear, light, beautifully unique shade of green and shone with an intensity that could be downright frightening if she was displeased. Her ex-husband whose surname she now refused to go by could attest to that. She stood nearly six feet tall and had an uncommonly commanding tone of voice, although no one still living had ever heard her raise her voice above it's normal soft register. Like all of Buck's executives, she didn't use drugs and rarely took a drink, even then only a glass of wine or two. That was where the similarities ended between her and her peers.

Ivory had a master's degree in chemistry and a P.H.D. in business management. She was cultured, extremely refined, and had grown up in high society. She was accustomed to having only the best of everything. However, when her ex-husband, a former financial guru on Wall Street, was sent to prison for embezzlement having swindled hundreds of people out of their life savings, her posh lifestyle temporarily came to a humiliating end. The bastard had used her family name and most of her substantial trust to leverage many of his shady deals, and she had been left with little more than the clothes on her back.

Unwilling to start over at the bottom in someone else's company and give up the life she was accustomed to, she was intrigued by Buck's offer of lucrative work if she could handle........extreme personnel. She met the crime lord at a party given by a mutual acquaintance. He, of course, knew of her reversal of fortunes due to the extensive media coverage. Impressed by her manner and always looking for people with superior management skills, Buck offered her a way to get her preferred status in life back. Used to being approached by men, and women for that matter, Ivory was impressed that there was no hint of the customary sexual overtures from the big man.

He was only, at least outwardly, interested in business, and that greatly appealed to her. She found it refreshing. Buck never treated her differently than any of his other lieutenants, unless it was to hold her up as an example to follow. She increased the productivity in the territory that was given her by over forty percent. All it took was the removal of some unnecessary personnel who were only in the organization because of their association with the previous manager.

After that, she identified a number of people whose habits were being supplied basically for free. Once these particular freeloaders and hangers on were cut off, she instituted extreme penalties for anyone deviating from her business model. It didn't take long for the message to spread. Now she was being given an opportunity to really move up. Lucky's position was one of only ten lieutenants, and word on the grapevine was that Buck was considering promoting one person that would handle these lieutenants and be accountable to no one but him, a Chief of Staff so to speak. Ivory was determined that it would be her.

She was on her way now to get the final details of her new position from the head honcho himself. Buck had to admit he was thoroughly pleased as well as very impressed with Ivory. She was keenly intelligent, superbly refined, and a damn good-looking woman to boot. Her generous natural curves appealed to him a great deal more than those of the plastically enhanced little Barbie dolls that usually approached him with silicone boobs, botoxed faces, collagen filled lips. Buck preferred his women more authentic. His relationship with the newly promoted former lieutenant had so far been kept on a strictly professional footing. However, as she sat across from him at The Paragon Supper Club, he seriously considered changing that.

 The Paragon was one of Dayton's finer eateries and one of Buck's personal favorites. The food was consistently delicious and flawlessly prepared. The atmosphere was romantic, yet still suitable for family dining. The walls of the dining area were a dark brown stone facade, and soft lighting came from wall mounted sconces. The main dining area was spacious, but still managed to convey a cozy feel.

The staff was attentive and efficient without being pushy or snobbish. Ivory sipped at a glass of Chardonnay while Buck's imported Lager sat untouched in its perspiring glass. Small talk had been dispensed with, and his new upper-level manager sat patiently waiting for him to get to the matter at hand. The expression on her face was attractive to him. She was not at all intimidated by his money and power, and she was completely comfortable waiting for him to begin. She showed no nervousness or anxiety, and she didn't fidget like many of his employees did in his presence. Breaking from his musings, he spoke in quiet tones, "Ok, so here is the way I see your position." Those lovely blue eyes gazed unwavering in full attention as he spoke.

 "Leon was, for the most part, competent in his position, but I always knew that he was as far as he would go in my organization. I see a different future for you if it's what you want."

"You do?" She asked.

Her voice was a rich sultry alto, and her perfectly straight, exceptionally white teeth flashed brilliantly when she spoke. "Why do you say that, and what exactly do you see differently?" There was a mild tone of caution lurking in her words that told Buck he needed to be very precise in his wording. He didn't want her to get the impression he was asking her to "sleep" her way to the top. He honestly respected her ability to get things done, and he admired her no-nonsense approach in handling her people. These were both traits he had found in rare supply in his chosen trade. The people working for her were happy because she paid them well with added incentives for productivity, and she treated them fairly. She allowed them time with their families if their production didn't suffer. The other side of that coin was that she came down hard on under achievers. She accepted no excuses and absolutely did not tolerate lies. If one of her runners got hemmed up by the cops or jacked by a competitor, she fully expected the shortfall to be made up immediately.

"Well first," Buck continued, "This position I've created was specifically designed with you in mind. I've never had the benefit of someone to help me cultivate allies both in the private sector and in government. With the connections you've made because of your station, you could prove invaluable to me in this effort."

Ivory placed her right hand under her chin, and Buck could see she was genuinely intrigued. "I like the sound of that so far." she said. And she did. The position he was describing was right up her alley, and it would put more distance between her and the grimy guts of the operation. She was waiting for the catch though. The one where she would have to earn this tailor-made post from the confines of Buck's bedroom. He seemed to sense this and immediately clarified the proposal.

"This position is largely autonomous. Although you will be accountable to only me, we won't be joined at the hip. The position is yours if you want it, if not I'll find someone else. I will tell you, though, yours is the only name I've considered so far." At that he smiled, and Ivory began to see how truly handsome he was.

She normally didn't care for long hair on a man, but somehow Buck pulled it off.

Ivory had at first taken him for simply being heavy, having only seen him in tailored suits. This evening he was wearing smart tan slacks and a light blue polo shirt that revealed the rippling muscles in his chest and arms. He was wearing an expensive cologne that spoke of a combination of citrus and spice that was very pleasant yet distinctly masculine and, if she was honest, very stimulating.

Ivory suddenly realized she had been staring at him in appraisal instead of merely paying attention. Considering his last sentence, she knew her open perusal could be taken the wrong way. Buck was aware of her scrutiny and seemed not at all put off by it. Not the type to blush, Ivory covered the momentary lapse by taking a sip of her wine. Placing the glass back on the table she got back to business. "What would you expect the daily duties to be?" she asked.

"I imagine the hours would be dynamic, as the need requires." he said.

He took a long pull from his cold beer, the glass dripped perspiration and he dabbed his mouth with a napkin. Ivory caught herself gazing at his full lips and silently chided herself. What the hell was wrong with her? Fortunately, this time he didn't notice.

"I'll take you on a tour of introduction. A sort of meet and greet with my more influential contacts, some of whom are in a position to greatly increase our scope of operations. That's where I see the need for a keen mind and sharp instincts to help with the expansion into new markets." Buck could tell she was still waiting for the catch. So, he decided to be candid with her and see what happened. "To be clear, I do find myself strongly attracted to you. To say I wasn't would be like serving you a bowl of bullshit and calling it chili. However, this position has no connection to that whatsoever. Regardless of your reaction to that fact, however, the job is still yours if you want it." At his honest admission and frank clarification, Ivory smiled, and her face lit up with the expression.

There was a demure quality in her lovely blue eyes that Buck found infinitely appealing in a woman of Ivory's stature. "I'm glad to hear that." she said, and Buck

could've sworn that her voice slipped into a completely
different register, and he wasn't quite sure exactly what she
was glad to hear. There was now more of a husky quality that
piqued his interest.

"Well, you don't have to sound so relieved!" he quipped, "Am
I *THAT* undesirable?"

"Not at all," She chuckled. "Quite the opposite, in fact."
Their server, a tall willowy redhead, came to check if they
needed refills on their drinks and to see if they wanted to
order anything to eat. They decided to have dinner. Buck
decided the decision to promote Ivory may just have been one
of his best. Little did he know she was thinking something
very similar. After dinner, Buck had Ivory meet him at his
office to finalize her appointment.

The drug trade in the territory Buck had carved out for
himself had always been very lucrative, but with the advent of
adding painkillers to heroin, he had been seeing profits that
dwarfed all previous years. He had just gotten off the phone
with a contact in Croatia that gave him incredible news.
Through a fortuitous tip from a relative working in a chemical
processing plant, the man had discovered a huge shipment of
pharmaceutical grade heroin bound for China.

Over 20,000 kilos were being shipped, and thanks to weapons
and mounds of cash for mercenaries supplied by Buck, the
entire load had been hijacked and was ready for transport to
the U.S. This cargo represented, literally billions of dollars on
the street! Buck was ecstatic. With Ivory's help, he would be
able to extend his power and influence further than ever
before. There would be no stopping the two of them as they
built a vast distribution network that would cover over half
the country. The best part
was that no one knew anything about it. The authorities in
Croatia had no leads on who committed the crime or where
the powerful drugs were now headed.

By the time anyone who could interfere found out, it would be much much too late. Buck sat back, taking a long drag from a fat, still illegal, Cuban cigar. He let the smoke out slowly, playfully blowing rings as the aromatic mist rose into the air of his opulent office. He jabbed a thick finger at the intercom button and told his assistant to send for Ivory. This occasion called for a celebration, and it just wouldn't have the same effect over the phone. After his assistant, Candy, acknowledged his request, Buck sat back and relaxed, putting his booted feet up on the edge of his expensive, hand carved, oak desk. After all, he thought, even God couldn't stop him from running the country after this deal.

****

Ivory was, surprisingly, very excited. When Candy told her that Buck wanted to see her, she felt an unaccustomed thrill pass through her like a charge of static electricity. She had no explanation for it, but the long absent sensation was a welcome change. She had become increasingly bored and totally disinterested in the predictable tedium of the so-called upper crust males. She was cruising North along State Route 741 headed toward Dayton. She was just south of the Dayton Mall having been at her condo in Springboro, a rapidly growing suburb between Dayton and Middletown, when she got the call. A few nights ago, following a second dinner with Buck, she had
willingly given in to the strong attraction she felt for the big man. The resulting encounter had been extremely satisfying for both of them.
Though long past the point of waiting by the phone for any man, Ivory was still pleased to get the call, saying that he wanted to see her. She knew that it was probably business related but found herself looking forward to seeing her employer again.

Thirty minutes later she sat on the other side of Buck's lavish desk trying to keep her jaw from dropping. The amounts of money Buck was talking about were staggering! This one shipment could vault him into the top tier of suppliers and exponentially increase his sphere of influence. This man who was quite obviously interested in her would soon be a major power broker on an international level, and she was as excited about it as an incoming First Lady of the United States. Pulling herself from the intoxicating visions of great power and influence, she refocused on the large man behind the desk. "Yes," she said, "If we can realize the entire street value you estimate, it'll buy us into both the House and the Senate, FEDERAL, not state."

Buck nodded in agreement. "That's exactly what I was thinking." Rising from behind the heavy desk, he said, "Let's have a drink." He walked smoothly over to the bar and poured a double bourbon for himself, and after asking Ivory for her choice, a single malt scotch for his guest.

"To grabbing the brass ring." He said raising his glass to meet hers with a clink. Ivory took a swallow of the rich expensive liquor and savored the tingling heat as it slid down her throat. Buck tilted his glass and threw the entire drink back in one swallow.

Just then Buck's mobile phone rang. The ringtone was a popular classic rock song that Ivory couldn't place. The big man answered and spoke just a few words to the person on the other end before ending the call. The smile on his face as he turned to her told her he'd gotten good news. "Our future has arrived," he said.

FIFTEENTH CHAPTER

The reason Buck was so supremely confident about this huge
new shipment of heroin was that one of his "Stompers" had
made a game changing discovery. Stompers were people
Buck employed to mix the powerful anesthetic drug with
other ingredients to stretch the supply or "step" on it.
One of them, totally by accident, discovered that if she added
a drug called Phendimetrazine to the formula of Heroin and
Fentanyl it could potentially prevent fatal overdoses. "Pmet",
as she dubbed it, was an extended-release stimulant, largely
prescribed for people with morbid obesity.
 When it was added to her heroin/Fentanyl hybrid, it kicked
in when body chemistry dropped to the point of respiratory
failure due to the increased acidity of the blood and pushed
the narcotic away from the body's chemical receptors. This
created a sort of safety net for addicts that allowed them to
reap the full benefit of the euphoric heroin high, increased in
potency by the efficacious pain reliever. This discovery would
set Buck's organization apart from all other suppliers. They
could give their customers the guaranteed assurance of the
absolute best high and grade-A quality with minimal risk of
overdose.
When word got around, their brand would become the
product of choice and the gold standard in every market they
could reach. Buck would become the Pfizer of illegal
pharmaceuticals. The increase in capital would be staggering,
and the effect it

would have on his personal influence would be immeasurable. The country would eventually be owned, at least unofficially, by one man. Then the real fun would begin.

The narcotics division of the Dayton Police Department was woefully understaffed and greatly overworked like most other large municipal departments. The huge influx of "Spiked" heroin had rapidly pushed an already out of control situation far beyond the breaking point.

Detective T'Mara Higgins ended the call on her smartphone and laid the compact device on her cluttered desk. She leaned on the desk with her elbows and closed her tired eyes. Putting her forehead in her hands, she sat motionless for a few minutes fighting the powerful urge to sleep. The information her C.I., or Confidential Informant, had just related to her made her feel like she was futilely trying to fend off a huge swarm of angry hornets with a broken flyswatter.

The rumors were true. Big Buck was about to make a move that would blanket the entire region in a virtual blizzard of the white poison known as heroin. Not only that, but it would also be a game changing formula that would skyrocket the drug lord's influence in the illicit drug market.

Higgins stood up and headed for the break room for a cup of strong black coffee. She was on the tail end of a double shift, and she desperately needed an infusion of caffeine. At least eight hours of sleep would've been preferable, but it didn't look like that was a possibility in the foreseeable future.

Higgins was not the typical picture of a homicide detective. She was black and very short, standing only a couple of inches above five feet. Her stature was what was commonly referred to in popular culture as "thick" or "curvy". The plentiful curves of her compact figure had at first made it difficult for her to be taken as more than "eye candy" around the department until she showed the male dominated organization what she was capable of. She had once stopped a man nearly twice her size with over a hundred pounds of weight advantage on her from brutally raping a barely teenaged girl. When the other officers on street patrol found out the guy had been sent to the hospital for three days before he could be placed in the jail, many took to calling her Cleopatra Jones. It was a reference to an old Pam Grier Blaxploitation film and a show of grudging respect. Her skin was the color of the steaming hot beverage she poured into a Styrofoam cup, if you added lots of cream. That skin was soft and smooth with a light sprinkle of freckles across the bridge of her small, delicate looking nose, across her prominent cheekbones and under her soft, dark brown eyes.

Her habitually clean reddish-brown hair, thick and full of natural curls, was currently pulled back in a ponytail that hung to a point just between her shoulder blades. Higgins had a well-known reputation for always being immaculately dressed no matter what time of day and that was fine with her. Her mother, a blonde, white woman, always stressed the importance of proper dress to all of her children which included Higgins, two older sisters and three older brothers. When they were young, their clothes were not the current popular fashion, but they were always spotlessly clean and meticulously maintained.

Higgins's father, a black man and a custodian by trade, had been killed in a botched home invasion when she was five. She could still vividly remember the tragic scene as if it had been burned into her mind's eye like the after image of the sun that remained after squeezing your eyes tightly shut.

James Higgins, having been awakened by an unfamiliar noise in the middle of an otherwise quiet night, found two men creeping into the small kitchen of his modest home, having easily picked the cheap lock. Throwing his full six foot two hundred fifty-pound frame into the move, he shouldered the door and slammed it shut against them before they could fully enter.

Higgins had quickly relocked it, turning the latch to secure the deadbolt, but before he could move back from the door, the quiet night erupted with the boom of gunfire as one of the men fired several shots from a nine-millimeter handgun through the aging wooden door. Two of the slugs struck the elder Higgins. One in the upper thigh, the other in his belly, just above his navel.

The would-be burglars hastily fled the scene in panic, and the Higgins family quickly converged on the kitchen having heard the loud commotion. Higgins remembered her mother, an emergency room nurse, being perfectly calm as she rapidly issued instructions to the older children. While Higgins's older brother held pressure on the thigh wound with a clean dish towel, her oldest sister did the same with the abdominal wound.

The warm slippery blood seeped past their fingers, and they were both crying but obediently did as they were told. Her father weakly groaned in agony as his family furiously worked together to keep him alive. In the midst of all of this turmoil, Higgins's dad locked eyes with her sitting terrified against the refrigerator, her knees hugged tightly to her chest. Even at five years of age, the little girl she had been read so much in her father's dark brown eyes; profound sorrow, deep regret, but most of all helpless anger. This was all so unfair. He clearly realized he would never see her grow up. Never walk her down the aisle. Never hold a grandchild in his arms.

Then, as she watched, the light slowly faded from his eyes, and his dark chocolate face went slack. Despite her mother and her siblings' best efforts, her father died right there on the linoleum covered kitchen floor. Right beside the heavy oak table where they all had sat for breakfast just that very morning.

Higgins knew, without a doubt, from that moment on, that one day she would be a police officer and a good one. She would dedicate her life to keeping mindless thugs, like the one who killed her beloved father off the streets. As she saw it, the path that created these merciless urban monsters could be traced directly back to rich self-absorbed men like Raymond Taylor. The new, lower risk drug would be an addict's Nirvana. Addicted men and women would go to great lengths to pay for it, including but not limited to robbery, murder, and prostitution. Now, according to her informant, Taylor was quietly promoting the most potent formula of enhanced heroin yet, with virtually no risk of overdose. If he could make good on that claim, people hooked on the powerful narcotic would sell their own mothers to get it.

Higgins took a cautious sip of the steaming coffee and grimaced. For some reason, whoever made what passed for coffee in the break room apparently thought it was supposed to taste like motor oil. And they, without fail, succeeded. It was loaded with caffeine though, and that's what she needed. Back at her desk the detective sat down heavily and slid her modestly manicured finger across the touchpad to wake up her laptop computer. There was a new email from a web address that she didn't recognize. Curious, after running the antivirus software, she clicked to open it. It was very simple and to the point.

Detective Higgins.

Within the next 48 hours there will be a large volume of ironclad evidence delivered to you concerning highly illegal activities carried out by Taylor Inc. It will be undeniable evidence, backed up by unimpeachable sources. These sources will be willing to testify in open court as to the accuracy of the information. You're probably thinking this is some kind of a joke or a prank of some kind, but I assure you it isn't.

In order to maximize your resources, you will need warrants for search and seizure at the following addresses as soon as possible.

There was a large number of addresses listed. One was in a residential area, but the rest were in business districts. Thoroughly familiar with the area indicated, Higgins knew several of them were most likely warehouses.

After reading the email three times, she sat staring intensely at the computer screen for several minutes, as if willing it to impart more information. For some unknown reason the brief message felt inexplicably genuine to her. For years she had prayed for some way to put Taylor's rapidly expanding operation out of business.

Unfortunately, although she instinctively knew he was neck deep in the illicit drug trade, she had so far been completely unable to prove a single thing. The man didn't have so much as a parking ticket. He couldn't be, even tenuously, connected to any illegal activities. But if the unidentified author of the mysterious email was to be believed, she would have everything she needed within the next two days. She told herself this had to be a hoax. Legally bulletproof men like Taylor didn't just drop into your lap gift wrapped with a big bow. As she often did when she was concentrating, Higgins unconsciously rubbed a small golden crucifix she wore on a thin gold chain around her neck.

The moment her fingers touched it, she felt a strong surge of energy course through her body, more energizing than ten cups of the 10W 30 crude oil laughingly called coffee in the break room. At that moment she knew with total clarity and unshakeable confidence that the unsigned email was completely authentic.

Galvanized into action, she hurried out to start earnestly lobbying for warrants.

SIXTEENTH CHAPTER

The big rig carrying Buck Taylor's highly illegal cargo was a sleek black machine built by a revolutionary company called Wolf. The futuristic, deceptively large rig was efficiently streamlined with a fully integrated matching trailer. At first glance it looked more like the aerodynamic engine of a bullet train. Buck had paid a positively obscene amount of money for both the patent as well as the plans and the demo model of the prototype, because it wasn't even in production yet. Once he'd laid eyes on it at a truck show exhibition, he knew he had to have it. He called the manufacturer directly and negotiated both the exclusive rights to the patent and a rush order for the prototype. Once he took delivery of the, literally, one-of-a-kind vehicle, he hired an international private security firm specializing in the installation of concealed weaponry.

Their clientele, outside of military contracts, were mainly high-end customers who because of the nature of their businesses couldn't always depend on traditional law enforcement agencies to protect their investments. Working in cooperation with the design engineers at Wolf, who produced the cutting-edge vehicle, the security firm's armorers diligently went to work customizing and upgrading the design of the truck. When their work was complete, the semi differed from an extremely powerful military tank and troop carrier only in its outer appearance, and it was infinitely better armed than most.

Its many upgrades included a nearly impenetrable, bullet resistant, armor plating, and next generation bullet resistant glass for the windshield and windows. It sported twin customized 60 mm cannons concealed behind the front grill that used "fire and forget" smart rounds. Laser guided, the high-tech ammo once locked on a target, could actually change direction nearly to the point of impact.

 The incredible rig was capable of accurately targeting and hitting a moving target while at a maximum speed of nearly 140 MPH, anywhere within a 360-degree radius around the vehicle. There were hidden armor shields that slid down over the huge run flat tires when needed and hidden missile pods on both sides of the cab, front, and rear. They fired the latest version of the lethal Hellfire missile.

Each pod held four missiles and there was a total of eight pods. In addition to back up these primary systems, there were 40 mm chain guns mounted below each missile launcher. Mounted on swiveling turrets and gyroscopically balanced gimbals, they created a virtual death zone around the lethal vehicle. That completed the rolling behemoth's partially automated, computer aided weaponry.

Then, inside, there were eight lockers mounted in the walls of the trailer, containing small arms, ranging from Heckler and Koch MP5 submachine guns to Smith & Wesson .40 and .45 caliber semiautomatic pistols.

There were also flash bang fragmentation and concussion grenades, as well as M2 50. caliber machine guns and LAW, light anti-tank weapons. An assortment of smoke and tear gas grenades finished out the complement of weaponry. The rig could carry twelve men, fully armed, seated in compact seats that folded down from inside the trailer's walls. An additional six men could be carried in the sleeper of the cab, and the cockpit of the tractor seated four. The inside of the cab was more reminiscent of a modern jet aircraft cockpit than that of a semi-truck. State of the art computer monitors for navigation and weapon systems control panels were packed into the surprisingly spacious interior. There were liquid crystal heads up displays, or HUD, on the inner surface of the broad windshield as well as above each monitoring station. It gave the driver, or pilot, access to all pertinent vehicle information and diagnostics ranging from fuel and available munitions status, as well as live feeds from internal and external, HD security cameras and several remote-controlled surveillance drones.

Weapons controls and ammo supply stats for automated and manually controlled systems were available by either touchscreen or voice command. The driver and passenger seats were ergonomically designed to maximize operator efficiency and comfort. Armrests also contained backup LCD touchpad controls for all systems. When all was said and done, the rig's final price was staggering eating up well over two years' worth of the entire organization's profits. But the investment had already proven to be worth every penny. In what was considered its "shake down" missions, it had been deployed against several rival factions. Shock and awe was a pitifully inadequate understatement to describe the brutal decimation inflicted on the unfortunate chosen targets. Something told Buck that now his huge investment in the flagship vehicle he came to think of as "The Bull" was about to pay off as never before.

About three months ago, an up-and-coming rival of Taylor's organization, named Juwon Tate was worried. Not just run of the mill worried but seriously, nail biting, foot tapping, gut churning worried. J.T. as he was known on the streets hated being worried. It made him feel weak and out of control the way he'd always felt as a boy. Both were unwanted feelings he had tried to leave behind for most of the ten years of his adult life, since dropping out of school at the age of seventeen. At that time, already two grades behind his classmates, Tate was probably looking at being a twenty-year-old graduate if he actually made it to graduation at all.

Raised in an aging government housing development, plagued with violence, known as The Desoto Bass Courts, J.T. learned from an early age how to either work the system or get worked over by the system. He had three "Baby Mamas" whom he used to scam the federal government out of welfare money, housing, and food stamps. They actually used something called EBT cards now. As soon as the children were weaned, he put the mothers back on the streets turning tricks. Most of that money went to J.T. as well. Having established that business model at nineteen, he branched out into dealing drugs and running a protection racket on the mostly impoverished Southwest side of Dayton. Over the years, he carved out a niche for himself by moving just enough product to compete without drawing the potentially fatal attention of larger, more connected suppliers. Oh, he made good money to be sure, but he knew where the line was drawn. J.T.'s sphere of influence ran along the west bank of the Miami River from as far south as Nicholas Road on the border of Moraine to as far North as Free Pike at the edge of Trotwood. Within that area were several prime drug consumption areas.

He supplied marijuana, cocaine, heroin and meth along with designer drugs like ecstasy to the college campus of the University of Dayton, the Veterans Administration complex, the downtown area around the Civic Center, and around the campuses of Miami Valley and Good Samaritan hospitals. This also included the Montgomery county Fairgrounds which provided a sizable income bump during the late summer when the county fair was in full swing. In addition, there were a number of low-income housing developments that provided opportunities for loan sharking and other scams. Although considered unemployed and having no reported income, J.T. had liquid assets in excess of twenty million dollars stashed in several secret locations throughout Dayton.

All in all, not bad for a high school dropout he felt. J.T. liked to live large, flaunting his "stacks" whenever possible. He had a sweet tricked out Range Rover with twenty-four-inch-deep dish Dayton chrome wheels. It was pearl white with gold pinstripe and luxurious white leather interior. The stereo system was premium Bose with sixteen speakers in addition to a huge subwoofer that took up the entire cargo compartment in the rear of the vehicle. J.T. no longer worried about being pulled over in his ride as he owned a few of the cops that were assigned to his area.

Even if he was given a ticket by an "honest" cop, one of the officers on his payroll would be sure to make the citation disappear. Unlike many other dealers, J.T. didn't move out of the hood when he started making serious money. He still lived within walking distance of "The Bass". He bought a small house along with a few similar homes on either side of it, then totally renovated and reinforced the interior. From outside, the small two-bedroom one bath house looked the same as many other buildings in the heavily gentrified area. Paint was peeling off in large flakes from the outer walls and the warped floorboards of the rickety front porch sagged giving the house a sad, worn-down look. The inside of the windows was covered with old, yellowing newspapers and the entire structure looked as if it should be condemned. The inside, however, was a totally different story. Tate had very little understanding of interior design opting for the more is better theory. The inside of the little house was crammed full of large, gaudy furniture and unnecessarily expensive electronics.

He had, however, had the forethought to have the load bearing members of the structure reinforced throughout the little home, as well as the floors, ceilings and the supporting framework for the roof. His taste in furnishings ran toward heavy gilt couches and chairs with thick leather cushions. Having been unable to find such items in any of the high-end furniture stores in the area he had them custom built.

J.T. also didn't believe in being uncomfortable, so he had the old house's ancient, radiant heat system replaced with an expensive top of the line central air unit. His "spot" as he called it was maintained at 70 degrees in the summer and a couple of degrees higher during the winter. Yes, J.T.'s life had been sweet as banana pudding until just a couple of weeks ago. One of his boys got a tip about some high-quality heroin or "H", changing hands up by the old Hara Arena on Dayton's Northwest end. J.T. asked his friend who would they be stealing from, but the man pointedly evaded the question, saying, "What difference do it make? We need to get dis money Man!"

So, against his better judgment, J.T. signed off on the plan. The crew picking up the drugs was more concerned about the sellers ripping them off than outsiders and were totally caught off guard by J.T.'s crew. They put up a brief fight and almost fought off the attackers, but in the end, J.T. and his men were victorious. It wasn't until the next day, when word got back to him that it was actually Big Buck's guys he had hit.

When he found out, the ambitious drug dealer and pimp's stomach felt as if it suddenly dropped into his shoes. J.T. knew this meant complete disaster. He'd spent the last two weeks, since then, nervously jumping at the slightest noise and searching every unfamiliar face for the slightest sign of aggression. He rarely left his house, and when he did, he was never alone. He had his people move all of his assets, including guns, drugs, and cash to a warehouse he owned off of South Gettysburg Avenue, one of the city's main North/South arteries.

The aging, expansive, multi-story building formerly housed auto and truck parts for General Motors. It had stood empty for years gathering dust, mold, and the normal detritus of birds and rodents. J.T. was able to buy it from the previous owner for next to nothing. He posted a virtual platoon of his most vicious soldiers in and around the building armed to the teeth and ready to shoot first and lawyer up later.

Tonight, he had his boy Bamma drive him to the warehouse in his tricked-out Range Rover. J.T. wanted to personally check on everything. He was extremely worried about Buck's people and also his own. With this much stuff in one place, it was a serious temptation for anyone, and his men were just as prone to grab some fast cash as anyone else.

The street raised thug harbored no false assumptions about loyalty when it came to looking out for number one. He felt somewhat comforted seeing all of his men attentively walking around the building with enough raw firepower to put down a hit by Al Qaeda. He was starting to think maybe he was just being paranoid.

Maybe, somehow, Taylor had let this one slip through the cracks. He was just about to tell Bamma that maybe they should start having everything taken back to its usual storage locations when he noticed a light gradually getting brighter shining through the windows on the East end of the building. The sun had set hours ago, and it was a dark gloomy and moonless night. Thick billowing clouds being pushed by warm humid air held the promise of a severe thunderstorm and blanketed the sky, blocking any light from the stars.

The light was rapidly getting brighter and brighter, and now J.T. heard a deep heavy rumble like a rapidly approaching train and the high-pitched whine of a powerful turbo engine, a very powerful turbo engine. The now blinding light blazed through the windows making it impossible to look directly at the source. J.T. and his crew could feel the cracked concrete floor vibrating as the heavy source of the blinding beams approached.

Sudden realization dawned on J.T., and eyes wide with fear, he abruptly yelled,

"MOVE!" The windows at the end of the building along with most of the wall and part of the second floor, erupted into the warehouse sending splinters of wood, jagged chunks of brick and razor-sharp pieces of glass flying through the open space. Two of J.T.'s men were too slow to move to cover frozen in place like deer on a country road. They were impaled multiple times and fell screaming to the floor writhing in agony.

J.T. waited behind the hulking mass of an old lathe machine for the deadly rain of debris to settle, then slowly raised his head, peeking over the top edge of the old machine to see what was happening. His mouth, full of gold capped teeth, dropped open in shock when he saw the massive futuristic semi sitting half in half out of the building.

It felt almost like a living breathing predator pinning him in its burning gaze, licking its chops in anticipation of the coming meal. As J.T. watched, the bright headlight beams switched to an eerie red giving the huge rig a truly demonic look like some huge beast from the deepest pit of hell. Suddenly the front grill slid up smoothly, and four wicked looking gun barrels thrust forward from the dark space behind it, locking into place with a loud metallic click. J.T. never believed in God and all that churchy mumbo jumbo his grandmother was always flappin' her gums about, but at that moment, he sincerely hoped he was wrong and said his first and probably last silent prayer for a way out of the warehouse that now threatened to become his tomb. Then the wicked looking weapons started firing, and J.T. doubted even God could hear him over the ensuing din.

SEVENTEENTH CHAPTER

Detective Higgins was totally swamped! She'd been given the daunting and unenviable task of wading into the shadowy world of Dayton's narcotics trade and making some attempt at significant high-level arrests. When she decided to transfer from vice to narcotics, she pictured herself busting the heavy product movers in the city to let the traffickers of poison know that not all cops were going to just throw up their hands and surrender.

Drugs were effectively destroying the city she loved and had grown up in, and she meant to do something about it.

Higgins had been fighting the typical stereotypes her whole life. Even though she had grown up on the violence wracked West side of Dayton, she was raised in a clean home with abundant love and compassion from BOTH parents in an interracial marriage.

Her father was a native of Dayton and met her British born mother while serving overseas in the United States Air Force. Both of her parents worked hard and diligently instilled the importance of that hard work into all of their children. Of all of her siblings, T'mara was the most driven to excel. Her brothers and sisters were all successful and productive in their chosen fields, but Higgins, in honor of her late father, was almost obsessed by the idea of living up to her full potential. She threw herself into every challenge with every fiber of her being to be the best.

She was active in cultural dance, soccer and volleyball in school and served on the student council in college. She also made time for charity work while earning her degree in criminology. She graduated at the top of her class in the police academy. In every endeavor, she consistently excelled. In her free time during college, she also earned a black belt in three different martial arts disciplines.

Every obstacle in her path was conquered with the same ruthless efficiency. She earned a nearly perfect score on her detective exam, soundly beating out any competition by an embarrassingly comfortable margin. Her career, up until her present assignment in narcotics, had been unblemished by failure. That made her inability to pin anything on Buck Taylor and his cronies that much more frustrating.

She was absolutely certain that the man controlled the lion's share of the illicit drug trade in Dayton, and she was fairly convinced that his area of influence spread much farther than the immediate region. Knowing it and proving it, however, were two entirely different things. So far she had been maddeningly unable to establish a connection between Taylor and the street.

She was sitting at her desk, piled high with case files, when the radio monitor, set to the patrol frequency, suddenly went berserk with activity. It sounded like World War Three had erupted in the warehouse district.

Grabbing her jacket from the back of her chair, she rushed to the elevator. Her every instinct told Higgins every able-bodied cop was going to be needed as soon as possible.

Arriving on the scene in record time, Detective Higgins' jaw went slack with shock as she surveyed the aftermath of carnage and destruction. One of the largest warehouse buildings in the area had been reduced to scattered heaps of burning wreckage. Several bodies were immediately visible, at least some of them were whole bodies, others, not so much.

Higgins stepped out of her unmarked police vehicle and took in the gruesome scene. The aging warehouse had been vast. It was situated at the corner of Keowee and East Fifth streets. It was a good commercial location with easy access to the railroad and only minutes from the I-75. Covering nearly three city blocks of acreage and four stories high, it had been one of the largest buildings in the area.

It had now been reduced to a vast field littered with burning mounds of debris and twisted steel girders rising up through shattered floors and collapsed ceilings. Higgins looked at what was left of the building and was struck by the notion that it looked as if the building had been built across the rail line and a freight train had smashed through it.

There was frantic activity all around the area. Firefighters were working hard to contain the raging flames and thick black clouds of smoke issuing from the huge, demolished structure. The decision had been made early to assume a defensive attack on the fire due to the obviously unsafe nature of what remained of the cavernous building.

There was also imminent danger from stored ammunition cooking off in the burning rubble. Apparently, there had been a large supply of weapons and ammo stored in the building. A patrol officer and a firefighter had already been hit by the unpredictable rounds.

Even so, medics accompanied and shielded by cops in riot gear were furiously searching the periphery and any accessible parts of the ruined warehouse for survivors of the devastating attack. The patrol officer who had been wounded was on his way to Miami Valley Hospital, a local advanced trauma center, by ambulance. The OIC, officer in charge, Captain Woodard, was unsure if the veteran cop would make it. He had been hit center of mass and had lost a lot of blood. The firefighter had what appeared to be a flesh wound. A round had ripped through his right arm but had passed clean through his bicep without striking the bone. It was a painful wound but not immediately life threatening. He had been attended to on scene by paramedics. His wound was dressed and bandaged, and he was back at work trying to keep the flames from spreading to other nearby buildings.

The medics tried hard to convince him to be taken to the hospital, but he'd stubbornly refused. They were shorthanded, he'd said, and insisted on staying until the job was finished. That was the kind of selfless courage and innate heroism Higgins had always admired in public safety workers. They invariably put the job first, their main concern protecting the citizens.

With so much going on around the destroyed building, Higgins, after checking in with Woodard, decided to do a foot patrol around the vicinity. She hoped against the odds that someone might have escaped the battle and was hiding until it was safe to escape the area. She was on Springfield street heading east.

She covered the area down to Findlay Street, then headed north to Monument Ave. She used her powerful LED flashlight to illuminate the dank urine-soaked alleys and shadowy trash strewn areas between buildings. She searched thoroughly in and around any building she encountered using the bright halogen beam to focus on any area a possibly wounded person might hole up.

Working her way toward Keowee Street, Higgins diligently combed the area. She was about to move to a different area when she spotted something that looked out of place behind a vacant house. She couldn't be sure, but she thought there was a glint of light reflected in her flashlight beam from something metallic on the ground near the corner of the building.

Drawing her Glock 20 service weapon, she cautiously worked her way toward the object. Closing the distance to about thirty feet, she made out what appeared to be the muzzle of a weapon.

"Police," she said in a voice that made it clear she meant business. "Leave the weapon on the ground and come out with your hands up!" There was absolutely no reaction. There was no sound of any movement, and the barrel of the weapon clearly visible now from only twenty feet away, did not budge. Higgins neared the corner of the building, pulse pounding with adrenaline, hoping she wasn't worked up over some teenager's airsoft gun. In a defensive move, she launched herself forward through the air, did a forward tuck and roll, and came up with her weapon trained on what looked to be the body of a man near the corner of the dilapidated house.

The man was lying on the ground at the foot of the steps to a back porch. Higgins moved quickly, kicking the gun aside, then feeling for the carotid artery on the side of his tattooed neck for a pulse. The guy wasn't dead yet, but judging by his weak, thready pulse, he would be soon. Higgins felt her right knee getting damp as she kneeled over the body, checking for any identification. Looking down with her flashlight, the detective discovered she was kneeling in a pool of the man's blood. Not wanting to further disturb the crime scene, she called it in on her department cell. She requested whatever manpower could be spared for a second crime scene and told dispatch to make it fast. Detective Higgins requested a medic, immediately, telling the dispatcher to be sure to tell them the condition of this patient was critical. Higgins needed this guy to survive. She needed to know who he was and what he may have seen, and she needed to know as soon as possible.

****

Higgins sat at her desk trying hard not to chew her fingernails. Her mother always told her it was a bad habit, and it made her hands look bad. Ever the dutiful daughter, she obeyed, keeping her nails short but manicured and proper for a professional woman. At times like these, however, it was all she could do to keep her hands away from her mouth. The detective was waiting on pins and needles for the doctor or at least a nurse at Miami Valley Hospital to call her back. The area's leading trauma center, MVH was the closest and best choice for Cunningham's survival. So far, the man was Higgins's only possible source of information as to what the hell happened at the warehouse. She had been practically chased out of the emergency room by the staff. She was told that her frantic pacing and incessant questioning every five minutes would not change the patient's prognosis. Higgins contented herself with trying to establish what could have been the motive for the brutal impromptu battle along with a tentative timeline of the brutal attack. A high-pitched ping from her laptop brought her attention back to the matter at hand.

She had executed a title search and discovered that the warehouse had at one time belonged to one Alfonso Dennison. Using a search engine designed by a nerdy tech friend of hers, she found that Alfonso was the estranged great uncle of one Juwon Tate. Higgins knew Tate was an up and comer who, word on the street had it, was taking an ever-bigger bite out of Big Buck's turf.

Higgins found that information very interesting. That certainly gave Buck motivation to eliminate Tate, but what could have done so much damage so quickly?

There was evidence on the scene that a large truck may have been involved somehow, but the amount of sheer devastation at the scene made her skeptical. It would be next to impossible for so much firepower to have been so accurately deployed from a moving semi. Higgins began a search for any semi-tractor trailer rigs that might have been stolen or recently purchased in the Tri-State area. After about an hour or so, she had a list of one hundred thirty-seven vehicles that fit the description.

With a deep sigh of resignation, she doggedly began going over the extensive list, weeding out the ones that were obviously not suited to the task. As she worked, a musical chime sounded, and a notification appeared on the screen of her department laptop. The brief preview pane that appeared with the notification told her the initial crime scene report was ready for review.

Gladly taking a break from the incredibly exciting world of eighteen-wheeler freight vehicles, she clicked open the attached report file and let out a soft low whistle. Higgins was amazed at the impressive amount of large caliber, high explosive ammunition that had, amazingly, been extremely accurate in targeting only the warehouse and the people in it. There were virtually no stray rounds outside the perimeter that had been established around the gory crime scene, and shockingly, no innocent bystanders had been hurt.

Witness statements indicated the entire battle lasted no more than three to five minutes. In that amount of time, this apparently single vehicle had laid to waste nearly an entire city block. The massive warehouse that had stood in that space had been four stories high, with walls made of steel reinforced cinder blocks. Its construction was the main reason the building had not been razed, due to the impractical expense of demolishing it. Now all that was left was a huge, shattered pile of wreckage with twisted metal supports reaching through the scorched, smoking rubble like the skeletal remains of a giant ravaged corpse.

Detective Higgins read through the entire report, shocked at the devastating extent of the damage. As she read, she grew increasingly skeptical that this could have been the work of any kind of civilian vehicle especially a commercial semi-truck. It looked more like the work of a small tactical military unit equipped with light armored vehicles, maybe even a tank.

With the exception of the severely battered thug she had found, all of the thirty- four heavily armed street toughs, both male and female, known to be associated with

Tate, along with J.T. himself, were confirmed dead. Most of them would definitely have to be closed casket funerals, many with not even enough left for a casket.

Higgins was about to close the report for now and head back to the hospital when an entry from a patrolman, one of the first on the scene, suddenly caught her attention demanding further scrutiny. One witness statement taken from an elderly homeless woman described\ what she called a "dragon from hell", zooming by her as she crossed the street pushing a shopping cart filled with her meager possessions. The bruising blast of wind from its passage nearly knocked her to the ground. It clipped her cart, sending everything she owned tumbling into the deserted street. Another second and she would have been smashed like an insignificant bug in its uncaring advance.

When the interviewing officer asked her to describe the, "Ummmm……. dragon."

She said it was as long as two or three train boxcars but not as tall. It's hide was black as pitch, and it soaked up the light around it like the pit of Hell it came from. It made almost no sound except the heavy rumbling of its feet on the asphalt roadway and a high-pitched whine.

The beast had six huge eyes that glowed so bright they nearly blinded her. The monster smashed through the chain link metal gate of the warehouse yard like a hammer through waxed paper. The way it moved with such awful purpose was terrifying, and the old woman could have sworn it roared like a ravenous lion.

The young officer noted a strong smell of alcohol on the filthy woman even over her stifling body odor, but something in the witness's statement rang true for Higgins. Jotting down the woman's name, she headed out to canvas the shelters and try to locate her. If what Higgins was beginning to fear was true, the situation in Dayton was about to become even more deadly than anyone knew.

EIGHTEENTH CHAPTER

In the wee hours of the morning, Buck Taylor awoke. He rose from his extravagant handcrafted king-sized bed and padded to his ensuite, stealthy and uncommonly graceful for a man of his size. After using the facilities, he washed his large hands and went back to bed. It was a clear night with ample light from a full moon. The soft bluish glow bathed the large opulent space.

Standing beside the heavy oak bed frame, Buck silently appraised the generously provocative curves of the woman lying naked on the bed. For what seemed like the one hundredth time, he drank in the details of Ivory's lithe form. She lay on her back, breathing deeply, barely making a sound. Her large, full breasts seemed to defy the natural droop of time and gravity as they rose and fell with each breath. Her head was turned toward Buck, and the angle of her long neck made it easy to see the steady throb of her pulse.

Buck's eyes appreciatively travelled down and over the gentle swell of her nearly flat belly taut with muscle. Having never given birth Ivory had no stretch marks to mar her perfect skin. When he had asked her why she had no children, she answered, matter of factly, that her former husband never earned the right to impregnate her.

As Buck's increasingly aroused gaze moved past the meticulously hairless area below her navel, he admired the well-toned splendor of her long muscular legs, a tribute to her personal fitness routine. All in all, she was a stunning, captivating woman.

The fact that her keen intellect and sheer guts were utterly intimidating to most other men was even more of a turn on for him. With that thought, he felt a familiar swelling in his groin, and slid into bed next to his companion. He slid his thick fingers through her soft silky hair, and as he reached the crown of her head, he gripped a handful of the white strands and gave a firm tug. Ivory's eyes immediately sprang open in surprise. Before she could react, Buck covered her lips with his, muffling the slight gasp that was about to escape. In the soft blue glow of moonlight, man and woman came together as one, for the third time this night. Several hours later, Buck sat at the large marble topped island, in his kitchen.

Sipping from a large, ceramic mug, he enjoyed his morning coffee while he perused the Dayton Daily News paper. Even in this new digital age, he still enjoyed getting his news from the morning paper. It was a ritual the big man refused to give up.

He normally started with checking the stock market to keep apprised of any changes he might need to address in his portfolio, then proceeded to the sports page before looking at national and local news. Today, however, there was a story on the front page that grabbed his full attention. The headline read, "Survivor of Mysterious Attack Conscious." Buck's thick manicured brows drew together in a sure sign of irritation. Since the maiden run of his armored assault cargo vehicle, every subsequent mission had been carried out flawlessly, no survivors, no witnesses.

That was exactly the way the drug kingpin wanted it. The less the authorities knew about the prototype urban juggernaut, the better. Buck had been sure the man, one of J.T.'s foot soldiers, would eventually succumb to his extensive injuries.

After all, he had been in a coma for three months now. If he could recall anything from the night of the hit on Tate and his crew, it could potentially bring more scrutiny to Buck's operations than he could afford at this crucial stage of his global expansion plan.

Just then, Ivory padded softly down the stairs leading into the expansive kitchen. She was freshly showered and ready for the day. She was dressed in a stylish, knee length floral print, skirt featuring earth tones with a matching short sleeved olive colored blouse. She wore a pair of knee high, chocolate brown, calfskin boots with low heels. With a tasteful diamond tennis bracelet on her right wrist, and her snow-white hair flawlessly groomed, Buck thought, once again, how much of an eye catcher the woman truly was. With the heels of her boots clicking on the Italian marble tiles of the kitchen floor, she approached the central island laiden with breakfast food. Eyeing the spread hungrily, she rubbed her hands together in anticipation. She glanced at Buck, who was once again looking intently at the newspaper. Noticing the expression on his face, she asked, "Something wrong?"

He looked up again at the sound of Ivory's naturally seductive voice and nodded his head. As a sudden thought occurred to him, a sly smile began to spread across his face, erasing the wrinkles of frustration from between his thick, blonde eyebrows. "I have something I need you to take care of for me." he said.

****

Detective Higgins stepped out of her unmarked police vehicle in the area designated for ambulance and police vehicles at Miami Valley Hospital. One of the two Careflight rescue helicopters on the rooftop helipad was just taking off on its way to pick up some unfortunate trauma victim. There was a light rain falling, and Detective Higgins held her soft sided leather briefcase over her head as she passed several private ambulances and a couple of patrol cars parked in the same area. There was a long, covered ambulance bay that always reminded her of a tunnel she associated with an old movie. It was wide enough for three full size ambulances to sit side by side and nearly as long as half a football field. Two City of Dayton squads were parked there, one of them still running.

As she approached the coded entry door to the emergency room, a three-man city EMS crew exited the building through the sliding glass doors, two of them maneuvering a wheeled transport cot between them. This negated the need for her to punch in the access code for entry as she passed by them and entered the typically busy hospital. Recently, there had been a great deal of new construction and renovation on the aging hospital, and the detective's destination was located in the newest part.

She stopped at the compact nurse's station and, after finding the specific nurse assigned to the patient, informed the woman of her intention to interview him.

"His doctor is in there at the moment, but I'm sure you can go in shortly," the nurse said, pleasantly. Higgins's brow wrinkled and her exceptionally sharp instincts kicked into high gear. She had just spoken to the patient's doctor on the way to the hospital to make sure there was no objection to questioning him. The woman was at her practice's main office in Cincinnati.

Higgins felt the familiar tingle of her gut instinct, warning her that something wasn't right, and drawing her service weapon, she dashed into the room holding her only link to the brutal massacre at the warehouse. Pushing the door open with her shoulder, she saw a very tall woman with short, snow-white hair firmly holding a pillow over the frantically struggling, obese thug's face.

 His flailing arms were weakening, and Detective Higgins knew his desperate struggle was almost over. "Freeze!" she shouted, aiming her service weapon at the medical imposter. The tall woman reacted with startling quickness. She released the semi-conscious victim and turned toward the source of the interruption. In a smooth fluid move, she threw the pillow she was holding at Higgins at the same time. Although the object itself presented no threat, Higgins ducked reflexively. In the confines of the relatively small hospital room, the detective suddenly found herself in close combat with the surprisingly strong woman.

The snowy haired amazon's first move was to close the gap between them, following the thrown pillow and quickly snag Higgins's wrist. She twisted it with stunning force causing the smaller woman to involuntarily drop her weapon. The gun clattered to the floor, and the big woman kicked it under the victim's bed as he lay gasping for breath.

Rather than further trying to resist the woman's move, Higgins went with the momentum of the twist. Using the close quarters to her advantage, the little detective nimbly ran up the nearest wall and executed a rolling somersault that turned her stronger opponent's momentum against her. Caught suddenly off balance by the move, Ivory lost her grip along with her balance, and crashed into a nearby tray table, then down to the floor. Before Higgins could recover her weapon or take advantage, however, the agile woman snapped to her feet. She charged the cop in an attempt to overwhelm her with superior size, but Higgins deftly anticipated the move, dropping to the floor and sliding between the taller woman's long legs.

Aided by the surface of the slick tile floor, Higgins came up behind the woman and shot a quick snap kick into the area behind her opponent's right knee. Ivory dropped to the floor again as the detective attempted to restrain her from behind. Just as the detective was about to gain the upper hand, the big woman's left elbow swung back and brutally smashed into her Higgins' temple. The vicious unexpected blow brought instant darkness and the detective slammed to the floor like a sack of bricks. Higgins desperately fought the overwhelming urge to vomit, gamely refusing to lose consciousness as she heard the would-be assassin making her escape through the rising commotion in the hall. Several nurses and aides came to investigate the noise and were bowled over as Ivory swiftly made her escape.

Shaking her head to clear the dense fog, Higgins retrieved her weapon and unsteadily rose to her feet. The room spun in crazy circles for several moments as hospital staff rushed in, checking on her and the patient. Finally feeling able to move without emptying the contents of her stomach, Higgins resisted the strong urge to pursue the white-haired woman and instead, went to question the patient. The man obviously knew something that someone did not want him to share.

NINETEENTH CHAPTER

Ray Ray Cunningham had been a morbidly obese man for most of his adult life. It was to this seemingly obscure fact that he owed his life. When the attack at the warehouse went down, Ray Ray was at the very rear of the building. Although he was not much use in a battle unless holding a gun, he had a sharp mind and an almost unnatural affinity for mathematics that made him a nearly indispensable part of Tate's operation. Also, since he was Tate's cousin, he had a level of trust with the boss that almost no one else could claim. In this capacity he had been keeping a close eye on his cousin's cash which had been stockpiled along with everything else in the building.

When the initial crash came sounding and feeling like a bomb going off, Ray Ray's prodigious girth prevented him from moving quickly to the main part of the warehouse to mount a defense with the other men and women.

Before he could get clear of the makeshift vault set up in the old building's boiler room, the entire wall leading into the main warehouse completely disintegrated along with a large portion of two floors above him.

Ray Ray had been told he was almost completely buried under nearly a ton of bricks, mortar, and iron debris. Shielded, in part by the boiler itself, It was a miracle he survived at all due to a void in the wreckage. Even so, he certainly did not come out unscathed. His injuries included numerous broken bones, a severe concussion, collapsed lung, lacerated liver, ruptured spleen and a perforated colon.

Infection from the latter nearly sealed his fate, but somehow, he pulled through. The staff at the nursing home he was placed in after his critical injuries were addressed, basically wrote him off the day he was admitted. To their shock, however, he held on to life with a dogged tenacity they simply couldn't believe.

He was in a great deal of pain, but it seemed the best he could hope for was a dulling effect of the pain meds. His condition was still largely touch and go, and his doctors were concerned that too much of the powerful medications would shut down his kidneys and his ability to breathe. To make matters worse, he was told he could not get his scheduled dose at the moment because a detective was on the way to question him about the night of the assault. The big thug made up his mind that he wasn't telling the cop a damn thing, and there was nothing he would be able to say that would make Ray Ray change his mind.

Detective Higgins entered Ray Ray's room when the injured man was trying to sleep. Until he could get medication for the pain, sleep was his only defense. The nurse who had shown the detective to the room went to his bedside and placing a gentle hand on the big man's shoulder, softly called his name. Ray Ray awoke instantly and firmly announced his intentions. "I ain't telling that cop shit, so give me my damn meds!" His voice was hoarse and gravelly from dryness and pain. Higgins almost felt sorry for him, except she had his extensive rap sheet committed to memory. She knew very well, there were many other people who had felt pain and, indeed, could no longer feel pain due to this man and his violent friends. However, something totally unexpected happened when she addressed him. "Mr. Cunningham, the sooner I can get the answers I need, the sooner you can get your meds."

Ray Ray's head snapped in her direction at the sound of her voice, and the stark surprise on his face spoke volumes. He had obviously been expecting a man and was completely thrown off guard when he saw her. Higgins was extremely proficient in adapting her manner to achieve the maximum effectiveness in an interview. It was a skill that some feminists disdained as shameless pandering to the male ego, but Higgins would use every tool at her disposal to do the best job she could.

The detective could be shy and demure, flirtatious and provocative, or fierce and tough as nails with equal ability. It was something she learned early in her career, and it had served her well over the years as she rose through the ranks of the police department, both with suspects and coworkers.

Ray Ray's meaty face was heavily bruised and swollen, mostly from fluid retention and follow up surgeries, and he still had bulky bandages around his head.

He was hooked by IV to several machines and monitors and had casts on both legs and both arms. Even so, Higgins could tell he was probably still an attractive man despite his considerable weight. An experienced and highly successful interrogator, she decided to play it soft for the moment, allowing a somewhat girlish quality to seep into her husky voice. "I apologize for bothering you Sir, but you are the only person to survive the attack on the warehouse and I really need to talk to you." she said softly, putting a slightly desperate edge into her voice. "I promise to keep it short so you can get some relief, ok?"

The tactic had the desired effect and Ray Ray's previously stubborn determination not to cooperate vanished like tendrils of mist in the wind as he took in every detail of the lady cop's appearance. Higgins's patient demeanor was pushed to the limit as the big thug's gaze brazenly lingered on the swell of her ample chest and her wide flaring hips.

She allowed the greatly inappropriate scrutiny with no outwardly visible sign of the deep disgust she felt inside and waited it out, knowing it would pay off in the long run. Although she would definitely need a long hot shower afterwards. Finally done with mentally undressing her, Ray Ray spoke. Although he was obviously taken with her physical appearance, she was still five-o, so he tried, unsuccessfully, to put a gruff tone in his voice. "What you want to know?" he said.

****

Jason sat quietly in a hotel room in Dayton. He was reflecting on all that had happened since he joined Gabe's holy mission. It was his way of staying grounded and keeping the many temptations of the world at bay. Ever since he met the man he now thought of as his closest, actually only, friend, things had been so different for him.

At first, he assumed Gabriel would be a stiff self-righteous kind of guy, like the judgmental people he avoided on the street. Always looking down on people and ever ready to criticize and correct any behavior that wasn't "Holy".

But as he got to know the man, he discovered almost the opposite. Gabe had a keen insight into the many factors that motivated people to do the things they did, but he was never judgmental. His manner was always kind, understanding, and empathetic. Surprisingly, he had a wonderful sense of humor and an infectious laugh, both of which he used often. He was just like everyone else with faults and weaknesses that he prayed every day to resist. One day, when Jason asked him about these things, the explanation he gave made perfect sense. "Jason," he said. "I am just like every other person on this planet. I don't have any special powers or abilities that you or anyone else don't also have. The things you see me do are not me, really. They are manifestations of the power of God, channeled through me.

You can do the very same things and so can anyone else. You just have to believe, without a doubt, that what you say or do will happen because God will make it so. Jesus told us in the Bible that if we have faith as small as a grain of mustard seed, we can move a mountain. That isn't hyperbole or symbolism. It is meant literally. You can do absolutely anything through the power of The Lord as long as you acknowledge where that power comes from, and you use it to protect and defend the children of God."

Jason had been trying to strengthen his faith and resolve in order to be more help to Gabe, but there always seemed to be just the tiniest bit of doubt in the back of his mind. He was determined, though, not to give up.

The sound of the hotel room door opening pulled him from his reflections. He had been sitting cross legged on the floor, in the middle of the room with the curtains drawn. As Gabe entered the room, Jason rose smoothly to his feet and opened the drapes to let in the afternoon sun.

The room was high up in the building and provided a good view of the shallow valley where the sprawling city sat.

Gabe's deep voice filled the room as he greeted his friend. "How's it going?" he asked.

"Not bad." Jason answered. "I was just sitting here thinking and reflecting. What's on the agenda for the day?"

"We're going to start closing the doors on Mr. Taylor's operations today." Gabe answered.

"Good! What do you want me to do? Jason asked, rubbing his hands together.

The two men sat at the small desk near the window and began making plans.

****

Detective Higgins was feeling cautiously optimistic. Over the past four hours, she had been able to secure warrants for nearly all the properties on the list in the mysterious email. True to their word, she had received a thick packet of information, two days after she got the email, containing clear digital photos of illicit activity, witness statements, and financial records that gave her more than enough probable cause to execute the searches.

The detective had then spoken personally to each, and every source listed in the packet and confirmed the information. To her delight, the evidence was rock solid. She was waiting for one judge to finish in court so she could issue the warrant, and she would then have everything she needed to get underway. She couldn't explain why, but she felt sure that it would be the start of a new era in Dayton.

She was no rookie, and she harbored no grand illusions that she could single-handedly eliminate the drug trade or end rampant crime in the city, but if she could bring down the, so far untouchable, Buck Taylor, it would send a glaring message to the other criminals and petty thugs who were not as well connected and thoroughly insulated. A new day was dawning. A day where accountability was on the rise and consequences were real.

****

After her interview of Little Ray Ray Cunningham, Detective Higgins had a working theory of what had transpired on that fateful night months ago. Taylor or someone in his employ had weaponized a tractor trailer rig and turned it loose on rival organizations and anyone else deemed a threat to Buck's enterprises.

There was no paper trail to follow without any idea of the manufacturer or point of sale. What she knew with certainty, however, was that it was large, extremely powerful, and armed to the teeth. The devastating destruction caused by this one vehicle was on a scale as yet unheard of in urban law enforcement.

When she tried tracing the origin of the mechanized destroyer, she had been told by every heavy transport in the country that no such vehicle existed or even could exist. The power needed to transport such a massive amount of ordinance was realistically beyond anything currently in production. So, she changed her strategy and began searching for conceptual vehicles that might not have made it to working models. She knew that often concepts looked fine on paper, but engineering sometimes could not realize the vision in practical application.

One evening about a week before, she had been sitting at her laptop in her apartment, near the point of giving in to sleep for the night, when her mystery email pal popped up on her IM application. At the time, she didn't know the author of that email would be the mysterious whistleblower from two days ago. There was a JPEG file attached to the brief message which read, "Pull the wolf's tail and see where it leads you."

When she opened the attachment, her jaw went slack, and her mouth fell open as if she were mesmerized. There, on her screen, were the technical specifications, a high-definition image of the original prototype and all proposed upgrades and modifications to the original design. The cherry on top, though, was the GPS frequency and scrambled codes for the proprietary communication system on the high-tech rig. Detective Higgins could not believe her eyes. Whoever her covert allies were, they were good, and they apparently had access to resources and equipment that the D.P.D could only dream of.

She didn't know who he, she, or they were, nor why they were helping her, but she silently thanked God, once again, that they were. There wasn't a judge in the country who wouldn't have issued the necessary warrants with such a wealth of evidence of illegal activity, especially when added to the previous information she had received about the truck. With the approval of her superiors, the tough as nails detective assembled the manpower and equipment for the blitz operation on Taylor's empire. She coordinated with S.W.A.T., the DEA, and the ATF, as well as the FBI and the regional HAZMAT team. Higgins had a little political diplomacy work to do with the federal agencies, because some of Taylor's operations and storehouses were across state lines in Indiana and Kentucky. All her assets were ready to mobilize as soon as they received the go ahead from her. The raids would be conducted simultaneously across Taylor's expansive empire to minimize the chances of his people sounding a warning to other locations.

The time was set for just after sundown. That would occur at about 9:25 P.M. In order to clear out civilians and minimize collateral damage, there would be simulated utilities emergencies where Buck's facilities bordered residential areas. They ranged from water main breaks to natural gas leaks and power failures. It was a massive operation. Several parts of it had been a logistical nightmare to put together on such short notice, but Higgins knew it would all be worth it in the end. The hardest and most exhaustive part had been personally coordinating with all of the team leaders face to face. Higgins knew the powerful crime lord had eyes and ears within the department, and she wanted absolutely no chance of Buck being alerted to her plans. As far as she knew, she had pulled it off. No one, outside of her superiors, seemed to have any idea about the covert operation. Higgins prayed it would stay that way for just a few more hours.

****

Ivory was nervous. Due to her extensive connections with upper-level society, in around the Miami valley, she had been able to put together a sort of grapevine for information that would serve her and her employer. Two days ago, she had received a tip from an old friend, working at the highest levels of city government, that a major operation was in the works to blindside Buck's business. Unfortunately, her source had no real details of the extremely secretive operation. They couldn't tell her where or when the raid was supposed to take place or the size of the force that would be sent against them. This put the highly intelligent woman in an extremely awkward position.

If she took the Chicken Little approach and warned Buck of impending doom with no real details to offer, it would seriously damage her credibility with an employer who valued her keen insight and ability. On the other hand, if she said nothing about it, and they got caught with their proverbial pants down, Taylor would, more than likely, feel betrayed and even suspect her of being in on the plan. She stood in Buck's spacious office staring blankly through the large ballistic glass window that overlooked the muddy brown water of the Little Miami River. She was uncharacteristically distant and pensive, absentmindedly chewing her bottom lip in thought. "And how are you today, Champ?" Buck asked.

The soft rumble of Taylor's deep voice behind her, using a nickname he had given her in reference to her superior sexual prowess, actually startled her. She jumped, turning around to face her boss who was standing right behind her. It never ceased to amaze her that a man of his size could move around so stealthily.

Taylor's icy blue eyes widened a bit at her atypical reaction. It was the first time he had ever seen the normally unflappable woman caught by surprise. Two of the things he had always admired about the striking woman was her quick wit and steely nerves. She had always been seemingly prepared for any situation, and Buck knew that there had to be something big on her mind for her to be so oddly distracted. The nervousness passed quickly, however, and she recovered her normal calm demeanor smoothly.

"Better now." Ivory said, mentally chiding herself for her earlier reaction.

"What were you in such deep thought about?" he asked.

This was the moment she had dreaded. It was do or die now. She flipped a mental coin and decided on caution. Without any solid intel, alerting her detail-oriented boss to a situation that might, possibly, be headed their way might do unnecessary damage to her solid standing with the man. It might even lay the groundwork for her to wind up eventually being replaced. In the Taylor organization, read the term "replaced" as murdered. Leaving people alive with intimate knowledge of his operations was an unacceptable risk for the big man. In order to give a credible explanation for her disconcerted reaction, she decided to stick with something that was true on a certain level.

"I was thinking about that little cop I had the scuffle with at the hospital a while back." Ivory said.

"I see." Buck said, his chin lifting in comprehension. He knew that Ivory's unaccustomed failure to get rid of Ray Ray before he could talk to the detective had rankled her on a very deep level. It was the only time she had ever failed to meet his expectations, and it took several days for him to convince her that she had taken the only course available to her at the time.

It would have been far more damaging for her to be arrested for attempted murder of a known felon and all but impossible to explain her motive for the attack without implicating Taylor at some point. Ivory was a total stranger to failure, and it was totally believable that she would have difficulty living it down in her own mind.

"Well, as I told you before," he said, "There was nothing else you could have done. I would have done the exact same thing myself in that situation. Put it out of your mind." Ivory breathed a mental sigh of relief as Buck began laying out the list of priorities for the day, and the things he would need her to see to. But at the back of her mind, she couldn't help but wonder if she had just made a grave mistake.

TWENTIETH CHAPTER

Gabriel sat with Jason on a park bench situated on the shores of the river. The two physically dissimilar men shared a bag of bread fragments they tossed to the birds populating the area. One thing Gabe always insisted on whenever they were working a mission, was taking time to rest and recharge in appreciation of life's small pleasures.

The first time Jason went on a mission with his now, closest friend, he had wondered aloud why they were wasting time instead of hunting, as he thought of it. Gabe explained that if they spent all of their time preserving and saving the lives of others without taking time to enjoy their own, it would be defeating the purpose of God's plan. God did not, contrary to popular opinion, expect Christians to live a bland sterile existence in His service. The reason that things were fun or pleasant, exciting or satisfying, was due to His design. He *wants* us to enjoy our lives to the fullest.

He loves us and wants us to be happy. So, whenever they got the chance, the Tools of Salvation, as they thought of themselves, would take the time to go to an art museum, or an amusement park, take in a movie, or even take young ladies out on dates. Neither of them had that special someone in their lives, but they both enjoyed socializing with ladies and having fun. One of their favorite activities was communing with nature in one way or another. It made them feel grounded and connected to every living thing since all life had come from God's creation.

As Gabe tossed out the last of the breadcrumbs, he stood and inhaled deeply. Although there were some odors in the air that were less than pleasant, he could also smell lilies at the water's edge, the various aromas of food from nearby restaurants, and the sweet smell of flowers from the grounds of the University of Dayton campus just across the boulevard from the park.

"Are you ready Bud?" he asked Jason, still seated on the bench.

"You know it." his friend answered.

"Alright then, let's get to work."

The two warriors climbed into the rented SUV they were using for this trip and headed into the city to bring justice to Buck Taylor and his crew of thugs.

****

The crew chief for 'The Bull' was a seasoned employee of Taylor's trucking fleet named Matthias Trask. He was one of only a handful of men and women who had been with the big boss since the beginning, nearly ten years ago. Buck knew Trask from his legitimate trucking business and had hired the man despite a criminal record for smuggling. At the time, Trask knew nothing about his employer's less than legal activities and had no idea he was being vetted for a position in those endeavors.

He was hired at a decent salary but still had to do what he could on the side to support one of his vices which was high class call girls. When Buck offered him a more lucrative position in the company if he was willing and able to keep his mouth shut about the contents of the freight shipments, he jumped at the chance. He quickly proved himself to be not only a highly proficient driver but a respectable tactician in his own right, having served many years in the military.

His unrivaled ability to adapt to any vehicle and avoid entanglements with police agencies moved him up the ranks in Buck's small inner circle. When the big man came to Trask with the plans for the ultra-powerful semi rig and appointed him as lead driver and crew chief of the vehicle's team of manpower, Trask was ecstatic.

The Bull was any trucker's dream, loaded with cutting edge state of the art instrumentation, incredible weaponry and firepower, and one of the most powerful engines and powertrain on the planet.

Its potential was limitless, and it was literally a one-of-a-kind vehicle. It drove like a dream and was a virtually unstoppable force in operation. During its initial testing and shakedown missions, the futuristic monster went far beyond proving itself, and Trask began to think of the devastating vehicle as his personal ticket to the life he so richly deserved. He developed an almost symbiotic relationship with the brutally powerful vehicle, pampering it and doting on it as if it were a living breathing entity. The men and women assigned to the vehicle's attack force and maintenance crew had learned the hard way about disrespecting or neglecting the needs of the prized vehicle.

Trask wasn't a big man. He stood just five feet seven inches tall and was thin but fit. He kept himself in exceptional condition for a middle-aged man, and he adopted the same mindset with the big vehicle. His manner was laid back in most ways but when it came to The Bull it was a whole different thing.

If the maintenance crew failed to meet his standards for keeping the vehicle spotlessly clean, in peak operating condition, or if he found any kind of trash or disarray inside the truck, his fury was unbridled. He would tolerate no backtalk or excuses, and anyone who valued their future would be wise to toe the line. Trask had Buck's full authority on anything involving the vehicle and its crew. Any resistance would create a situation that could become life and death at the drop of a hat.

Today, Trask was preparing for a run to one of Taylor's warehouses in Indiana to pick up ammunition and other supplies for The Bull. He wished he could take the vehicle on the run, but Taylor was adamant about keeping it hidden during daylight hours or utilizing it for anything other than high priority assignments. Trask understood that a great deal of the effectiveness of the truck was the air of mystery that had sprung up around it. In the past few months of its operation, The Bull had become an almost mythical object.

Taylor's many rivals and even more numerous enemies had been made painfully aware of the almost obscene power wielded by the Taylor operation in the form of a weapon that once deployed would more than likely be the last thing its targets ever saw.

So, Trask pulled out of the fortified warehouse facility that housed his pride and joy in a standard tractor trailer rig. The big Kenworth semi rig was modern and exceptionally comfortable itself with all the amenities an OTR driver could possibly want, but in Trask's mind, it was a poor substitute for his baby.

Trask left the garage facility and headed out to make his way to Interstate Route 70, which he would then take West on his way to the pickup. The time was just before seven p.m. Trask had no clue that an unmarked ATF helicopter was shadowing him from several thousand feet above. Part of Higgins's task force, it was one of two surveillance crafts keeping an eye on the building suspected of housing Taylor's weaponized semi. The other chopper was tasked with watching the facility for signs the assault vehicle was being deployed. At the first sign the big truck was headed out, Detective Higgins would be notified. The wise detective had her own contingency plans ready to implement if that happened.

As the day passed and evening came, Ivory was becoming more and more worried. She had been second guessing her decision to keep quiet about the tip regarding an impending assault on Buck's operation. She had completed everything he asked her to do and was now on her way back to see him. It was Friday, and she would be meeting him at his home for dinner and what would probably turn into something much more intimate afterwards. It was a pattern the two had established as the official beginning of their weekend. It unfailingly proved to be mutually pleasing to both of them and was becoming a ritualistic but non-obligational way to finish the work week.

Halfway through a scrumptious meal of sea bass with new potatoes and fresh salad, she made up her mind and broached the sensitive subject. "Buck," she began hesitantly.

As his pale blue eyes met her own green ones, she forged ahead before she could lose her nerve. Taylor had known there was something weighty on her mind since this morning, but he had decided to let her bring it out on her own terms. "I have a confession to make." Ivory said hesitantly.

At this, his eyebrows lifted in curiosity, but he waited patiently for her to continue. It was unlike her to be so indirect. Seeing no negative emotion in his eyes she continued.

"Yesterday I got a tip from a friend of mine in the mayor's office. He told me that he overheard the mayor talking to a judge on the phone, and that they were discussing a raid on your businesses. I was going to tell you this morning, but that was all he knew.

He didn't have any specifics on where or when or what the searches were looking for, so, I didn't say anything, because I know how you hate incomplete information. I've been thinking about it all day, and I just didn't feel right not telling you."

Taylor sat quietly for a minute or two, and she met his gaze unflinchingly. She could see that sharp mind of his working intently behind those clear, intense orbs.

When he finally spoke, his voice was calm, measured and totally without malice.

"I understand." he said, and Ivory relaxed, only then realizing she had been holding her breath. "And you're right, I don't like vague information. But in this case, I think you've made the right decision. This stage of our plans is critical, and we can't afford to take any chances. Better to be prepared unnecessarily than caught unprepared." The big man picked up his mobile phone from the table and began making calls. Ivory felt like a huge weight had been lifted, but she only hoped she hadn't waited too long.

TWENTY FIRST CHAPTER

Six, Taylor's right hand man, was enjoying one of his favorite pastimes when his cell buzzed. As a way of working out his biological urges as well as keeping his interrogation skills sharp, the diminutive enforcer had set up a system to indulge his unique tastes and skills. He employed several people whose sole function was to locate, procure, or more accurately kidnap, and deliver to him women of a specific type for his use. His detailed requirements for these women were that they must be at least six feet tall or taller. He preferred brunettes, redheads and blondes, in that order.

The height requirement was crucial as he needed to be able to completely dominate them to compensate for his own below average height. He preferred to rotate them, according to hair color as well as the color of their eyes. In this regard, his desires were very precise.

Brunettes had to have dark brown or black eyes, redheads green or hazel and blondes must have blue. He also had specific body types for each category, although this was the only area where he was a bit flexible. He preferred curvier, hourglass body types but pear shaped would be acceptable as well. He even had exacting specifications for bust, hips and length of hair.

Six despised short hair because it was more difficult to pull and control any particular movements of the woman's head. Brunettes could be tanned, but redheads and blondes had to have fair to pale complexions. This was to maximize his stimulation by making scratches, bruises, and welts much more visible. There were several other standards that had to be met such as shoe size, appearance of their teeth, hands and fingernails, and they absolutely could not be smokers.

This extensive list of requirements was the main reason he needed a staff of people to find, locate. and acquire these women. He simply didn't have the time to locate them himself. The first time he assembled his "grab crew", as he called them, two men and one woman made the cardinal mistake of laughing at the difficulty of finding such exact victims, and victims they were since none of them would ever be seen again. Six made the rest of his assembled crew watch as he "corrected" the offending personnel.

Since one of the specialties Buck relied on the man for was torture, both physical and psychological, usually to extract information, the correction took hours. When it was over and the quivering remains of the foolish, potential crewmembers had been disposed of, the message was crystal clear and not a single person ever repeated the error.

The woman who was currently "entertaining" the vicious little man was a formerly beautiful, buxom, twenty-eight-year-old brunette that had been "pleasuring" him for nearly twelve hours.

She stood six feet four inches tall, although, at the moment, standing was a feat she was completely unable to accomplish. The dark-haired Amazon's thick glossy hair fell nearly to the middle of her back, though it was now badly tangled and thickly matted with both dry and fresh blood in some areas. Her formerly seductive, dark brown eyes were now bloodshot and the left was swollen shut.

The unfortunate object of Six's desires had deeply tanned skin which, prior to her capture had been flawlessly smooth and totally free of blemishes, was now covered with dark blue and purplish bruises, and a host of lacerations ranging from an inch or so to nearly a foot in length and of varying depths. Her full pouty lips were now dry, cracked, split, and swollen. Her small Greek type of nose was clearly broken, and a thin trickle of blood trailed from her left ear.

She lay, all but naked on the bare concrete floor of Six's "playroom". Curled into a fetal position on the grimy floor, wearing only the torn and tattered remains of a filmy negligee provided by her torturer, she silently suffered, twitching in such unbearable pain, she no longer even had the strength to cry.

Normally, at this point, Six would put his "playmates" out of their misery, then call for removal of the body. Naked as well and spattered head to toe with the poor woman's blood, he methodically picked up a wickedly sharp blade from a collection of knives laid out on a long waist high metal table along one wall, similar to what one might see in a surgical room.

Six preferred to grab the used-up wretches by the hair and yank them up to their knees. He would then make certain they were looking at him as well as they could, as he slowly slid the sharp, cool metal between their ribs and into the heart, savoring the exquisite terror in their dying eyes. It was only at that point that his own, earth-shattering climax would occur. Just as he roughly grabbed his latest victim's tangled hair and snatched her up to her knees, his mobile phone, lying on the same table as the assorted cutlery, vibrated with an incoming call. He knew it was Taylor because no one else would dare disturb him when he was in the playroom. His carnal mood was now thoroughly broken. Six angrily shook his head, growling with intense sexual frustration.

He dismissively tossed the broken brunette aside. Six callously left the seriously injured woman on the floor, like a dirty fast-food wrapper. The cleanup crew would handle her entry into the sex trade. He picked up his mobile phone from the table, no trace of the seething rage he felt reflected in his voice as he answered the device. "Sir?" he said simply.

****

Taylor's second call was to Trask. The strike crew leader was just nearing the state line between Ohio and Indiana, the blue arch marking the transition rapidly approaching ahead. Trask was a careful driver on these types of runs due to the vigilant presence of the state patrol of both sides of the line. He knew that Taylor would be anything but forgiving if the authorities were made aware of the illegal aspects of his businesses because of something as stupid and utterly avoidable as a speeding ticket.

The consequences of such a thing would be severe to say the least, and Trask not only liked his job, he enjoyed breathing immensely. Taylor's message was brief and direct. "I need you back here immediately." he said. The intense, serious tone of Buck's voice told Trask all he needed to know about the urgency of the statement.

The Bull's crew chief pulled over at the welcome center, just over the Ohio/Indiana state line and parked the rig. He secured the cab and activated the intrusion alarm, then went to the rear of the trailer and pulled up the cargo door.

Inside, there was only one large crate, permanently secured to the corrugated metal wall. Unlocking the heavy, case hardened, padlock on the door of the crate, Trask reached inside and pressed a small black button on the inner surface of the crate. The top, front and side panels of the crate opened with a soft electronic whirring sound. Inside was sleek black Ducati 959 competition rated sport bike.

Trask kept an exact duplicate of the powerful two-wheeler on every commercial rig. Should the need ever arise to ditch a load or any unforeseen entanglement with law enforcement, Trask wanted an escape ready and waiting. After securing the trailer, Trask fired up the motorbike, appreciating the throaty rumble of the Italian racing machine.

The awesome racing machine was capable of speeds approaching one hundred seventy miles per hour and was definitely not for the faint of heart. Making his way to the next off ramp, he reversed course and headed back to the east on I-70.

Rolling back on the throttle, Trask held on tightly, leaning forward as the powerful bike shot forward like a cruise missile, its front wheel climbing into the air for nearly one hundred yards. He would be back in Dayton in record time, ready for whatever Taylor would demand.

****

Six was ready for action. Having stopped at his apartment to grab a shower and remove the dried biological evidence of the past day's activities, he was now dressed for combat in a snugly fitting, black Kevlar mesh bodysuit and tactical cargo pants of the same color.

Armed to the teeth, he carried an efficient looking pump action shotgun slung across his back on a leather bandolier with plenty of extra shells across his chest. He also carried a Beretta, 9mm machine pistol hanging under his left arm in a custom holster and a huge .44 Magnum, Smith and Wesson revolver on his right hip. Special pockets on the sleeves of the bodysuit and the cargo pockets of the tactical pants held extra magazines of ammo for the automatic weapons and speed loaders for the Magnum.

There were a pair of nine inch long, razor sharp, combat knives carried in a nylon sheath affixed to his belt at the small of his back. The former soldier also carried a Walther .380 caliber semi-automatic pistol in an ankle holster on his right leg. Finally, there was an Asp, a telescoping baton, carried in a customized forearm sheath on his left arm. For added protection, he wore a vest made from the latest innovation in lightweight Kevlar body armor. In the trunk of his car, he had a tailored running suit designed to conceal all his armaments with virtually no sign of what was concealed beneath it. However, he didn't think he would be needing that tonight. Stepping out of his car, he approached the warehouse where the heroin shipment was being stored until it could be modified by Taylor's "cook". Buck told Six that he was preparing to defend against a possible raid by unknown agencies. Taylor's right hand man noted the glaring lack of information about this attack and knew his boss would be on edge. The big man despised incomplete information, but a Taylor didn't get to where he was by ignoring intel no matter how light on details it might be.

The shipment, waiting in the huge building in front of him, represented a true game changer for the big man, and he wasn't about to leave anything to chance before that change could place. Accordingly, every man and woman working for Taylor was on high alert. For Six, it was reminiscent of pre-combat readiness when he had served in the military.

After making a visual check around the entire perimeter of the vitally important building, Six began posting personnel at key points of defense around the structure, both out in the open and concealed. He went inside to the office and checked to make sure every surveillance camera was operating, as well as hidden microphones and motion detectors installed all over the facility. He didn't know who or what was coming, but whoever or whatever it was, they would be ready for it.

TWENTY SECOND CHAPTER

Trask made it back to Dayton and the hangar housing The Bull in just under 20 minutes. Although travelling at such a high rate of speed was exhilarating, he hadn't been able to enjoy the ride. As fast as the bike was, his keen mind was running circles around the purring machine. He was checking off the list of things he would need to accomplish when he got back. He made sure that the weaponized semi was always prepped, loaded, and ready to deploy at a moment's notice, that wasn't his concern.

His main focus was personnel deployment and support of The Bull's mission, whatever that might entail. He had several smaller vehicles, armored SUVs, vans, and cars outfitted with bullet resistant glass and special ports in the windows and doors that could be used to fire weapons from a protected vehicle. He was thinking to himself who would be best suited for each assignment.

In addition, he would need to check current weather conditions, traffic patterns, and street closures due to construction, in order to determine the best routes for deployment. He would also run diagnostics of all of The Bull's computer enhanced systems to ensure there would be no technical glitches or software failures that could potentially cripple the high-tech monstrosity. Trask knew Taylor was depending on him, and he was well aware of the heavy price of failure in the big man's employ.

****

Detective Higgins was fully outfitted and prepared. Dressed in tactical gear, she made a final check of her weapons and equipment. Even though she was practically compulsive about keeping her weapons clean and in tip top working condition, she checked them again anyway.

It was nearing time to move out, and the detective had a "big game" feel coursing through her whole body. She had received reports from aerial surveillance that Taylor's troops were mobilizing. She was, at first, furious, frustrated, and completely baffled at how word had leaked out. As reports came in from different agencies and assets, however, the picture began to clear a little.

It was obvious Taylor didn't have any specific information about the raid. The helicopter tailing Trask alerted her to the man's sudden bailout from the semi and subsequent high-speed return to "The City of Neighbors". The crew staked out on Six's place informed her of his return to his apartment, and his departure after a brief period.

The teams on Taylor reported the arrival of a tall high class looking woman with short snow-white hair at Buck's home. Shortly after she entered the sprawling estate, she and Taylor both left in his vehicle and headed out to an airfield, adjacent to the Dayton International Airport.

The two of them then boarded a private jet and left almost as soon as they arrived. Checking the filed flight plan, Higgins discovered the jet was bound for Canada. Rats deserting a sinking ship she mused. If something went wrong in his eyes, Taylor didn't want to be anywhere near the fallout. Well, she thought, she would deal with them later. After all, she owed Taylor's tall frosty haired companion a rematch, and she would be ready for her this time.

Her sharp mind returning to the matter at hand, Detective Higgins made a sudden discovery that totally wiped her earlier anger from her mind. With no precise information indicating the possible target of the raid, Taylor and his henchmen made a crucial error. There were any number of buildings among Taylor's holdings, but the drug lord's minions were apparently circling the wagons to protect one particular location above all others. The thugs had unwittingly pinpointed the exact spot where the huge shipment of heroin was being stored and gave her the primary target of her assault.

Prior to this information, the raids would have been a huge game of Whack-a-Mole, but now they had a bullseye location. Higgins decided to stagger the raids, now, in order to throw the criminals off balance and make them unsure of themselves. Confusion in the ranks of her targets could only help. With that in mind, she issued some last-minute instructions to all department heads and team leaders.

In a sudden flash of inspiration, Higgins decided to put out a bit of disinformation to help with the uncertainty among her opponents. The detective went to see her captain and having previously sent him a heads-up text, she angrily stormed into his office, purposely leaving the door open behind her. She then made a huge production of being beside herself with rage at the last-minute exposure of her supposedly secret operation. Uncharacteristically raising her voice and gesticulating furiously, she pointed a finger at him, and all but accused her appropriately defensive supervisor of being on Taylor's payroll and asking who else was on the take.

Having been fully prepared for the contrived confrontation, her boss played his role perfectly, even ending the loud clash by pointing his own finger in her reddened face and yelling at Higgins to get the hell out of his office before he sent her home with the contents of her desk in a cardboard box. Higgins left the Captain's office in a huff, making an elaborate show of slamming the door behind her, hard enough to shatter the pane of glass with his name and rank on it. Oops, she thought to herself, that might have been a tad over the top. She made a mental note to buy her boss a bottle of his favorite scotch as she stormed through the squad room, fists clenched and red faced with fury. Judging by the shocked, wide eyed, looks on the other detectives' faces and the near palpable silence in the room, she was sure Taylor would get word before long.

****

Gabe and Jason sat on either side of the small dining area table in their hotel room. As was their habit before a mission, their hands were clasped in front of them and their eyes were closed as they prayed for strength and spirits of mercy, going into tonight's operation. Having spoken to detective Higgins by instant messaging, or IM, they were up to speed on all developments as of 30 minutes ago.

When the detective informed them of the possible leak of information, Jason assured her that it would change nothing. The two warriors had eaten a light dinner a couple of hours ago, cleaned up after themselves, and changed into their "work clothes".

His faith not quite as unshakeable as Gabe's, Jason petitioned The Lord to guide his efforts tonight. He knew that everything would go according to God's plan but that didn't mean it would necessarily unfold as he and Gabe envisioned it. Finishing his communication with his higher power, Jason opened his eyes and marveled at what he saw.

No matter how many times he had seen it, Jason was always awestruck by what happened when Gabe made his pre-mission petition as they humorously dubbed it. When Gabriel began his prayers, he would close his eyes. A few moments later his eyelids opened and in place of his clear hazel eyes was a soft, yellowish white glow, like the light of a soft light bulb in a table lamp. As Gabe's prayers continued, the glow became brighter and brighter until it was difficult to look at directly, like the noonday sun.

Jason looked away so as not to blind himself and a moment later the bright glow faded and his friend's familiar eyes, clear and free of worry returned. The motel where they were staying was only a stone's throw from the designated target of tonight's operation and as such was within walking distance. The late evening air was thick with humidity and the smell of rain. Dark clouds, pregnant with the promise of a summer storm, slowly approached from the west.

Gabe looked into the distance at the foreboding cloud cover and thought to himself, Mr. Taylor along with all of his thugs and operatives, were indeed about to face a violent tempest. What damage was left in their lives after the storm passed, would be solely up to each one of them.

Buck's unofficial CEO was feeling much better about the relationship between herself and her employer. She had received updated intel from several informants at police headquarters that the lead detective, the woman who had very nearly captured Ivory in the hospital those months ago, was badly rattled and beside herself with rage. One woman had even been near enough to the Captain's office to overhear some of the details about the raid. According to her, Buck's precious shipment of heroin was mistakenly assumed to be in the wrong location. The task force raid would be focused mainly on the building which housed Buck's high tech rolling juggernaut.

Apparently, the cops assumed the massive load of the potent drug was located there as well, in order to be protected by the proven lethal machine. That building, at Buck's instruction was more heavily guarded and defended than any other structure he owned. It was a clever strategy on the drug kingpin's part, and, by all indications, it had paid off.

Taylor's private Lear jet was smoothly winging over the state of Michigan, and as it banked, in a nearly imperceptible turn, Ivory had a magnificent view of Niagara falls. The popular tourist attraction was all lit up and majestically impressive, in the rapidly fading glow of the setting sun. Now that her nervous fears about giving Buck such an indistinct picture of the impending police action had been allayed, she was more relaxed and comfortable in the big man's presence again. Taylor, for his part, was not as quite as relaxed as his companion, due to the decidedly unwanted scrutiny of his business empire. A bright spot in the gloom of his thoughts, however, was the fact that the police couldn't prove anything criminal simply by discovering The Bull. After her aborted attempt at damage control in the hospital, Taylor had told Ivory to give it a couple of weeks for the attention from the unsuccessful attempt to blow over, and she had done just that.

Three weeks after his admission, in the middle of the night when the staff was typically far less vigilant, Ivory slipped quietly into the nursing home. Ray Ray had been sent there for physical rehabilitation. Totally undetected, the tall snowy haired assassin efficiently corrected her previous error. With her, she carried a large syringe, equipped with a long needle, commonly used for removing blood from the sac around a patient's heart.

Ray Ray's resonant snoring droned loudly in the cramped room, effectively masking any errant sound the long-legged woman might make. Covering the fat man's mouth, Ivory swiftly pushed the sharp needle through the flab covering the left side of his ribcage. She injected a bubble of 50 cc's of air directly into the man's left lung. Concealed from view in a fold between layers of fat, the tiny puncture would likely go unnoticed.

The next morning the nursing staff found Ray Ray during their rounds. His flaccid, fleshy torso was visibly mottled and bluish from mid-chest up to his head. His thick coated tongue protruded from his slack mouth, and his glazed dead eyes stared unseeing at the ceiling of the cramped room. It was quickly assumed the morbidly obese patient must have succumbed to a pulmonary embolism during the night.

Since such an occurrence was not out of the ordinary following extensive surgery, particularly if the patient was unable to actively move around to prevent blood clots, there appeared to be no reason for further inquiry into the man's death. An autopsy was performed, but since the overworked coroner's office had a perfectly plausible cause of death, there was only a cursory attempt to find any other cause for Cunningham's abrupt demise. That tied up one, potentially troubling, loose end and made anything the man might have told the police totally irrelevant since he could no longer testify as to the accuracy of the information. Although Buck's legal team, some of the finest attorneys in the country, would completely dismantle any effort to tie their client to illegal activity, it still angered the big man to have such a public light shined on his, up to now, off the grid criminal ventures.

With a Herculean effort, Buck dragged his mind from such distressing thoughts. He took a sip of top shelf bourbon from the crystal snifter in his hand and directed an appreciative gaze at his lovely companion. Starting at her surprisingly dainty feet, clad in expensive designer heels, he let his eyes travel slowly up her smooth, muscular legs.

Her cream colored, linen skirt cut off the view from just below her knees, and he continued up to the plunging neckline of her snugly fitting teal colored top. The first three buttons of the top were undone, and the big man's eyes lingered on her generous cleavage. When his eyes finally met hers, there was no discomfort from either of them at the raw scrutiny. It was obvious she had watched his entire visual inspection and knew full well he was more than satisfied with what he saw. Ivory's enticing green eyes sparkled with the promise of carnal delight, and Buck allowed himself to relax a little

More. After all, this was just a minor speed bump on the road
to his unavoidable, and complete domination of the drug
trade on an international level. Yes, he thought, his eyes
locked with Ivory's, openly flirtatious gaze, what could
possibly stop him now? Buck decided it was time to admit
Ivory to his own personal mile high club. He stood from the
comfortable, custom designed seat. Holding direct eye contact
with his beautiful companion, he wordlessly invited her to the
more intimate sleeping section of the sleek aircraft.
The smoldering look in his icy eyes, however, informed Ivory
that the big man was definitely not interested in sleep. With a
seductive smile, she stood and happily followed him to the
lushly appointed bedroom located in the rear section of the
plane. As the amorous pair entered the airborne boudoir,
Buck slid the pocket door closed for privacy and dimmed the
lights.

TWENTY THIRD CHAPTER

Trask was in his preferred element now. Having received new instructions from Taylor, he was now on the road with a full strike team in The Bull. His new instructions from the boss were to keep the powerful semi on the road, prepared to immediately respond to wherever it might be needed. Travelling a similar pattern to the state police, they patrolled around the Dayton area, moving along the interstate and state highways.

Trask stayed off the surface streets as much as possible for two purposes. First to avoid being stopped or detained by city police, and second, to prevent being tied up behind any traffic jams or vehicle crashes. The last thing the crew chief wanted was to be delayed in responding to any request for backup from the big rig. Something like that could be hazardous to one's health working for Buck.

The futuristic vehicle was loaded for bear and fully stocked, both with manpower and ammunition. With its current contingent, the deadly vehicle could lay waste to a small army, let alone the woefully understaffed police department of Dayton, even if backed up by the city's highly efficient S.W.A.T. unit. The hardened men and women of Trask's strike force were confident and ready to take on anyone that might stand in their way. All of them were expert marksmen and superior fighters in hand-to-hand combat. They had all proven themselves both before and after being assigned as the dedicated assault team augmenting the incredible destructive capabilities of Taylor's one vehicle army.

From their inaugural mission and on every assignment since, they had shown themselves to be vicious and without mercy for any who stood in their way. Trask had supreme confidence in both them and the nearly indestructible eighteen wheeled destructive force called The Bull.

On their fifth circuit of Dayton and the area immediately surrounding it, the anticipated call for assistance came in over the communication system. One of the warehouses Buck used to store weapons and some of his own personal collection of high-end cars was under attack. The men assigned to defend the building did not know how many cops were in the assault force, but it sounded like a substantial threat, enough to warrant the services of Trask and his team at least.

The Bull was currently travelling westbound on U.S. State Route four, near the Dayton Children's Hospital, and the designated location of the attack was very close to their current location. They could be on site in just a few minutes. At the team leader's direction, the driver of the powerful truck took the closest off ramp which would bring them out on Valley Street and within just a few blocks of the warehouse. Boy, did those cops have a rude awakening coming, Trask thought to himself.

Detective Higgins, dressed in full tactical gear, sat in her unmarked city vehicle. The radio traffic coming from the dash mounted radio in her car, informed her that the bait had been taken, and Taylor's urban assault crew was now enroute to the desired location. As soon as she received word that the big truck was nearing the location of this initial phase of the police raid, she would order the assigned personnel to withdraw, and the next phase would begin.

The idea was to keep the lethal asset and its highly skilled team of killers on the move and off balance. It was crucial for the cops to not get pinned down by the big truck since they had nothing that could defend against an assault from the brutally destructive vehicle. There had been no time to request and coordinate assistance from the federal government for military vehicles and soldiers from the national guard or the army reserves assigned to the Dayton area.

Detective Higgins wasn't at all sure that they would have been able to stand against the damn rolling arsenal anyway. Her only viable option was to keep the armored semi and its crew on the move and off balance to give her people time to close the net on Taylor's operation.

As for her own role, Higgins assigned herself to the team that would raid the site where the heroin was stored. Hopefully, her spur of the moment campaign of disinformation would be enough for her and the team backing her up to regain at least a portion of the element of surprise. No one was more aware of how high the stakes were than Higgins.

The weight of a very real life or death situation rested squarely on her shoulders and hers alone. She silently sent up a heartfelt prayer that her unidentified ally was right about all of this. Her reputation, her job and the lives of everyone involved in this operation were on the line.

Sending out the predetermined radio signal for the next phase of the operation, Higgins checked and rechecked her weapons and extra magazines of ammunition for the third time since leaving headquarters. She literally could not afford to have anything go wrong at this crucial stage of her plan. Shifting her car into drive, the resolute detective headed out to rendezvous with the rest of her multi-agency team for the assault on the drug lord's well defended storehouse.

****

Gabriel and Jason stood in the deepening shadows in a small cluster of maple trees on the edge of the commercial property line between the warehouse and a salvage yard, used mainly for metal recycling.

They had arrived just as detective Higgins's personnel began their approach, on foot, to the side entrance of the large building. Reconnaissance teams had confirmed that it was the least protected and provided the best access to the interior of the target structure.

The two men watched in silent observation as two thugs stationed on either side of the standard size metal entry door were swiftly incapacitated by the police special tactics officers. The pair of gangsters were dispatched with such quiet efficiency that if Gabe and his partner hadn't been watching, they probably wouldn't have noticed.

As four of the extensively trained cops entered the building, Gabe sent Jason to his assigned tasks, and the big, robed man headed for his own pre-determined mission.

Both men understood no one, not even Detective Higgins, was aware of their presence, and that put both of them in the direct line of fire from both the police and their well-armed adversaries.

Neither man showed any sign of fear or anxiety at the dangerous situation. They were both confident in their abilities, the righteousness of their cause, and the protection of God's power. Whatever was in store for them, they were resigned to their fate and ready for whatever came their way. Six had been diligently listening to the perplexing traffic on the two-way radio net his people used to communicate. So far, in the past forty-five minutes, there had been three aborted attacks on the same number of locations. In each case the cops were on approach to the target building, but for some unknown reason, they pulled back at the last moment, before even a single round was fired. What were they up to? Six wondered. Surely, they weren't utilizing such a large number of people just to harass or intimidate Taylor's businesses. There had to be a legitimate reason for the deployment of such extensive resources.

The sharp mind of Taylor's chief operational lieutenant was working overtime to decipher the confusing strategy and attempt to predict what might happen next. He was beginning to get frustrated when a sudden powerful wave of clarity washed over him like dust blown from the cover of an old book.

The cops were playing an elaborate shell game. All the broken off attacks had been wild herrings. It was an intentional distraction play, designed to keep his people off balance and second guessing themselves. A chill of dread seeped into the vicious man's spirit as he realized it might be too late to do anything about what he feared was coming.

Up until that point, Six had been content to monitor the numerous digital cameras covering every inch of property outside of the high priority building in real time. The highly valuable drugs, stored on plastic wrapped wooden skids, filled the vast storage areas of the huge warehouse from nearly floor to ceiling. The estimated street value of the stuff after being modified by Taylors' chemist was astronomical. To say there was a lot riding on this bold plan of his boss would be an incredible understatement. Spurred by the sudden realization of what the cops were attempting, Six jumped up from his seat at the desk in front of a wall covered with a dozen monitor screens so quickly that the two other men in the room were startled enough to grab for their guns. Not taking the time to explain, Six dashed from the security room and raced for the access ladder to the roof at breakneck speed. He bowled over several people with the misfortune of being in his way, and reaching his destination, darted up the ladder like a spider monkey. Flinging open the hatch to the roof, he made his way onto the flat, rubber covered surface. The advantage of his new position was the unobstructed view of the area surrounding the building for several blocks in any direction. From this new vantage point, he could see several police vans and other vehicles staged about three blocks from where he stood.

Swearing out loud, Six pulled his mobile phone from his pocket and sent two speed dial alerts, one to Trask, the other to Buck. The predetermined code informed the two men that the shit was about to hit the fan.

When Trask received Six's coded message, he sprang into action. He ordered The Bull's driver to pull over immediately, and after the man quickly complied, his boss pulled him from the driver's seat and replaced him at the controls of the big rig. Seconds later, the rolling arsenal was barreling through the streets of Dayton at high speed. All the usurped driver could think was he pitied anyone who happened to get in the way as the big vehicle sped through town.

Detective Higgins kept her head down and her assault rifle up, intensely focused on eliminating any targets that might pop up after the tactical team in front of her moved, cautiously but rapidly, through the target building. The power to the warehouse had been cut, as requested, just before the police entered the building, and with all of the windows having been previously covered to deter any curious passersby, the expansive building was dark as pitch.

The S.W.A.T. officers were all equipped with night vision goggles, and the team leader had given Higgins one of their spare sets. The tough little cop was thankful for the tech as they turned a corner visually sweeping the area ahead for the telltale heat signatures of hidden gunmen. Just then a deafening explosion erupted in front of the stealthily advancing officers. Higgins saw at least two men go flying as she dove for cover behind a parked forklift.

Her ears ringing and every sound totally muffled, she shook her head several times, desperately struggling to get her bearings. Trying hard to suppress the sudden intense wave of nausea, Higgins cautiously peeked around the edge of the heavy forklift. Her eyes widened in shock. The little detective blinked away the swirling dust from the explosion and beheld the sickening mass of destruction before her. Through the thick fog of settling brick dust and dark billowing smoke, she could see several small fires burning and at least four of the eight-man tactical team in front of her lay wounded and bleeding on the cracked concrete floor of the warehouse.

As some of the smoke began to clear and the choking dust began to settle, she saw that the team had been moving through a narrow hallway connecting one part of the big warehouse with another, like a breezeway. The heavy brick walls on either side of the approximately thirty-foot corridor had been completely blown away.

The ceiling, which was actually the floor of a room on the next level up, showed definite signs of impending collapse. Checking on the wounded, disoriented officers, who had been closer to the blast than herself, Higgins gingerly moved forward through the mounds of debris. She made her way to the shattered edge of one of the exterior walls and spotted the source of the sudden blast.

Incredulous, she stared aghast at what had to be the homeless woman's dragon, its bright angry eyes pinning her in its hungry gaze. An icy chill ran down the detective's spine as she watched another pair of high explosive projectiles belch forth from the mouth of the mechanical beast. There was no time, even to pray, as the stubby metal instruments of her imminent death sped toward her. With no options left to her, Detective T'Mara Higgins closed her eyes and waited for the end.

****

Jason kept up with his taller friend's long legged pace as the two men dashed into the darkened building. They entered from the opposite side of the warehouse from the firefight. The telltale sounds of gunfire being exchanged drew some of the men guarding the main entrance into the cavernous building to help the others repel the unwelcome guests. The two guards that remained turned their attention back to their post just a fraction of a second too late. Gabriel and Jason bowled them over like tenpins and continued, unfettered, into the combat zone.

They were homing in on the distinctive sounds that were gradually getting louder. Passing an old freight elevator, the two men rounded a corner and stopped short, in the nick of time, as a vicious blast took out a short section of the building, apparently some sort of passageway.

Gabe saw furtive movement on the inside the ravaged tunnel and identified several police officers down, wounded on the debris strewn floor. He also spotted detective Higgins, covered in brick dust and spatters of blood, stubbornly moving forward determined to complete her assignment. The big man admired the relentless tenacity of the dedicated detective. He was just about to move toward her to offer help if it was needed. At that moment, however, Buck's heavily armed fortified semi-truck sitting about 60 yards from the building, launched two more missiles straight at the police detective, momentarily blocked by wreckage and debris. The big man's eyes glowed brightly as he quickly lifted his right arm, the palm of his right hand spread out towards Higgins. Had anyone else been watching the impending tragedy, they would have seen the compact detective stand, eyes closed in grim acceptance, as two missiles streaked towards the spot where she stood.

Unerringly arriving dead on target, one of the stubby projectiles actually appeared to pass right through the incredibly brave young detective's body, as though she suddenly had no solid mass for it to strike, like a ghost or an apparition.

Inexplicably unobstructed, the now impotent, missiles sailed on, straight through the huge, ragged hole created by the first salvo. Then, in defiance of all physical laws, the missiles simply vanished. Nodding to Jason to follow, Gabriel struck out in a different direction. Backtracking on their previous path a bit, they turned down a corridor on their right and sped through several cargo bays filled to capacity with Buck's record-breaking stash of heroin. They passed through another wide doorway with a roll up type garage door, retracted in its cylindrical housing above them. And as the saying goes, all Hell broke loose.

Six was on the move. His battle trained ears catching the unmistakable growl of The Bull emanating from the south wing of the building. He conscripted a half dozen fighters, and together they hurried off in that direction. He wanted to be sure to get in on the kill and send a clear message to the idiot cops that Big Buck Taylor was definitely not someone they wanted to tangle with.

As he and his impromptu attack force passed quickly through one of more than a dozen bays filled with skid after skid of pure heroin, they came to an abrupt halt. Standing, maybe fifty feet in front of them, were two unfamiliar men.

Obviously not police, both were fit muscular and didn't appear to be the least bit intimidated by the heavily armed contingent of violent criminals facing them. As far as Six could tell, neither of the men were armed, though the taller one could possibly have some hardware hidden under, what appeared to be a long flowing robe.

Something about the strange pair just didn't feel right to Taylor's chief henchman, and he wanted more definitive intel before deciding on a course of action. "Who the hell are you two clowns and what are you doing here?" he called out.

The answer came from the bigger man in a deep commanding voice that reverberated through the cargo bay as if amplified by some type of powerful public address system. "Who we are is unimportant, but what we want is to give all of you a chance to change the direction of the lives you lead from this day on." Gabe answered.

The group of street toughs, all with long histories on the wrong side of the law, exchanged amused looks with each other and laughed, clearly of the opinion that the two nut jobs had, unwittingly, stumbled into an incredibly dangerous situation and obviously had no idea how close to death they stood at this very moment. Six wasn't laughing it up, though. Something in the big man's voice was strangely familiar. He just couldn't place where he had heard it before.

He did, however, have a reputation to uphold and a job to do, so he responded. "Look, I got something of a soft spot for people like you, you know, special people." Some of the men behind him chuckled softly at that. "I don't know what you think you're doing here, but I'm telling you now, get your asses out of here, lickity fuckin split, or both of you get an express ticket to the city morgue, you get me?" To illustrate his point, Six pulled the big .44 from its leather holster on his hip and pointed it directly at the guy who was doing the talking for the strange pair.

In these situations, Jason always allowed Gabe to do the talking. Never having been much for appealing to the kinder nature of people who wanted to do him harm, the younger man had no idea what to say. He simply prepared himself, mentally and physically, for the inevitable response to his friend's heartfelt appeal.

Without fail, even if some repented and pledged to change their ways, there was always, at least, one who just had to use the occasion to try and carve out a valuable chunk of street cred for themselves. Gabe truly believed no one was unredeemable, and Jason would be forever grateful to his friend for that, so he gave all their opponents every opportunity and every benefit of the doubt possible. Gabe decided to narrow his focus to the man speaking since he was clearly the leader of the group.

The gangster's face was obscured by a black knit half mask embossed with the image of a white skull. It was the type motorcycle riders wore to protect them from the wind. He also wore tinted, impact resistant, goggles that were clear to the wearer's view but dark and reflective for anyone observing them. He also wore a plain, black, ball cap, turned around backwards, on his head. All of these measures were taken, primarily, to obscure his face and prevent it from turning up on any police body cams or vehicle dash cams.

He could not risk his face, which was quite often seen with Buck, showing up on police video. Also, since it was known that he worked for Taylor, who was well respected in the area, it would bring unwanted attention to his upper crust employers' business. That, of course, was something the dangerous little man would not allow. Gabriel seemed to sense something unusual about the other man as well. Although the exchange between the two opposing men took only a few seconds, the rest of Six's goons were obviously growing tired of all this jaw jacking.

One of the men, standing off to the side of the man in charge, leveled his weapon at the two strangers standing in their way and, seeing his action, the rest followed suit. Now all of the men facing them were aiming death dealing weapons at Jason and Gabe.

"Last chance." Six said, thumbing back the hammer on his Magnum with a loud series of clicks. "The choice is yours." the big guy said. "You don't have to throw away the rest of your life. There is more out there for you than you know." Without any additional warning, the Magnum bucked in his hand as Six pulled the trigger on the huge revolver. At the deep, resounding boom of the powerful .44, the rest of the men opened fire and the cargo filled area was filled with the thundering sound of deadly gunfire.

TWENTY FOURTH CHAPTER

Detective Higgins was moving swiftly in the direction of a sudden, new, outburst of weapons fire, being careful, all the same, to check corners and other suitable spots for a gunman to hide in ambush. Totally unable to explain how she was still alive, she mentally put a pin in the thought and continued on with her search. After she made the call of officers down, radio traffic became much more hectic and exceedingly difficult to decipher.

She switched to the backup radio frequency, laid out in the mission briefing, but either no one else had done the same or no one else was able to answer, either because they were injured or because to break radio silence would compromise their position. Higgins fervently prayed it was the latter. She held herself personally responsible for every cop injured in the operation so far.

If she didn't manage to nail Buck and shut down the kingpin's operation, their blood would have been spilled for nothing. As she neared the area where the fierce firefight was taking place, the deafening barrage abruptly trailed off, then ceased altogether. Seconds later, it was replaced by the unmistakable sounds of close quarters combat. The distinctive sounds of flesh striking flesh and combatants grunting or crying out in pain, were easy to make out.

She reached the room where the down and dirty battle was taking place and risked a quick peek around the corner of a door frame to assess the situation. She felt like she was developing an unhealthy habit of letting her jaw go slack and her mouth drop open. There, in front of her, surrounded by murderous thugs were two men, one very tall and powerfully built and a shorter one similarly built but on a smaller scale. The strangely dressed pair were gamely fighting off the group of hired killers, and, incredibly, they looked to be winning! As she watched, surreptitiously, from behind the door jamb, she was totally astounded at the highly skilled and efficient combat skills of the two, clearly outnumbered, defenders.

Who in the world were these guys? Where did they get their training? And what the hell were they wearing?

Whoever they might be, they were effortlessly tossing hardened lifetime criminals around the room like throw pillows. On top of that, Higgins could see that the warehouse floor on one side of the room was all but covered with spent shell casings, and the two men skillfully tearing through Taylor's men were, as far as she could tell, unarmed. How in God's name was it possible for career criminals to expend that much firepower at such close range and miss? It was totally unbelievable.

Higgins spotted Six, the man her evidence indicated was Taylor's chief lieutenant. He had just tried to stab the bigger of the two opposing fighters with a nasty looking blade pulled from a sheath on the back of his belt. The blinding speed of his potentially lethal strike should have been all but impossible to avoid, yet the big man deftly slid out of the way with a fluidic grace that belied his impressive size. He allowed Six's deadly lunge towards the left side of his abdomen to pass beneath his arm and within mere millimeters of crippling contact with his body.

Six lost his balance when the blade unexpectedly failed to penetrate flesh and bone. The surprisingly agile man in the flowing robes caught his attacker's right wrist in the powerful grip of his left hand and continued spinning around to his left expertly allowing Six's forward momentum to aid him in slinging the smaller man into the air and across the bay like a lawn dart.

Six crashed awkwardly headlong into one of the plastic wrapped skids loaded with heroin. The sturdy wrapping held, however, and Six visibly stunned, slumped painfully to the floor. The other member of the two-man wrecking crew, although smaller than his companion, was calmly wreaking havoc as well. Having already incapacitated two of his attackers, he was now facing off against a third. Two other thugs among those who had initially squared off to face him broke off and charged across the bay to Six's aid.

A sudden flash of intuition revealed to Higgins that these two men must be her mysterious cyber informants, or at least associated with them. With that knowledge now abundantly clear to her, the loyal dedicated detective couldn't just stand idly by while these civilians did her job for her. The pair of larcenous cronies heading to assist Six then found they had a new problem, as Higgins charged into the room and assumed a defensive stance with her service weapon drawn before her. "Hold it right there." she said, with authority her hands steady and sure. The two gangsters hesitated for a second or two, apparently trying to decide if they could rush the lone detective and disarm her before she could shoot both of them. "I wouldn't try it if I were you." she said with a sly smile as if reading their minds. After another second or two, the two men realizing they had no other workable options grudgingly raised their hands clasping them together on top of their heads.

"Good call guys." Higgins said. She quickly moved in and placed heavy plastic riot cuffs, like zip ties, on both men's wrists. With that done, she made her now cooperative prisoners assume positions on their knees with their legs crossed behind them. She then turned, hoping to get some much-needed answers from her clandestine allies and discovered she was alone, except for the other felons sprawled insensate on the floor. Then she noted with irritation Six was also nowhere to be seen.

TWENTY FIFTH CHAPTER

Trask was at a loss to explain how the missiles fired at one of the cops could have possibly failed to destroy their target, not only that, but the rounds evidently had not exploded at all. The cop had rushed back into the comparative protection of the building and the opportunity was lost. Shaking his head in frustration, Trask shifted the powerful rig into gear and headed towards the other side of the building. His thermal imaging monitors and directional sound sensors indicated a heated battle taking place over there.

There was a chain link fence ahead separating a fueling station from the rest of the asphalt parking area surrounding the warehouse. Angry at having somehow missed a sitting duck target, Trask didn't even bother to avoid the barrier.

The sturdy fence bent like wheat waving in a summer storm, and The Bull passed over it without losing so much as one horsepower in the collision. The high-pitched whine of the truck's mighty turbine engines wailed into the darkness as the semi picked up speed. The big truck rounded a corner of the building just as Trask's HUD and other sensing equipment indicated that the men in this section of the building had been soundly defeated.

The thermoscan showed a heat signature with a distinctly feminine outline, placing cuffs on the only two men still able to move. The others were all still alive based on the readings Trask was getting, but they were undeniably out of the battle.

His communications man informed him that the S.W.A.T. officers had overcome the other men and women assigned to defend the storehouse for Buck's heroin and they were now in custody. It was a catastrophic defeat.

There was no chance that the crews guarding the other buildings could possibly make it here to reinforce Buck's people before the cops had everyone rounded up.

Buck's standing orders in this situation were emphatically clear. Every single person on site was ultimately expendable when it came to safeguarding the precious anonymity of his criminal enterprises. Trask gave his dejected crew the order to brace themselves as he prepared the final onslaught. He would launch an overwhelming barrage of deadly ordinance into the doomed building, then utterly obliterate it by blasting through it in the nearly invincible semi. There would be no survivors save him and the men and women inside the truck with him.

The Bull's commander lined up his targeting grid on the heads-up display in front of him and resolutely pressed the buttons that would launch an unsurvivable hail of firepower into the ill-fated building and…. nothing happened. He pressed the buttons again as his eyebrows threatened to climb off his forehead in shock.

The state-of-the-art foolproof systems of the one-of-a-kind vehicle had never failed before. It was positively unheard of. Trask feverishly racked his brain to find the cause for such a large-scale system failure, the powerful roar of The Bull's turbocharged diesel engines began to diminish as if the mechanical dragon was now tired and wanted to rest. A moment later, the unstoppable vehicle was dead in its tracks.

Trask looked through the windshield, now devoid of the HUD and no different than a standard windshield. He spotted two men standing about twenty feet in front of the now powerless semi. The shorter of the two was holding some type of device in his left hand. It was roughly the size of a tablet computer, and as Trask watched, the man tapped it a couple more times and the interior of the invincible massive assault vehicle went totally dark.

"Kill those bastards!" Trask screamed with unrestrained rage. His people quickly headed to the egress door, located in the side of the trailer section and lift the release control. The female squad leader for the strike team spoke up with more unexpected bad news. "Umm, Boss?" she said, sheepishly. "The door won't open."

Trask nearly fell on his face as he leaped from the driver's seat in the dark interior of the lifeless truck and rushed to the door. It was true. The high-tech systems of the futuristic truck were all dependent on its redundant electrical system. When the modifications to the prototype were made, the manual systems for entry and several other functions had to be sacrificed to make room for the vehicle's armaments and armor plating. As ridiculous as it sounded, they were all trapped inside one of the most advanced engines of destruction ever built. There was only one thing on Trask's mind now. They were all dead.

Jason was practically bouncing with glee. His computerized shutdown of the systems on the assault rig worked like a charm. With access to the technical schematics of the vehicle, he was able to find its Achilles' heel. The overzealous armorers had overlooked a basic necessity when they modified the vehicle's original plans. Since the big vehicle had a backup power supply considered to be hack proof, they placed entirely too much dependence on electric powered devices.

Despite themselves, they unintentionally gave Gabe and his tech savvy partner a way to effectively put the vehicle and its entire crew out of action. Now there was only one task left. That was to land the big fish. Looking to a cracked and neglected expanse of asphalt behind the warehouse grounds, Jason tapped more commands into his controller.

Buck Taylor was nearly hysterical with dangerous, murderous fury. He had just been informed that the warehouse, the key to his expansion plans, had been successfully raided. All the men and women on location had been taken into custody, save those transported to the hospital or the morgue. His extravagantly expensive ultimate weapon and its elite crew had been rendered helpless, and the vast store of precious heroin had been seized. It was the largest such seizure in Dayton P.D. history. Ivory, still in the bedroom section of the jet upon hearing the big man's anger erupt, hurriedly got dressed.

Apparently, their energetic sojourn into the mile high club hadn't been able to sooth Buck's nerves enough to bear such devastating news. As she entered the main cabin, she heard Taylor ask the pilot how long before they reached their destination? The pilot told him they were on approach now. Ivory wordlessly took her seat and gazed out the window. She instinctively knew not to disturb her employer when he was in such a foul state of mind.

In fact, she thought, she couldn't remember him ever being in such a state in her presence. As she wisely elected to keep her immediate concerns to herself, something odd caught her attention. She knew the airstrip at their Canadian destination was in a largely unpopulated rural area. As the sleek jet came in for a landing, she could see buildings, bridges, and traffic congested roads, alarmingly close to their flight path. Taylor had not yet taken his seat, even though it was standard procedure for landing, and she certainly was not going to be the one to tell him the pilot had brought them to the wrong destination.

Just as that thought passed through her mind, she heard the boss's baritone voice crackle with total incredulity behind her. "What the fuck?" he shouted, his normally smooth and soothing voice breaking like that of an adolescent teenager. His anger now had a focal point, the pilot, stuttering and stammering as he tried to make sense of what happened.

"Where the hell are we? What are you trying to pull, you stupid sonofabitch?" Buck's voice had a frightful air of danger in it now, and the beleaguered pilot suddenly looked as if he was seeing his landing zone for the first time. The plane's landing gear touched down, immediately buckling on the broken asphalt. The terrified pilot was unable to answer his employer's questions since all his attention was now directed towards keeping the jet from a catastrophic landing. The surface of what he had expected to be a well-maintained private airstrip was full of cracks, uneven surfaces, and it was dotted with large potholes. Taylor was thrown to the deck as the jet rocked and slid crazily to one side then the other as the pilot desperately fought to maintain control of the badly swerving jet. A shower of sparks filled the view outside Ivory's cabin window, and she could see the tip of one wing scraping along the ground. The deafening shriek of metal on concrete penetrated the cabin along with the horrifying sounds of parts of the plane being shearing off.

Ivory held on to the arms of her seat with a death grip, and she could see Buck on the floor being bounced from one side to the other like a giant human pinball. The stench of something burning and clouds of acrid smoke invaded the. formerly pristine cabin of the expensive aircraft. After what seemed an eternity, the smoking wreckage of the once luxurious aircraft slid to a screeching halt.

The pilot made his way to the hatch in the side of the cabin which was miraculously still intact. He turned the release lever and jumped out onto the ground. Ivory unbuckled her seatbelt and followed the pilot to the ground outside. Their exit from the ruined jet was facilitated by the jet lying, tilted on its side, at about a thirty-degree angle. As they both looked around to get their bearings, they simultaneously reached the same conclusion. They were back in Dayton. Ivory's green eyes ignited with full intensity as she looked at the pilot with undisguised suspicion. Ignoring the look of shocked surprise on his face, she asked the obvious.

"Did you fly us in a fucking circle?" The pilot opened his mouth to reply but, before he could utter a sound, his forehead erupted like a smashed tomato. Ivory reflexively snapped her eyes shut as hot blood and chunks of brain matter splashed her face and drenched her snowy hair.

Wiping the gory muck from her face, she opened her eyes to see Buck standing over the corpse of the unfortunate pilot, his semiautomatic pistol trailing smoke from the barrel. Not having the first clue what to say, the disgusted woman was spared the need.

"Drop the weapon Taylor, you're under arrest." Detective Higgins called. She was standing about fifteen feet away from the big man, her unwavering weapon pointed directly at him. Keeping her attention on Buck, the detective shot a sidelong glance at the tall, gore-soaked woman standing not ten feet from the drug lord's right side.

"You too, Snow White", she said' "hands up."

Ivory made a show of complying with the cop's command and began to raise her hands. Just then, Buck tossed his weapon in a high arc towards Ivory. The unexpected move put Higgins in a quandary. Her training told her to track the weapon and take out the most immediate threat to her life. The second she took her eyes off of Taylor, he darted around the mangled nose of the wrecked aircraft and bolted towards the nearby warehouse.

Ivory stood stock still as the gun landed not six inches from her left foot. Higgins kept the woman covered with her weapon, taking the gamble that Taylor wasn't faking her out to circle around behind her. She had two choices as she read the situation. She could order the woman to kick the weapon away and move away from it or she could order her to back away and secure the weapon herself. She was painfully aware of just how fast the big woman could move, and either choice carried significant risk.

Determined not to make it easy for the cop, Ivory stood motionless, eyes locked with the little detective as Higgins made her decision.

"Kick the gun towards me." she ordered. "No tricks, I don't want to shoot you, but I damn sure will if I have to." she said. The look in the cop's eyes told Ivory the shorter woman was not bluffing in the least. There was a chunk of aircraft wreckage on the ground near the gun. It was about the size of a large serving tray, and there was a bundle of torn wiring attached to one side of it. Ivory had been careful not to look directly at it, and the detective had all of her attention on her suspect. Ivory knew that in the back of the cop's mind, she had to be worried that Buck would suddenly reappear, and she would be at a distinct disadvantage.

Ivory moved toward the weapon; her hands still held high. Higgins kept the woman pinned in her unflinching gaze.

A sudden loud bang from the doomed jet and a hissing sound startled both women, but Ivory was in a better position to see it was just something inside the wrecked plane. Higgins turned her head for a split second which was all Ivory needed. The white-haired woman kicked the piece of wreckage, sending it sailing straight at Higgins's head.

The detective instinctively ducked to avoid the object giving Ivory just the break she hoped for. The taller woman followed the airborne piece of wreckage and as the detective ducked out of the way of the projectile, Ivory plowed into her shorter opponent full force. Both women fell to the ground and the detective's gun went flying. Ivory tried to get her hands around the cop's neck, but Higgins rolled out of the way and came to her feet in an impressive show of agility. Ivory quickly got back to her feet, and the two faced off.

Not about to let the big woman dictate the terms this time, Higgins went on the offensive. She closed the distance between them with her arms spread wide as if she intended to tackle her opponent just as the white-haired woman had done. Ivory prepared herself to trap one of the cop's arms and take her to the ground, planning to slam her face to the asphalt.

At the last second, Higgins changed tactics, lunging forward, she tucked herself into a tight ball and somersaulted into Ivory's legs. There was a loud sharp snap as the taller woman's left leg bent in the opposite direction for which it was designed. Ivory let out an involuntary shriek of pure agony, but to her credit managed to stay on her feet as Higgins rolled through the move like a gymnast. Tears sprang from the crippled blood-soaked woman's eyes, making streaks through the grime and gore on her face.

Higgins rapidly followed up her advantage by shifting laterally, side to side, knowing it was a motion the injured woman would be unable to duplicate. Ivory was basically standing on one leg and was rapidly losing mobility. As Detective Higgins moved to the side of the injured leg once more, the taller woman faltered and nearly fell.

Higgins used the opportunity to the fullest. Leaping into the air, the detective launched a spinning, reverse kick catching her larger opponent squarely in the jaw with her boot heel. As the dazed woman began to fall forward, Higgins brought her right knee up to meet her face. Higgins felt the cartilage of the white-haired woman's nose shatter against her knee Ivory dropped to the asphalt, hard. Breathing hard, Higgins took a second to catch her breath, then put cuffs on her captive, securing her to part of the wrecked jet's door frame. The detective looked around, recovered her weapon, and wondered where Buck went. She radioed for someone to come and take custody of her snowy haired prisoner and headed off in the direction she had seen him run.

****

Buck was livid. How could this have happened? Everything was going so well. What could have gone wrong? Making his way around the corner of the warehouse, the big gangster kept to the shadows, quickly ducking to the ground at the approach of any cops. So far, he had managed to stay undetected. If he could just get across the main road to the railroad yard, he was sure he could get away.

He stood as two cops disappeared around the end of the building and prepared to make a break for the road. Just then, he heard a soft call, barely a whisper, off to his left. "Boss."

He peered through the darkness and spotted a hand waving from behind a large clump of shrubbery. As he spotted the signal, a face emerged. It was Six. Buck made his way to his man's location. Keeping his voice low, he spoke to his trusted aid.

"What the hell happened here?" he asked.

"I'm still trying to figure that one out myself." the man answered. "All I know is two guys showed up after the cops and everything went to shit! I thought you were on your way to Canada." Six said.

"So did I." Buck replied cryptically. "What two guys?" he asked. "Who do they work for?"

"I can answer that." said a deep voice from very close by. Both men turned and stood face to face with Gabriel and Jason. Although he was staring directly at them, Buck couldn't make out the features of their faces. But a sharp intake of breath from his trusted lieutenant told him that wasn't the case for Six.

"Gabe?" Six asked, not believing his eyes.

Jason saw a look appear on Gabe's face he had never seen before. Shocked surprise and something else, profound sadness. "Jimmy?" the big man asked, his own disbelief evident in his voice.

Before Gabe could react, which was another thing Jason had never seen, Six drew a small pistol from a holster on his leg and brought it up in one swift move, aimed at Gabe's heart. Before he could pull the trigger, Jason leaped forward, turning midair in a somersault, he connected with both feet flush on the man's chin. Six dropped to the ground like a sack of wet cement.

Buck tried to use the sudden distraction to his advantage and rushed the big man. As soon as he started to move, he realized it was a mistake. The momentary confusion in Gabe's eyes had vanished like wisps of smoke in the wind. Buck launched a furious series of rights, lefts, and uppercuts to no avail. No matter what he did, the guy never seemed to be where he directed his punches. After a couple of minutes, Taylor began to grow weary, years of soft living taking their toll. Breathing hard, he stood facing the robed guy who wasn't even sweating.

"This is your turning point, Mr. Taylor." he said. "There is nothing stopping you from leaving this life of violence and death." Taylor abruptly stood up straight, his fatigue totally vanishing.

"That's where you're wrong." he said. His voice was completely different. It didn't sound like one voice at all, more of a chorus of voices, both male and female. Then, the big blonde man's eyes began to glow red as the molten core of a volcano. "Don't worry," he said, at the look of confusion on the big man's face.

"I'll see you again…. very soon." Then, he smiled with a mouth suddenly full of long razor-sharp teeth. Throwing his head back, he began to laugh, and his laugh chilled the blood. As Gabe and Jason watched, the big, fanged man began to sweat. Black oily looking fluid oozed from every pore, and a roiling cloud of black foul-smelling smoke vomited forth from Buck's mouth, eyes, ears, and his nose. The filthy cloud rose into the night air, trailing from the man like a snake leaving its skin behind.

When the last foul wisp left his body, Raymond Buchanan Taylor dropped to the ground, eyes wide open and staring like a corpse. He stayed that way for a few seconds, then went into a fit of coughing as he rolled over and struggled to his knees. He opened his mouth to speak and vomited a vile black stream of what looked like tar more than anything else. When the purging was finished a few seconds later, he found his voice and looked bewildered at the two men standing before him. "What happened?" he asked in a weak shaky voice.

"What do you remember?" Gabriel asked him.

Taylor frowned in confusion as he frantically tried to recall his last memories. "I was sitting in my living room," he began, "I was watching the news."

Gabe's voice was gentle and understanding as he asked the next question,

"What was the story on the news?" he asked.

"The World Trade Center was under attack by terrorists, they were saying." Buck said. Jason looked at Gabe, bewildered but the big man seemed to understand completely. "What about this guy," he said pointing to Six, lying unconscious on the ground. With the saddest expression he had ever seen on his friend's face, Jason heard the words but almost couldn't believe what the big man said. "He's, my brother."

EPILOGUE

Higgins was bone tired. She had finally finished her report and submitted all evidence pertaining to the arrest of one Big Buck Taylor. She had no explanation or sympathy for the man's assertion that he had total amnesia going all the way back to 9/11.

That was for lawyers and the courts to decide. She had done her job and gotten a record shipment of heroin off the street before it could poison countless lives. She had broken up a major criminal operation which included drugs, human trafficking, illegal arms sales, prostitution, illegal gambling, and racketeering. That was just the bullet points. There would be indictments for a host of other crimes and a number of corrupt politicians would be scrambling for cover as the gavel of justice slammed down.

T'Mara Higgins headed home. Trudging wearily through the door, she kicked off her shoes, slid out of her holster and laid her gun on the coffee table. Yawning, she went to the bathroom and started a tub of very warm water running, pouring in her favorite scented soap beads and some soothing bath salts. She went into the kitchen, poured herself a glass of wine and turned to head back to the bathroom. She stopped dead in her tracks, facing a man so tall that he almost needed to bend over to avoid bumping the ceiling in her small apartment.

Ordinarily, she would have dived for her weapon and gone on the attack, but for some unexplained reason, she wasn't at all afraid of this total stranger, standing uninvited in her living room. In fact, she felt more at ease than she did a few moments before.

"I just wanted to tell you how important you are." he said, cryptically.

"I don't understand." she managed to say. "Who are you?"

"My name is Gabriel. My friend and I sent you the information on Taylor's operation.

"Thank you." she said, mentally chiding herself for such a lame response and wondering why she wasn't spitting out any one of a thousand questions she wanted to ask. "You have made a very big difference in Dayton, Detective." he said. "But I have an offer for you, If you would like to make a difference on a much larger scale."

Higgins found herself curious to find out what the big man meant by that. She knew she should be terrified that a huge, total stranger just appeared unannounced in her home, but she was completely at ease. "I'm listening." she said.